DIARY OF A VIGILANTE

DIARY OF A VIGILANTE

SHAUN CURTIS

EST.   2019
BLKDOG

PROLOGUE

Why? Why not?

Like Shakespeare's Romeo and Juliet's famous, 'To be, or not to be', I say, 'Punish or be punished'. Yeah, yeah, I can hear all you literature buffs with no sense of humor and politically correct whine asses saying, "Oh no, how dare he use such a beautiful piece of literature in a book such as this?" To this I say, "Fuck You"!! Oh, and by the way, just in case all you PC ass hats were wondering, the 'Fuck You' was meant to hurt your feelings. It's a form of expression, which is why, of all the harsh words out there, this is my favorite. The reason I say favorite is because it's nearly impossible to misinterpret. No need to hear the 'oh my god, that was so mean, and it hurt my feelings', no need to wonder anymore, it was both mean and meant to hurt your feelings. I am not trying to be mean in so many terms; I just felt that if you can't take a joke or have your feelings hurt from time to time than maybe you should just go play in traffic. Save the world some valuable air, and just live your life and yours alone.

The 'system', as I call it, for the most part works. It at least tries to anyway. The concept was, in the beginning, a great idea and worked. It's really quite simple even. You do stupid, and you pay for it, nothing more, nothing less. Even biblically there was crime and punishment—'Eye for an Eye and Tooth for a Tooth' ring a bell? Essentially, you reap what you sew. Now however, there are so many laws within laws that almost give the criminals an advantage if there are smart enough to play the game right. I want to change the game for those that think they can play our judicial system in the wrong way. In a way I too am playing the game, but I am neither profiting nor using the breaking of the law to my advantage. I am just trying to get some of those people that are screwing with it out of it. Examples of the things that are pissing me off are as follows: people getting any kind of a lengthy sentence for smoking dope or doing any kind of drugs. The way I see it, if you want to shove that shit into your body so be it. In time, the garbage you put into yourself will get its own revenge. Do not, however, sell that shit to kids. They are not old enough to make the kind of responsible decision that would allow them to partake in such things. To them, the fact that they could see their childhood heroes actually flying through the air or doing drugs, that might make them popular cause it's 'cool' is often times good enough for them. If you do choose to sell or push these drugs to the innocent, then do not be surprised if one day I show up on your doorstep.

Now, a person that rapes, murders, or molests a child can receive little or no punishment if they have the ability or money to work the system. This type of justice is what set this whole series of events in motion. Don't get me wrong, I do believe in the system, however, it has just become a shell of the way it used to be—enter 'The Vigilante'. This type of person or persons takes the law into their own hands and becomes judge, jury and executioner. This is the path I took after a series of events in my life left me realizing that I could no longer take it anymore. I could no longer watch as people I knew got hurt or were about to get hurt by people that should not have ever even been there to hurt then in the first place. If I hadn't had something in my life affect me on a personal level, I may have never ended up doing what I had done and continue to do to this very day. While my ways may be unorthodox, cruel, and yes illegal, I couldn't think of any other way in which to deal with the problem. So, I decided to solve it myself.

When there is a problem and you need a solution but no solution presents itself, what do you do? You remove the problem, right? If no problem exists to trouble you, then you have no problem at all. So that is what I decided to do. Now I find myself in the position of removing problems that our court system does not, cannot, or for whatever reason will not solve. As an exterminator goes about their job of ridding the world of pest that we dislike, I too am an exterminator of sorts. The difference between me and a traditional exterminator is that my pests walk upright and speak. I consider it a service to all persons who have been wronged and never received the justice they deserve. Some people may disagree with my methods and may say I am insane, however, believe me when I say that I am in full control of my actions and sanity. I know that what I am doing is wrong and immoral, but I just got tired of caring about the morality of it all when the justice system can't or won't.

I do believe in God and realize that my actions will probably send me straight to hell. This, however, is on my soul and mine alone. I will have to deal with it.

The people that I exterminate—or for all you PC cry me a river because he said boo wanna-be do-gooders, 'murder'—are in my opinion a drain on society. They are no more than a warm gut-sack, sucking the life out of this world. One such example of said gut-sack are child molesters. Now there are a weird bunch of fuck monkeys if ever I have seen one, **KIDS, REALLY??** What you do is not love, it's sex, plain and simple. It is sex with an innocent child—a child that after you are done 'loving' is no longer innocent and now has the rest of their lives to try to reverse the trauma that you inflicted upon them. That being said, you all are high up there on the get rid of list. Another example are rapists; that bunch suffers from a real lack of imagination. If you want to dominate something there fifty shades of fuck-up, then go buy a nerf football and some Vaseline; cut a hole in the ball, lube well then violate and dominate the shit out of that. If you are not satisfied then like so many shampoo bottles say, 'rinse and repeat'.

Now some of you, I am sure, would love to ask me what makes my life more important than those I kill. Hmmm…, aaa, NOTHING. Well, except for the fact I do contribute to society by paying my taxes. As far as I am concerned, taking a little evil out of the world is a nice fringe benefit to humanity. Now before all you head shrinkers start psycho analyzing me, I did not have a traumatic childhood event or any late-night sneaky uncle that screwed up my life. By all accounts, my childhood and upbringing were just fine. I learned right from wrong, and etiquette. I also learned all those traits that made me, well at least the working father and husband side of me that is, who I am. As for the killer side of me, guess you will have to keep reading in order to find out. No worries, it's a good story.

CHAPTER 1

Well, where to start? There is nothing real spectacular to say about me, just the simple fact that all people have a point at which they have simply had enough. I was at that point when this all started. I am your average Joe who just so happens to have come from a family that was better off than most. My father owned a chemical engineering company that was very profitable and allowed us to live very well. Neither of my parents spoiled us. If we wanted something, we earned it. It was my parents' belief that a good work ethic would get us far in life, and I, to this day, still believe that. Being around the chemistry side of science all my life, I naturally took an interest to it and all that it encompassed.

In high school, I was in the science club as well as the on swim team and played football. While in high school, I met the girl that I would end up spending the rest of my life with. Oh shut up Alice This is not wonder land; I just happened to find a woman and we clicked. Jill and I attended the same collage—she on a full academic scholarship, while I attended on a combined swimming and academic scholarship and received my degree in chemical engineering. Jill's degree was going to take a bit more time than mine was; she was training to be a General Practice

Physician. While Jill completed her medical training and before joining my fathers' factory, he encouraged me to join the military and become a man—his words. As I look back, it indeed was a life changing decision.

After completing OCS (Officer Candidate School) I was assigned to an NBC (Nuclear Biological Chemical) unit. I served my country with honor and still to this day would die for it. Jill finished her med school studies and went to work in private practice with some people whom she had attended school with. Just before I left the military, Jill and I were married. I was hired at my father's factory and as per his orders, had to work my way up the 'honest' way, no hand-outs for this pup.

Jill and I were happily married and had two kids that took after their parents in the brains department. We gave them every opportunity to succeed academically and allowed them to choose their own path in which to follow in life. We had our friends that we hung out with, one of which was a lady by the name of Melissa. Melissa was a person I met working at my father's factory and became friends with. She and her husband would come over and BBQ, and we adults would go out from time to time in order to blow off steam or just catch a show. Melissa's family is the one that ultimately threw me into the place I am today, or at least, what almost happened to them.

Melissa was about to marry a very bad man. While I actually have no idea whether or not I would have eventually gone down this road or not, I can say that the ordeal with my friend ushered things along quicker.

Melissa is a great person—full of life and spirit— the type of person always there to give a hand if needed. Until two years ago, Melissa was happily married to Jim, an ad executive from a well know agency. Together, their life was like a storybook tale of love and happiness. Jim made enough for Melissa to stay at home and care for the kids full time which she had always wanted to do. I first meet Melissa at our mutual place of employment. We got along well as did she and my wife, a definite plus. We often hung out with her and Jim when they were engaged and even after they were married. As is often times the case, when people start having kids they sometimes part ways, not so much because they lose interest in the people that they spent time with but usually due to the fact that life can get very busy very fast.

When Melissa decided to quit work in order to stay at home and fulfill her dream of being a full-time mother and wife, she was noticeably happy. While we would miss her at work, we were also happy that she was able to chase and catch one of the things that she had always wanted.

"Good bye sports car, hello SUV," Melissa had said on her last day at work.

I just smiled at her and said, "Jill and I hope you have the life that you had always wanted and please keep in touch." We said our goodbyes and agreed to try to keep in touch.

"That would be great," Melissa said, and she walked out the door on her last day of work and off to her new life. She had a noticeable spring to her step indicating that she was indeed a happy woman. Ok, ok, so I checked out her butt, what? She has a nice butt. I'm married, not dead. Smiling to myself I turned and went back to work.

As you can imagine, we never really did stay in touch like we had planned.

For five years, all was as good as could be expected in Melissa's life. Jim went to work in the mornings and would come home in the evenings. Melissa would do what house wives do, which is pretty much everything. I once read that your typical house wife, on average, should earn around $250,000 a year if you were to take into account all the services that they provide on a day to day basis. For example: restaurant owner/operator, daycare provider, taxi, nurse, counselor, fashion consultant, part-time cosmetologist, and last but not least, professional home cleaner. Melissa did all this and more when needed, and the whole time, she did it with a smile on her face. Then as life sometimes goes, tragedy struck.

As was often the case, the morning was like most other mornings for Melissa. Get up, make breakfast, blah blah blah... you all know the routine. As life often does when you are not looking, you get a curveball thrown right into your face and the whole world seems to go to shit. Suddenly, things that you would only think could happen to someone else happen to you.

Melissa heard the phone ring and went to answer it.

"Hey you," Jim said.

"Well hey back." She said.

"Just called to say I was on my way home and should be there in about half an hour."

"Sounds good, see ya then," Melissa said to him and hung up the phone.

Melissa sat on the couch and read her book for a while when she realized that it had been quite a bit longer than a half an hour. They always went out to eat after he had gotten back from his business trips given the unpredictable time in which he would often times show up.

That's weird, Melissa thought to herself. She waited for a few more minutes and decided to call him. "Hey, you have reached Jim please leave a message." She tried several more times and repeatedly got his voice mail. Now she was getting worried; she had made up her mind to call the police when a knock came from the front door. Two things happened just then; she got both a chill down her spine and a jolt of relief. Jim either had something in his hands and could not open the door, or her worse fear had come true, something had happened to him.

She turned the door handle and slowly opened the door.

"Mrs. Haley?" The officer asked. "Mrs. Jim Haley?" He said again. Melissa just stood there not knowing what to do. "Ma'am?" the officer asked.

Getting her wits about her again she said, "Yes that's me, Mrs. Haley. How can I help you officer?" She prayed that she was being served with some kind of lawsuit, or that someone had broken into their summer home up state—anything but what she feared was coming.

"Ma'am I am afraid I have some bad news for you."

Still holding out hope she replied, "Yes, what is it?"

The officer took off his hat and said, "Mrs. Haley, I am sorry to inform you that just a short time ago, you husband, a Mr. Jim Haley, passed away after being involved in an automobile accident."

Melissa looked up at the officer and blinked a few times. "Ma'am?" the officer said again. "Are you alright? Is there any one that we can call for you?"

That started to bring her around a bit. The ringing in her ear that had for the last few minutes made her all but deaf was subsiding, and she could hear the officer again.

"Yes. I mean no." The officer looked at her again, knowing that it was a lot to take in. This was unfortunately not his first time with a death notification. He knew that the initial blow was always the hardest and that she would be coming back around again in a second.

"No, I do not need you to call anyone, and yes, I will be ok."

The officer nodded his head and said, "Very-well, I do need you to come down to the hospital in order to make a positive identification of your husband's body."

Melissa looked up at him and said, "Um, ok. I need a few minutes to make a phone call to get someone here to help with the kids."

The officer replied, "No problem Ma'am."

The investigation revealed a garbage truck's brakes had a catastrophic failure. Life has its way of doing things that you would rather not have happen to you or a loved one, and Jim was going through the intersection at the same time the garbage truck's brakes failed while he was trying to stop for the sign. According to the police report, Jim was killed on impact, the truck having enough force and momentum. The driver was not charged because it was a true mechanical failure and in no way a fault of his. Melissa met with him. The driver was emotionally distraught, and she knew that he would suffer with this for some time to come. This being known, she made a point to tell him that she knew it was not his fault and forgave him.

"Melissa," I said to her at the funeral. She looked up and came over and gave me a big hug.

"Jack," she said, "long time, no see." Releasing me from her hug she looked me over. "Still the same old Jack. Are you ever going to age?"

Laughing I said, "Only if forced."

"Thank you all for coming, how have you all been?"

I nodded my head a few times and said, "We have been real good. I want to say how sorry we are to hear of your loss. If there is anything that Jill or I can do for you, please do not hesitate to ask."

She smiled. "Thank you for your concern; it means a lot. It will be difficult for us for a while, but we will manage. Jim had the peace of mind to make sure that we were well taken care of financially if he were to meet an untimely death."

I saw the tears begin to well up in her eyes. "You do not need to talk about it Melissa, this is hard enough I am sure."

She composed herself and said, "No, no its ok. I was just thinking how thoughtful Jim was insuring that we would be taken care of, even if it wasn't by him in the flesh."

I again nodded my head and said, "He was a very good man, and he will be missed."

Melissa nodded her head and said, "It was very nice to see you again. I hate to cut this conversation short, but I need to see to my other guests."

I said good bye and repeated my offer of help anytime she may need it, and she was gone. My wife Jill and I looked at each other and agreed that under the circumstances Melissa seemed to be doing alright.

Not too far in the future, I ran into Melissa at the grocery store. Melissa saw me before I saw her and said, "Well hello stranger."

I looked up, saw who it was and said, "Well hello to you, how have you been?"

Melissa smiled at me and said, "We are doing well, thanks for asking. The kids are adjusting, and things are going as good as can be expected."

"That is good to hear," I said.

She asked how the wife and I were doing, and I told her all was good on the home front.

"That is so good to hear. I have met someone, and we have been seeing each other for a while now. I think it may be leading somewhere good."

I looked at her and said, "That is great news, you will have to bring him over. We can barbecue, or if that brings back too many memories, than we can just shoot the shit or something."

She smiled and said, "That will be a fantastic idea, thank you for the invite."

"I will tell Jill and you both can make arrangements that work well for the both of us."

We said again how good it was to see each other and that we looked forward to our get together.

As we walked away, I turned around and said, "You still have the same phone number?" She nodded her head and we said our goodbyes.

I got home that night and told Jill about running into Melissa and our conversation.

"So, who is he and what does he do?" she asked me.

I gave the typical male response, "Ahhh…Well I guess we will just have to have that barbecue and ask him those very questions in person."

"Is it all men that just forget to ask more than 'hey how ya been', or is it a particular defect in your DNA?" she asked me.

"Yep," was the best I could do, trying to get back some of my humanity I lost.

About two weeks later, Melissa, her two boys, and Frank joined us for a barbecue. We greeted Melissa and the others and she said, "Everyone, I would like you to meet Frank Morris my fiancé."

I walked over and offered my hand and we all made our acquaintances. Melissa and Jill were sitting at the patio table catching up on old times and all other manner of missed gossip and life. The kids found things to do while Frank and I talked.

"So, Frank., Melissa says you are in the law profession?"

"That I am. It's a bit boring, but the pay outweighs the crap part of it all."

I laughed. "I can see where a good paycheck can deter some of the monotony of the job. So what type of law do you practice Frank?"

Frank took a drink of his beer and said, "Corporate Law… really bland but I like it, and someone has to do it."

I looked at him and said, "So contracts, buy outs and things like that?"

Frank nodded his head and said, "Yeah, that and all things big business, from mergers to acquisitions, to hostile takeovers of one company by another."

"Bland you say? That seems a little less then bland to me, but I suppose that after awhile of doing the same-ole thing, anything can get boring."

To that Frank said, "Indeed it can, but as I said the paychecks make it a lot easier to overlook the boring and monotonous."

I turned the burgers and Frank asked me what it was that I did. "I am a chemical engineer and I too can say that sometimes the job gets monotonous. However, my checks also compensate for the boring."

"That does not sound like a boring job at all. What all is exactly involved in doing what you do?"

I looked at him then to the burgers then to the sky, "How exactly do I explain what I do? Well shit, Frank, that's a good question." I said laughing. "In a nut shell, we take chemical compounds and combine them into other things that, in the end if all goes well, turn into everything from medicine to plastics and what not."

Just then Jill called out to us, "The monsters are about to eat the fence and all that is around it. How much longer till we can feed them?"

We all sat down to eat and catch up on old time as well as new ones. "So, Melissa, how did you and Frank meet?" Jill asked.

Melissa smiled and looked at Frank. "Well, really by accident. You see, he was handling the business end of some of the investments I had made with Jim's insurance money. I was hoping to be able to make enough so that the kids will be able to attend any college that they choose. Post graduate college that is." Melissa continued, "Anyway, over the years and many visits later, Frank asked me to have some coffee and I agreed. The rest you could say is history."

Jill smiled as Frank and Melissa look at each other. "We are so very happy for you two."

Melissa looked over at Jill and said, "Thank you, Jill, that really means a lot to me."

"So, if this is not too personal…" Jill began to ask.

I interjected and said, "Yeah, that is a real good way to start a conversation." We all laughed.

Jill continues, "As I was saying, if it's not too personal, how are the kids handling a new man in mom's life?"

Melissa looks over at Frank then back to us before and said, "Not too personal at all. The kids seem to be adapting rather well, and Frank just loves them and treats them like they are his own. I couldn't ask for better. I never would have thought after losing Jim I would have found someone like Frank."

We all chit chatted about various things for the rest of the evening until well into the night. We all decided to call it a night and say our goodbyes. Before Melissa and Frank left, we all decide that we should do it again and agree to keep in touch.

So", Jill said, "Frank seems like a nice guy."

"He sure does," I said.

"I sure hope things work out for those two. Melissa has had enough to tragedy in her life for one person." Jill responded to me. As she spoke about Melissa, Jill sat on the bed, and I heard her say, "Well fuck me running."

Hearing it, I looked out the bathroom door and said, "Can I just fuck you laying down on the bed?"

Laughing, Jill said, "You are such a perrrvvv…"

"Well thank you my love," I said to her, "but really, what's the matter? Did your laptop crash or what?"

Jill looked up at me and said, "No, I just get sick and tired of all the stupid adds and shit I get all the time that have absolutely nothing to do with me, my age group, or even anything close. I mean come on really, do I look like I am old enough for **AARP**, or do I look like want or need a sexy young Russian vixen to liven my nights?"

I looked at her with as serious of a face as I could and said, "You definitely do not look old enough for **AARP**. However, if you are willing, I would share the sexy Russian vixen with you to make our nights lively."

Jill chucked the pillow at me. "God, you are such a pervert, does your mind ever leave the gutter even for a minute?"

I look at her smiled and said, "Nope, I am the master of my domain. Hell, perverts come to me for advice." She just shook her head.

"Here is a dandy of an ad," Jill said shortly after I got into bed.

I rolled to my side and said, "Oh really, what is it selling?" She opened the ad and began to read.

"Find sexual predators in your area. They may be living next door, and you may not even realize it. Are your children safe?"

I looked over at her and asked, "So how does it say you can find out who is a bad guy and who is not? According to the ad that is?"

"Seriously?" Jill asked.

"Hell ya, why not?"

She shook her head before really thinking about it and said, "Oh hell, why not?"

"That's the spirit." I said to her. We both laughed and thought about a name that we could put in.

"I am coming up blank," Jill said.

"What about Frank?" I asked.

"Frank?" Jill asked.

"Yeah, Frank Morris, you know, the guy that was here with Melissa tonight?"

"Oh my God Jack, are you serious?"

With a shit eating grin on my face I said, "What, it's the only name that comes to mind right off the top of my head." With a giggle Jill typed the name Frank Morris into her laptop and hit the enter key while I turned back to my news program on my iPad.

'DING', I heard Jill's e-mail notification chime go off. Still tuned into my program, I heard her say, "Oh my God!"

To this I respond, still looking at my iPad, "Nice try smart ass, but I am not falling for that one."

She tapped me on the side of the head and said, "Believe what you want to, but Frank is on this website."

"You better not be messing with me or I will be forced to tickle you until you pee." Jill turned her laptop toward me, and the picture that I saw made me freeze where I sat. The man that we had just hosted in our house, who ate our food, and hung out with our kids had his picture front and center on the sexual predators' website. The charges were listed as 'two counts of sexual misconduct of a minor'. The two kids that he had assaulted were both young boys.

"Melissa has two young boys," I said to Jill. "The same two boys that not more than a few hours ago Melissa said got along well with Frank—the two kids that Frank loves like they were his own."

Jill looked at me and said, "What do we do?"

"Kill him, I'd say."

She just continued to look at me and said, "No, really?"

We both sat on the bed for awhile stunned by what we had just discovered. Jill spoke up first and said, "We should make up one of those fake e-mails and send Melissa this sexual predators' warning, so she can at least know who she is about to marry."

"That's a great idea," I said. We cut and pasted the warning from the site and attached it to Melissa's e-mail on our newly formed ghost account and sent it off. The response that we got back in return was nowhere near what we had expected. Given the straight forwardness of the e-mail, I would never have thought that we would have gotten the response that we did. I knew then in the deepest darkest part of me—the place everyone has but never has the need or willpower to tap into—that I was going to kill that man. I would kill him, dispose of the body, and hopefully get away with it—all this, before he harmed a hair on their bodies.

CHAPTER 2

Jill was looking at her computer waiting for the response to the email when I heard her say, "Uh Oh, Jack?"

I came in and asked her what is wrong. She looked at me and said, "The email we sent to Melissa has a response."

"Is this the reason for the uh oh?" I asked.

"The uh oh is putting it mildly," she said.

"Ok?" I said.

"Just come and look," she said.

I walked over and read the message and took in a small breath. "Yep, uh oh is putting it mildly," I said. The response reads something like this. 'Whoever this is, it's not funny. The man you say has done these things HAS NOT!! Nor is he even capable of doing such monstrous things. So, whomever did this photo shop shit can go straight to hell. If I see another one of these emails, I will have the IP address tracked and pursue any and all punishments to the full extent of the law."

Jill looked and me and told me that we should just keep ourselves open to help her if and when the time came that she may need our help. I just kept staring at the screen and realized I could not in good conscious stand back and wait for that freak to hurt those kids. I would do anything and everything in my power, and then some, to stop this.

What blows my mind is how the 'system' could let this guy off with only two years of probation and a fine for two counts of child endangerment instead of sexual molestation of a child. Obviously, this was a rich man's version of justice. The 'system' has become so screwed up that a person trafficking marijuana can go to prison while a child molester can get off as lightly as Frank had.

I looked at Jill and said, "Yes, we should be there for Melissa when and if things get ugly." I then sat back and planned on how to go about killing Frank. While I believe in my heart that anyone can do anything to anyone at any time, including the act of murder and torture, not everyone can go through with it or believes that they can actually do it, regardless of the circumstances. I myself never even thought of it until that guy came into our lives via Melissa. Whether or not he intended on harming those kids was beside the point. He could not be aloud, to harm them at all. That family had suffered enough.

I got the urge for what people call 'vigilante justice'—others call it murder, while I called it a need. I needed to right a wrong. I needed to show others that, while they may not go to jail, there were still consequences for the actions they had done—actions that were far worse than jail could ever even come close to.

How I thought of, and the way I was able to carry out, such awful atrocities to another human being, all the while carrying on a seemingly normal life with my wife and children, I have no idea. However, it did seem almost as if I were born to do it.

Like any good hunter I stalk my prey, not unlike animals, humans can be and are very predictable. They follow patterns and have routines, often times following the same route to and from work, frequenting the same dining and drinking establishments. Note to self: diversity is the spice of life, or for that matter, can save your life. I followed Frank, observing, making notes of his movements and favorite places to frequent. I wrote all this down and repeated it until a pattern appeared. This being done and seeing a pattern, I planned for the take down. Due to immense and still growing anger and hatred I have allowed to fester toward this man and what will come to be all of my targets, my plan was to abduct, relocate, and then have a little fun with them prior to killing them. In my mind, the pain I would inflict on them was a mere freckle on a canvas compared to the pain they had caused to their victims and their families.

In this case, he who likes young boys also likes donuts and coffee on his way to work each morning. This is good for me, not so good for him however. Actually, the doughnuts are probably bad for him also, if you sit back and think about it. They weren't as bad for his body as I was going to be for it, but nevertheless. I laughed to myself, "everyone's got to be a comedian." I said. "Now the fun begins."

It started slow, a note on the window of his car saying. "I know who you are and all about your past. If you lay a hand on either of those children, I WILL KILL YOU.", or "So you like them young do you?" Of course, all the notes were on clean paper. (By clean I mean, I had never touched them as to not give a way to be tracked back to me.) All the hints and suggestions were just enough to get him thinking—thinking that someone may be watching and may in fact know who he really is and what he has done. If you have ever been afraid of anything and had the real chance of running into what you fear, then you know how it felt.

Fear in itself can be healthy, as it can help you to think about doing something that you may not really need to do because it could be harmful to your very survival. While a natural part of life, fear can also be debilitating, making you pay more attention to the thing you fear more than everything else around you. My hope was that it would make him paranoid and get a little uncomfortable—uncomfortable enough that he became irritable. This would make my snatching him the way I planned a whole lot easier.

The day was planned and came quickly. I made preparations, as I always do, and began the game. This part of the game is always a little different; I say different due to the fact that everyone is different and can change their plans at a moment's notice. The reason for abducting him, as opposed to just killing him, was that I planned on having a little fun before I ended his life. Now, don't go saying what a psychopath I am. I take no real pleasure in harming another human being; it's just a little pay back for the pain and suffering that they put their victims through and then got off virtually free of any and all reasonable punishment that should have come with the crime committed. I almost always take my marks after dark, because let's be realistic, so much can go wrong during the day. In today's society, everything seems to get recorded. While I should be put behind bars for my actions, I am in no real hurry to get there. So doing my deeds in the dark will lessen risk of discovery. Now, if I choose to go to a marks house in order to carry out the kill, well, we will have to cross that bridge when and if we get there, but that's another story for another chapter.

As predicted 'Lester the Molester', sorry to all you out there that have the name Lester, but it's just a name that I had heard some time ago and have held on to. Anyway, sick-o left the bar following his usual evening cocktail—"fuck this guy is predictable," I laughed to myself. Frank got into his car and headed to what I have noticed was Melissa's house. By this, I mean her primary residence where her and the kids live, sometimes with and other times without Frank there. Halfway there at a planned intersection I made my move. The light turned red and Frank stopped his BMW and waited. I slowly rolled up behind him and tagged his bumper, not hard enough to do a lot of damage but enough to make him aware someone had hit him and piss him off. As predicted, Frank got out of his car, and in one of those 'I am better than everyone else attitudes', said, "How the hell did you hit me?"

I sat in my car and acted like I was concerned, while inside I was laughing my ass off. I said, "I am so sorry, I got distracted."

Frank said, "are you blind? This is a BMW; it cost more than you probably make in a year."

'WOW!' I thought to myself, 'did he really just say that?' Guess Frank just made the asshole list also, and on that note, I'm not sure that I could handle another immature mouth shitting, so I tazed him. "Damn, that really looks like it hurts," I said laughing. Realizing who it was that just tazed him he said, "Why?"

I respond, "Really, chimo (child molester)? You have to ask why?" I shook my head. "I will put it very simply, NO SEX WITH YOUNG KIDS. Was that simple enough for you, Mr. BMW?" I said, just before giving him some more juice. I was not worried about killing him; the extra juice didn't bother me. In fact, I started laughing as I watched his body shake and jolt. Yep, that had to hurt. I loaded him in my car and headed off to the place where his life was going to get real, painful.

When chimo woke up at our location, he immediately went into a tirade. Frank started saying, "You know who I am? I have rich influential friends!!!"

"Yes, Frank, I know exactly who you are, or what you are I should I should say." I continued in my attempt to drive the point home by saying, "Blah, blah, blah, even if you have these friends, do you really think you are going to get out of here alive? Once the truth of who you really are and what you have done to those kids comes to light, do you really think they are going to care that you have gone missing?"

Frank gave me a stare that told me it had finally sunk in. He said, "You're are going to kill me." It was said more as a statement than as a question.

I looked him right in the eyes and said, "Yes, that is exactly what I am going to do Frank. I guess there are some functioning brain cells in that head of yours after all, and just in case you were wondering, it is not going to be fast. There will be lots of pain and suffering involved, like the pain and suffering you inflicted on those two young boys and who knows how many other children." Just for kicks, I tazed him again. I laughed hysterically and said, "Damn, that never gets old." I sat in a chair across from Frank and waited for him to wake from his last electrically induced coma. As he started to come around, he looked all around, realized that this was in fact was not a dream, and to my despair, or maybe pleasure, he started his tirade again.

"You know," I said, "if you would tone down the amount of asshole spilling out of your mouth this might go faster. However, I may get to have more fun with you if you keep it up. Sooo, I'll let you decide how this goes, for now." Would you believe I had to taze that mouthy bastard three more times to get him to shut up? Stubborn little prick. When Frank finally calmed down or realized that the approach to the situation he was in was not working, the lawyer part of him decided that another way was going to have to work—introduce, 'the negotiations' yep, he tried that.

"Frank," I said. "Stop it, nothing you can say, do, or pay, will get you out of this situation."

"Why?" he asked.

I looked at him and said, "Are you fucking serious? You really feel the overwhelming need to hear the why of this? After all the notes about knowing who you are and what you did to those kids, you feel as if you don't know why this is happening to you?"

Frank looked right at me and says, "I never hurt any kids, I loved them."

That was a touch too much for me right at that moment. I hauled off and gave him a beautiful right hook.

I will admit that my first kill was a little rougher than I had thought. Not that I lacked the will to do it, just making my hands do what my brain wanted them to do was lacking a bit, at least, until the first bit of torture. Then, to my surprise, it came very easy, almost as if I where predestined to do it and do it I did.

As you can imagine, Frank was not capable of keeping his mouth shut. He just kept saying how much he loved those children, and if you knew what it was like you would understand. Blah, blah and blah.

"You know Frank, you are a real pain in the ass," I said. "By the way, that little 'If you knew what it was like' statement just cost you two fingers." I told him as I went to the table and retrieved a pair of hedge trimmers. "How dare you stoop so low as to actually believe that what you and all those other chimo perverts could believe any of us even want to imagine what it would be like to have sex with a child" I said. "You fucking disgust me."

I walked over to Frank with the hedge trimmers, and can you believe it, the man sitting in front of me actually started to piss his pants. Mr. big nuts lawyer is nothing but a big softy. I laughed softly and said, "Unlike what the doctors may say when they try to ease the pain, you know, 'This will only hurt a little', well stud, this is going to hurt like hell."

Frank, apparently not believing what was actually happening sat there in his own urine, stunned look on his face and completely silent.

I looked at Frank and said, "Yes this is really going to happen.". Still stunned, Frank sat there as I walked over to him and said, "Any particular finger you would like to part with first? Oh for shit sakes Frank, I realize you are used to having the upper hand in most cases, but really?"

A sound like that of a mental patient strongly dosed on Thorazine (a strong antipsychotic) emanated from his lips, ahhhhh. "Never mind," I said. I walked over grabbed one of the fingers on his hand and fitted it into the hedge trimmers. With a swift motion, I took off said digit and immediately after that, the one next to that one. Surprising as it may seem, it sounded very similar to the sound the trimmers where meant to make if the actual item they were intended to clip off were in them. It was kind of a wet crunchy sound, maybe like that of crunching bubble wrap under water. The amount of blood was astonishing, not as bad as his scream, but I knew that was coming. I got out the torch out and cauterize the two fingers to keep him from bleeding out before the fun was over.

I gave Frank a bit of a rest and went back to the table to retrieve a three-pound sledge and headed back. "So, buddy, you still think you were showing those kids love, or are you still living in the world of delusion?"

Would you believe it, instead of small talk or anything near admittance of what he had done, he looked me right in the eyes and said, "FUCK YOU!!"

"Ahh," I said, is that what that expensive law school education taught you?" So, I took my finger and thumped one of his recently departed finger stubs. Just to set the mood really. Then in a swift motion I brought the sledge down on his other hand. This time he didn't make a noise. Rather, he made a squeal mixed with a groan or something like that anyway. No matter what it sounded like even an idiot could tell it was a sound of excruciating pain. "Oh damn! Now I know that had to hurt," I said to him, laughing out loud. I thought to myself that I really should not like it as much as I did, but nevertheless, I did. I especially took enjoyment as I thought of the pain that those children must have felt at the hands of that monster.

I then moved to his lower extremities and hacked off a toe with a rusty old steak knife I had found. I will admit that it turned my stomach a bit. The knife was not at all what you would call sharp, so it took a bit of sawing to remove the toe. By that time, Frank was past the weeping and had moved to all out screaming and carrying on. I punched him in the twig and berries again. Why, you might ask? The answer to that would be, because I could. Now, that there is a part of the body I never get tired of striking, It looks like it hurts like hell every time it gets struck, so that is the one place I continue to strike.

I asked Frank, "So, is what you give those children still love? What's the matter Frank? Cat got your tongue?" I allowed a laugh to escape my mouth. 'I is way too easy,' I thought to myself. "Frank!!" I said a little louder. "If you don't answer me, the cat having your tongue will be a blessing you sorry excuse for a human skin sack. I'll pull that little child molesting tongue out of your cock sucker, Frankie boy."

He looked at me and shook his head and actually said, "You will never understand."

I looked at him and said, "I don't ever want to understand, you sick-o." Realizing I would not make any headway with this tard-ass, I took my sledge and struck him in the side of his head near his temple. His head slumped, and that was it.

Now, I know you may be saying, how did someone with all that anger built up be able to do the things I did and only take off a few fingers and toes and just end it with a swift blow to the head. Well, I can say that thinking about doing those atrocities and actually doing them are two completely different monsters. Given the fact that I actually was able to kill him in the end was the clincher for me. Becoming more creative in my work was something only time could change. Have no doubt, it is not as easy as one may think, regardless of how pissed off you may be, besides, I ws new at it so give me a break. I did know that there was more to come. So, stick with me, it does get better. Well, better as I see it. LOL.

CHAPTER 3

Getting rid of a body is a whole different matter; that's something you have to put a lot of thought into. You have to do it in a way that gets rid of both the body and any and all evidence that you may have left behind. I have no intention of going to prison, AT ALL!!

I mean after all, it's not like you can throw it away. Well, I guess you could, but you risk giving away your location by revealing any number of things. For example, the disposal site can give the police an idea of where you are and where you may be coming from. Lots of criminals work in what is called a comfort zone—a place where, as it implies, is a place that the criminal feels comfortable. I have no comfort zone. I live around a conglomeration of large cities and am not afraid of leaving said area to take care of my personal vendetta against the criminals I target. Does this make it impossible for me to be captured? Hell no, it doesn't. I will say I plan on staying free for a good long time however. Prudent planning and carful disposal will help me in this, I hope.

My plan to rid the world of the remains of my victims is very important, and in my opinion, a good one.

1. Remove the limbs
2. Place limbs, torso, and head in a chemical bath of Hydrofluoric or Phosphoric acid or use lye and water, bringing it up to a proper temperature (approximately 300 degrees Fahrenheit.) This will effectively break down the body and bones into sludge.
3. Strain the sludge into a fluid, removing all other pieces.
4. Collect any remaining pieces, such as teeth and some undissolved bone.
5. Grind up all solid pieces into a powder.
6. Dispose of the powder and sludge in a place not to be discussed. Sorry y'all, but I am still doing this thing and would rather not give anyone any ideas beyond this. The short and skinny of it is, with a little forethought disposing of a body is a real possibility.

Never dispose of all the remains in the same place. I love reading cases of serial murders where the killer places the bodies or body parts around themselves or even in some cases under their house or kept as trophies of their kills in their homes. Dumb Asses. There have been many disposal methods in the past. For example: burying parts of or the whole body in the woods or in any number of places. This can be affective as long as you know it will never be found. This means deep, deep, deep in the ground, and again never near where you reside. Shallow graves can and will be discovered, so you may as well leave your contact info so the cops can collect you when the body is discovered. Then there is the grinding and feeding them to animals thing, except for that whole DNA thing. Oops, busted.

Don't get me wrong, I'm not saying my way is the best, just that it leaves nothing left for anyone to wonder about if done in the right way. Maybe DNA but that's it. In saying this, you for sure don't want any of the disposal method to get on you. It can easily eat your body just as fast as the victims. It would be hard to tell the cops you're innocent when you have acid burns on your skin. As a chemical engineer, I have worked with all sorts of chemicals and know very well what they can do. If all else fails and the whole disposal method I speak of doesn't work or takes too much time, then I will change my game. There are all kinds of methods of disposing of a body that can be done right as long as you take the time to do so the right way.

All in all, I would say that my first kill went well. As sick and twisted as that sounds, it's true. What may be more disturbing is the fact that I am anticipating the kill. I do not believe I will deviate from my vigilante style of killing; I have no desire to take the life of an innocent—AT ALL. However, I cannot wait till my next kill. Whether or not it is because deep down I am just as bad as those I hunt or because I take great pleasure knowing that I am removing a certain person or persons from society that truly do not need to be here, I don't know. It may be an uphill climb, but I will try my damnedest to rid the world of pond scum left floating on the surface of our lives. Left to their own means, they carry on their nasty deeds on society with

CHAPTER 4

s you can imagine, not all crimes are committed by men. There are plenty of women that do some less than admirable things. One of those things is in fact murder hidden under the guise of post-partum depression. Now, I am not saying that, in fact, there is no such thing as PPD as I will refer to it. It's just that, when a disease is used for a criminal to either get a lesser sentence or to put said criminal in a hospital to rehabilitate them, there are a line of criminals just waiting to use it to their advantage.

One such case is that of a woman whose little boy went missing and was later found dead. It turns out that the mother was, hmmm, a slut. Yes, that is the word I am looking for. In fact, the mom was out doing her fuck me dance and drinking while her little boy was at home alone and ended up getting into some cleaning supplies. He died from ingesting the aforementioned cleaners. When the mother came home and found her boy dead, she swiftly put him in the trunk of her car and disposed of the body, fearing that she would get into trouble for letting her little boy die. A valid fear and she should have indeed been in trouble. The story and truth behind it all finally came out, and she was charged with child neglect and sent to a rehab to help her with her drinking problem. As they say while texting, LMFAO (laughing my fucking ass off). Yea, that will help her all right.

I looked into the case and found out where the woman was living and began to observe her. I wanted to see if she had indeed learned from her mistakes… I am all for the human beings' ability to rehabilitate and make themselves better and be a productive member of society. It just so happens, that it doesn't happen all that often.

Side by side, I believe that a woman can be far more vicious and deceitful than men can even dream. Sure, guys can be super fucked up, but we generally wear pure screwiness on the outside. Well, most of us anyway. There are those really mentally fucked up individuals that are master manipulators, but they are in a league of their own.

For example: unless your gay—a man walking up to another man and flirting with him—there are a few things that will take place. One: you get your ass kicked, two: you manage to be a lucky fella, and you found a gay man who welcomes the flirt, or three: you get yelled at and told to get the fuck away from me, or you may get your ass kicked. I see a pattern forming.

Now on the other hand, a woman could walk up to a man and within a few deft moves, touches, flirts, etc. can have the man in bed. Or, with the promise of something great, she can lead said fella just about anywhere she pleases. Oh, and please guys don't say, yeah right. Both you and I know we think with our dicks most of the time, except for when we are eating. Unless we are eating with a woman, then we will probably think about the sex that may come after the meal. Lol.

You see a woman can be like a real good fishing lure if the fish are guys, well now days I guess they can be men also. But anyway, women—unlike men—can simply lure their victims to where they need to be to do what they intend to do. Unless the guy is like Ted Bundy and have a way with women; that just makes them all hot and bothered and willing to do whatever, whereas men have to usually resort to violence or some other such means.

There are benefits to living in a big city; the main benefit is, they are a target rich environments. I started the observation stage of my little game as always. Observe, note any regularities that may lead to a pattern, and then plan the takedown. Some of you may be wondering how I can do my observations and other things in my trade and stay unsuspected. That is a very easy question; I don't change much. I go to work; whether I get there or not is a whole other thing. I go home at night and spend time with my family and then repeat. If I need to work some night hours, then I plan a business trip. As a chemical engineer at my fathers' company things are a little easier. However, in my professional trade we work weird hours anyway. If we get on a project that requires tons of hour to see through to the end, then I am all but never home anyway. So, as you can see, I have an almost natural camouflage for my little side business.

As I was saying about my new victim, she is a real study in freaky. I would say nut fuck crazy, one tit short of a great rack maybe, or any number of cool crazy saying that you may want to use. My first day of following little miss crazy, I saw her peruse the gambit of drug houses, bars, and various other less than reputable establishments. I even watched her blow some dude in an ally for no other reason than it looked as though she wanted too. Can't lie; I did get a little rise in my Levi's. What? I'm still a guy. It's kind of like a live porno.

Anyway, the way she was servicing this guy made me bet she could suck start a Harley if she put her mind to it. Hell, for that matter, I was wondering if she was going to suck the guy's eyes out of his head, not a terrible way to go I suppose. The man groaned, a groan of pure satisfaction, mind you, no missing eyeballs via the man straw. I watched little miss crazy stand up wipe her mouth and knees and walk off. Un-fucking believable, but wait…

The second day was better. As Jill and I were talking I said, "I have to go out of town for a couple days, but I will let you know when I will be home. We can go out and grab a bite to eat at that New Greek restaurant."

She said, "Do you need anything packed in specific?"

"No, I'll just grab an overnight bag and call it good," I said.

Jill came over and gave me a kiss and said, "Be sure to say by to the kids."

"Will do," I said and walked up stairs to pack.

Going out of town is not unusual for me; whether a conference or a continuing education event, it's never very long. I packed my bag and stopped in to say goodbye to the kids.

"Hey guys", I said. "I have to go out of town 'til tomorrow evening. Make sure you help your mom with whatever she needs, and get your homework done also."

"OK dad," they said in unison.

It goes without saying that my wife is one hell of a woman. Some people may wonder how I can love someone and care for anything and then go out and do the things that I do. That is an easy one. When I kill the scum that I do, in my mind I have absolutely no thoughts on the matter at all. To me, taking these people out of society so that they cannot harm anyone else is nothing more than taking out the trash at my house so that it doesn't stink up the place. As I said earlier, the day that I decided to do what I am doing, something just snapped. I no longer had any feeling for the people that I was taking out of this world.

On my second night of following little miss 'fuck me cause I want you to', my interest was piqued. I watched her talking to someone at a house I assume was her new place of residence, or at a minimum, a place she frequented often given the laidback manner in which she held herself and acted around others. She was talking to a man that I would say was just slightly older than her, acting chummy as though she had not a care in the world. Little miss 'you want me and you know it' stayed at the place for around an hour and then she was off.

'Oh boy this ought to be good,' I thought to myself. Given the fact that it was Friday night and she was on the prowl, only the Lord himself knew what she would get up to, but I was going to find out. No matter how long this night would take, I was going to get to know this lady and how I might get close to her and remove her from society. Of course, there was one way. I could always just pull out my johnson and say, "Hey good looking, you hungry." Laughing a little to myself I thought about it and decided that whatever STD (sexually transmitted disease) she may or may not have could probably jump right off her and on to me.

So, little miss wanna-be free internet porn star be bopped her way from place to place doing and/or getting whatever it was that she needed through the day even pausing for a time to nap, yes, nap, under a tree in a park. She acted as though nothing bothered her, not a care in the world. As the sun went down, we moved to the downtown scene. "And the fun begins," I said to myself as she made her way into the first club. I could only imagine the show I was in for tonight given the show I saw last night.

It has always amazed me how some people can act as though nothing they have done has affected them in the least at all. The woman I was watching was obviously one of those people. She acted as though the death of her son had freed her more than it hurt her. In my mind anyway, the difference between what I am doing and the things my victims have done, while equally horrific, can be said is, I am removing a drain on society. In doing this, I am stopping another crime from being perpetrated by said individual.

So, little miss hot to trot let them all in my twat was a study in absolute party animal perfection. I could see where a child would get in the way of her lifestyle. She had no time to be a social butterfly, no wait—butterfly slut nugget—and raise a child at the same time. The nighttime events got kicked off with a bang. The first club was so-so, however, it did not take long to see my living blow-up doll start her thing. Between her insatiable appetite for booze and dancing, I also saw she is a firm believer in casual sex. Wait, not casual sex, liked sex in general. I say 'just sex', because she fucks like the energizer bunny on steroids. This walking sex machine drops her pants anywhere, anytime, and as near as I can tell, for anyone. She is like a walking porn expo. She has sex and the pursuit of sex down to a fine art.

One such case was her walking up to a guy and dancing with him. I am pretty sure she lipped to him, as she rubbed her hand from his sack to his bellybutton, "Do you want to put that there thing in this here thing?" pointing to her already half bared vaginal area. I would have been disappointed if the guy said, "sorry, not on the first date." However, give it up for the reliability of the male species. His head bobbed up and down like a dog waiting for a bone that was being waved in front of its face. With the menial formalities out of the way, she dropped her pants. It's no surprise she had no under clothes on. They began to kiss as she undid his pants and he began to finger her. Oh yea, might I add this is all taking place in front of God and everyone, in the middle of the dance floor. When she felt he was properly aroused she told him to pick her up, and in doing, so she slid him into position and had herself lowered onto him. Well that's one way to do it, I thought to myself.

Apparently, he was not the only lucky guy this night. Dropping the last guy like a bad habit, little miss holy hot crouch disappeared into the bathroom for a few minutes and then to the bar where she had a drink, and I assume a small rest, before her next escapade into sexual voyeurism began. She did not disappoint, in fact, she hit the floor running.

While she was at the bar, she must have found her next play toy to please her. She went up to the man and with a deft move, flung the petite thing hanging on him off and out of the way. Something was said between the two and they began to dance, the aforementioned petite thing forgotten as if she never existed. The beat went faster and so did their dancing and what can only be described as foreplay. They began to kiss, and the sexual escapades stepped up a bit. By a bit, I mean the kissing began along with the groping. Her hands went down the front of his pants and started moving up and down in an all too familiar motion. Judging by the way his face was contorting, she was doing something right. The kissing got more passionate and down went the pants. She wiggled out of her clothing, and he spun her around and entered her. The thumping music set the scene for the sexual escapades. He thrust into her over and over again as she threw her head back. When he drew back, she bent forward in anticipation of him filling her up once more with all he had. When both parties had climaxed, he withdrew and she re-clothed, kissed him and was gone.

"Well fuck me," I thought. Where was she when my hormones where raging. The night went like that for what seemed like an eternity. Drinking, dancing, fucking, and not always in that order. As the weekend went on, I was about one hundred percent positive that if her liver didn't give out from the booze, her guts may fall out of her vagina due to lack of its ability to stay in her body. I was sure, however, I had a plan of attack for this victim. I will admit however, after watching all that sex, it was impossible to keep it out of my bedroom. At the very least, the wife and I made love like we were teenagers again.

"Well," Jill said, as we rolled off one another and lay they're breathing hard and sweating up a storm, "that was something else."

"Yes, it was." Were the only words I could say.

We were both wondering where we got the energy to do it. I looked at Jill and she looked at me and we both said, "Who fucking cares," and went at it again.

The next day, I went to work 'til around 2:00 and went out to track down our little sexual firecracker. As I figured, it wasn't very hard—oh people and their patterns. I found her at the house I had spotted her at before. Deciding I was still a bit tired from the vigorous sex with the wife and the late nights the last weekend, I would just swing by the house the next couple of days and see if, indeed, it was really going to be this easy. Then I went home to spend some time with the family and get ready for the weekend ahead. She did not disappoint; she was there every afternoon when I went by. If I hadn't been planning on putting our little walking STD out to pasture, I am relatively sure she would have died of AIDS or some other unnatural death. I decided that this weekend would be the weekend I would take out this little vixen. There will be blood, lots and lots of blood. Little miss she devil was about to meet the real devil. ME!!

When the weekend came upon me, I decided her days of mayhem and partying were over. Her biggest mistake was choosing lifestyle over the care and upbringing of her own child. I set things up so that there was an event to attend that would take me out of town that weekend.

"Hey Jill, is there anything you want while I am out of town?" I asked my wife. "Anything special or something that you can't find or get here?"

"I am about out of that perfume that you get me if you can find me some of that," she said. I said I would look, then said my goodbyes to her and the kids.

I took my car to a paid lot and walked to where I was hoping my little miss can't keep her pants on would be that night. I was rewarded with a very short wait. She came into the club wearing a skirt that was not much more than a cloth napkin wrapped around her waist. My guess was the only reason that she had any clothes on at all was because she had to have something on. As much as I despised this chick, remembering the times I had observed her and her overabundance of sexuality I could not keep a small stirring from happening in my own pants. If I hadn't been married and loved my wife, the way I did I am sure I would have had some fun with her before I turned out her lights for good.

I let her get her drink and watched her do her rounds seeking out her next romp. I stared at her the whole time and our eyes meet a few times—sewing the seed, one might say. That last time our eyes meet I saw that my crops would be plentiful.

I made my way onto the dance floor and worked my way to my new plaything. "Well hello there," I said.

"Hello yourself," she said, looking me up and down as if she were appraising a piece of art.

"Like what you see?" I asked.

"Indeed I do," she said.

We started to dance and rub up against each other. Even though I hated everything about what I was doing and tried to think of only my wife, I got a raging erection. She apparently noticed.

"Looks like someone wants to come out and play," she said.

"Oh, he very much does, but he likes to play rough," I said.

"Do you think you can handle a good working over?" I asked.

She looked up at me and said, "The real question is, can you handle me?"

I was fairly sure, given the opportunity, she could get a gay man to convert to a heterosexual. Not only that, but she could get him to deliver where, when, and how much or as often as she deemed necessary. While observing her in the last few weeks, I noticed that it looked like she was rough and demanding on her mates. This was not the case, not even a little.

As we danced, the sultry way she did everything was as if it were right out of one of those harlequin novels. She would whisper things in my ear about what she wanted me to do to her, and I began to wonder if I would mess myself right there on the dance floor. She told me how she would slide me in her and ride me nice and be slow bringing me to the limits of my sexual tolerance before slowing down and starting all over again. If I wanted, she was even willing to do anal if that is what pleased me. You always hear about how guys are all horn dogs and that is all that we think about all the time. Well boys, this woman makes even the horniest of men pale in comparison. She wanted me to use her like my own personal sex doll—do as I please for as long as I care to. Like a hippy in a pot field, I got a grin from ear to ear.

"Let's go," she said. Then she grabbed me by my raging manhood and led me away like a dog on a leash. We ended up in the lot in a dark corner between some cars, and she had her hands down my pants before I could even react.

The warmth of her hand on me stroking in such a sensual way was so perfect and overwhelming it took everything I could do to not cum right then and there. I guess there is something to be said about 'practice makes perfect'. I moaned and realized she was heading downhill, as I had no intention of cheating on my wife, I did have to play the part to a certain extent. Realizing what she was about to do and knowing how many other men's Johnson's had been there, I was not letting her get a hold of me with that mouth. You know, there are a lot of places that I am not willing to put my dick. For example: meat grinder, any acidic solutions, bears mouth, but definitely not the toilet that she calls a mouth.

Now if my cock had a brain, it would for sure be less than impressed with my next decision. After all, I wasn't here to get laid, however, I do feel for my wife, whom I am sure will be on the receiving end of this particular need for sexual release. As she started to unzip my pants and release the beast, or should I say eat the beast, as observed in the past, I clocked her upside her head and she dropped like a sack of potatoes. I sighed, as well as my manhood probably did, and drug her to my old beat up pick up that I used for my little garbage transfer and disposal vehicle.

CHAPTER 5

I have this little place in the middle of nowhere that I take my victims. It's an old shack on some private property, heavily wooded and impossible to see from the air or road. This is where I take my victims and teach them the real meaning of punishment.

When the little devil girl woke up, she found herself tied to a chair and completely immobile. As with most people that find themselves in an unfamiliar place bound and unable to move, she began to struggle, cry, and wonder what the hell was going on. I let her do this for a while and finally said, "You know you are really getting on my nerves with all that carrying and completely useless struggling?"

She looked at me, and yes as you can guess, she asked what everyone would think she would ask, "Why?"

"Really?" I asked. "Can you, by any chance, stagger a guess as to the why of this whole scenario? Or is it just the mind of idiots that you all are incapable of the simple concept that actions have consequences?" She looked at me with that 'duh, who me' look. I just shook my head and said, "Yea, that's what I thought. Well, let me explain it to you." I said to her, "You see, it goes a little like this, you like to fuck, and sometimes when people fuck, they make little people. Just in case this doesn't quite ring a bell, the rest of population calls them children. Ringing any bells yet?"

She continued to stare at me like I had something stuck in my teeth. "Didn't think so. That pussy of yours seems to work well, however, you seem to come up a few cans short of a six pack in the brain department."

Still looking a bit befuddled, she says, "I thought you liked me?"

Ok, now it was my turn to look dumbfounded. "Let me get this right, and by all means please correct me if I am wrong. You are sitting here bound, naked and probably not in a position that is looking very good for you, and all you have to say is, I thought you liked me? Am I missing anything here?" I said all this with a bit, no that's not the right word, a shitload of 'are you fucking with me' laced in my voice.

The waterworks came on and I looked at her and wondered if she really was fucked in the head or just screwing with me in order to see if I might let her live. When I laughed at her and said, "Is it really possible for someone as good looking as you to be as fucking stupid as you are?" I was rewarded with the real she-devil slut mouth that I knew she had in her. All pretenses of 'poor little me' and 'oh I thought you liked me' flew out the door like a person with a case of the water ass.

"You mother fucker. If I get out of here, I will chop your balls off and feed them to you right after I stick them up your ass."

"Well now, there you are my sweet, and such beautiful mouth you have to my dear," I said. "Guess that mouth of yours can do something more than suck cock." I said this with a great big smile on my face. Then I looked at her and said, "You do know that you are in no real position to make threats, right?" Just to get the point across I took out a small blade and made a few well-placed cuts on her arm before burying the blade in her thigh. "Now that we have established who is really in charge here, care to fathom a guess as to why you are here?"

Of course, as always, the look of shock and disbelief on her face was priceless. She may only be my second, but I had a sneaky feeling that that look was never going to get old no matter how many times I witnessed it.

"So, to be clear, you do still remember your child correct? The one that you put your overwhelming desire to having your pussy filled in front of, instead of just staying home and caring for?" I said to her, looking right in her eyes to drive home the point which I was trying to make. She looked up at me and just spat at me. "I will take that as a yes. Any chance you'd like to plead your case to me? Not that it would really do any good, but I am a good listener. While I will listen and try to understand, the end result is still going to be the same. However, it may help to clear your conscience."

With a smart-ass look and tone, she said to me "Oh yeah? And what might your so-called result be?"

Without hesitation I said, "DEATH." That seemed to catch her attention.

"Death?" she said.

"I didn't stutter," I said. "The only thing explaining your actions will do for you is reduce the amount of pain that is involved in the process."

She just smiled at me and said, "You don't have it in you. You are nothing more than another man that is all talk and no action, except that of which you can use your cock to perform."

I laughed a little before saying, "Somebody has some man issues. I can assure you that if you tell me who it was that fucked you up so bad, I give you my word that I will also kill that person. I assure you little miss thing, my 'cock', while it does fine on its own, is hardly all I am capable of using in a fashion that may or may not determine what I may or may not be capable of. Just so we are very clear on this matter I will give you an example." I selected a framing hammer and one fast motion I brought it down hard onto her kneecap. Satisfied with the crunch it made and the scream that came bounding from her mouth, I was sure that at a bare minimum she had to be at least thinking I was serious. She then passed out.

When she started to stir again, I said, "Welcome back. Any chance you would like to rethink what I may or may not be able to do?" To my surprise she nodded her head a little bit. "Well now that's good," I said. "Please think carefully before you answer this next question? Why did you let your child die instead of staying home and caring for him?"

With a whimper she began to speak, "He was not supposed to be born, for that matter even conceived. I have a problem with sex."

I snickered and said, "A problem is not an accurate definition of what you have lady."

"I know" she said, tears beginning to fall from her eyes.

I wasn't sure right at that moment, but I did have a feeling that I was about to hear a story about her being abused as a child repeatedly until all she knew about love is that it came in the form of sex. True to form, that is exactly what came spewing out of her. While I do sympathize with this and have no idea how damaging it may be, in my book this is no reason to destroy, by means of neglect, another young person's life—especially if that young person is your own son or daughter. While she was carrying on about how bad she had it, I took notice of the leg wound I gave her. The wound was flowing a little too fast and I thought I must have knicked an artery with a bone fragment or something.

"Well shit", I thought. Little miss mobile porn show is going to get off way too easy if she bleeds out. So, I grabbed some salt and poured into the wound. This stopped her 'pity me' story quickly, if for no other reason than it is terribly hard to talk and scream at the same time. "Oops," I said to her. "Does that hurt? Cause it sure in hell looks and sounds like it does." Laughing as she screamed, I wondered if I was actually enjoying this. She yelled so loud I thought that she would tear her vocal cords apart when I smashed her other knee.

"So, have you had enough?" I asked her. "Are you ready to end this by saying you are sorry for what you did. While I can forgive you, I can't let you live. I can say that God will forgive you if you ask and mean it."

"Go fuck yourself," she said.

I laughed out loud and said, "You must have taken a fall from the stupid tree and hit every branch on the way down. However, if this is how you want it then so be it." I went to retrieve a pair of hedge trimmers and proceeded to take off a few of those lovely little fingers—the very fingers that not so long ago had a firm grasp on my manhood. I took every other one off and stood there till she passed out. When she came to, I looked at her and said, "Ready for more?"

She stared back at me and said, "Please no, I want to live."

"Oh really," I replied. "You want to live? You know who else wanted to live? Your boy, that's who also wanted to live. Live to become an adult and have children of his own to love and cherish. If, that is, he had survived the upbringing that you would have given. I can only hope that he would have done a better job raising his children than you did in the short time he was alive. You robbed him of the chance to even try to have a family."

She just sat there and let the tears fall as I continued to chastise her. "As it is, he will never even get a chance to try or even see what life has to offer." With a little more feeling I said, "BECAUSE YOU KILLED HIM!!" Feeling as though I had done enough and the very real mental anguish I was going through just thinking of how a mother could completely ignore her child to the point that he ended up dead, I took the knife and slit her throat. Damn, I really have to get that whole anger thing under control. I shrugged my shoulders and said to myself, "oh well."

Satisfied with what I had done, I cleaned up a bit and changed my clothes, turned out the lights and went home. I returned home around one thirty in the morning, took a shower, climbed into bed and went fast to sleep. All thoughts of vigorous sex with my wife had vanished. Yes, I went to sleep. There is a certain amount of satisfaction in doing a deed you believe in. This is why I sleep just fine. The next day I went to the shack and disposed of the body. The stink of the corrosive material and the body being broken down into its disposable goo was getting on my nerves. Not that it was the gruesome event itself, because I knew that what I was doing was, at least in my mind, justified. Not to mention, I think I want to make a statement. I mean, while taking out the trash of humanity is a good thing, where is the deterrent to not commit the crimes if no one knows that there could be deadly retribution for doing the bad things that people do.

I suppose by trying to make a statement, I could end up getting caught. This however, was a chance I would gladly take to get my point across. I would just have to be a lot more careful how I kill and dispose of the bodies. I would need to put them in a place that they could be discovered and somehow have a note, either hand written or carved into the body. I haven't figured out the how just yet. There were going to be some changes however.

I wondered as little miss thing was bleeding out if anything good was going through her head. I was hoping that maybe she was thinking back about her child, alone and dying as she was out partying. Now that the tables had turned, she was the one alone and dying. Eye for an eye, life for a life.

CHAPTER 6

ife—now there is a word. It can have many different meanings I suppose. As I see it, it means to live, starting at birth and ending with death. In that time, a whole lot of shit can go down both good and bad. You can live well, or you can live not so well. I think for the most part, we decide how we do it. God gave us free will, with it we are able to make the decisions we do, either good or bad. If god wanted a bunch of mindless drones, we would have never left the garden. Having free will, we are allowed to make decisions; right or wrong, they are still ours to make. What is a right decision you may ask? Shit, lot of good it does to ask that. If I had to stagger a guess, I would say that it depends on your morals. There is a right and a wrong thing to do in every situation—period.

My life, by all accounts, is normal—well, normal minus the whole murder thing of course. I have a wife and kids, all of whom I love with all my heart. On the outward appearance, I lead a normal life, you know, house, job, family, and bills. My secret life is a little more complicated. How does a person start to do the things I do you may ask? I explained a bit of it earlier in the book, but just so you don't get to thinking along the lines of most serial killers stereotype, I'll break it down a little more.

I did not grow up hurting animals or dreaming of killing people. I had a rather normal life. Grew up with a good deal of money around me, but not spoiled. My folks did not believe in giving us everything just because we wanted it. We had to earn it doing various chores or save any money we may get on birthdays or Christmas. I did, and my parents let me, watch horror movies, which I thought where quite amusing. My parents, however, always taught me that it was not real, and that there is a line between real and not real, so keep it straight. Keep a good head on your shoulders, and make wise decisions. Be fair, but always true to what you believe.

Growing up with money gave me the opportunity to experience life. My family did and saw all kinds of things, from rock climbing to skiing and travel. Having access to what the world had to offer is a helpful tool to get invested in life and all it has to offer. One of the most memorable experiences of my life was a trip to a science museum that had all kinds of hands on activities. One such activity was simple. You added baking soda and vinegar in paper-maché volcano mock up. The reaction that took place between the two materials with each other absolutely fascinated me. So, I took an interest in the sciences.

School for me was never hard, yeah, yeah, I was one of those people that never seemed to pay attention, but still made good grades. I was active in sports and dated the same girl throughout school and even college where I received my PHD in chemical engineering and she her MD. Now, I know you all may say that shit doesn't really happen in the real world, yeah well, maybe not in your world, but it did in mine. College was made easier, I believe, due to the fact I was dating my, to be wife. You may ask, "Why would that make it easier?" The answer is really quite simple. I could spend time studying instead of chasing all that scattered ass.

My brother on the other hand was a textbook story of what most people thought college life might be like. Beer stands, keg parties, half naked co-eds and lots and lots of sex—if didn't know better, I would have thought my brother found a class on how to be in and succeed in the porn industry. I also believe that it was his personal goal to hit every piece of ass on the female roster, student and teacher alike. How the hell the word slut only managed to stick to the female side of our society is beyond me. By all accounts, my brother was a male slut, through and through.

If you're not familiar with what a chemical engineer does, I'll tell you. As described by Wikipedia, a Chemical Engineer is a branch of engineering that applies physical sciences (physics and chemistry) and life sciences (microbiology and biochemistry) together, with applied mathematics and economics to reduce, transform, transport, and properly use chemicals, raw materials, living cells, microorganisms and energy into useful forms and products.

Both my wife and I make good money and love what we do. If you were to look at us on any given day, you might see what you would in any household. We get up in the morning and get kids ready for school, eat breakfast, and head our separate ways. As I said before, my job only takes me out of town from time to time and Jill, my wife, works in private practice, having a regular schedule minus the occasional emergency. So all in all, we live a normal life, or at least normal as I see it.

As for the whole murder thing, I can't tell you what you want to hear. The only thing that drove me to do what I do was the injustice, as I interpret it, and a strong desire to right a wrong. The judicial system was running ramped with all the laws, and laws for the laws and the bylaws for the laws, that keep the laws ....fuck, now I don't even now, how to explain it. I, on the other hand, as I have said before, am an eye for an eye type in absence of a functioning law system. The PC (politically correct) ass hats might say that you can't do anything that might be cruel and unusual to someone that has committed a crime. Fuck all that. With crime comes punishment; this is not a hard concept to grasp. You do something wrong you pay for it; you do not get off on a technicality like throwing out evidence because someone didn't submit it in a timely manner. If there is evidence that is not tampered with, USE

IT. All you lawyers just stay the fuck out of the conversation please. No offense, but this is my book.

The way I see it, if I can take some of those weirdo freaks off the street before they can repeat their atrocious crimes on another person, well then yippee for society and me. I decided to take a few weeks off to rehash how to proceed with my plans. I also wanted to keep things looking as normal as possible. You know, home, work, home, work, and home again. I sought out and attended some out of town educational charity work to give me an excuse to continue my extracurricular hobby when I resumed. I rolled through the sex offender's list and the newspapers, online of course. Does anyone even get paper news anymore?

I decided to do some research on the two people that I had dealt with. Ok fine—the two that I had killed, are you happy now? My victims if you may. Laughing my ass off, I think, in order to be victim, wouldn't there first have to be the implication that they were innocent in the first place, and innocent they certainly where not.

The woman was mentioned nowhere. As for Mr. child molester, as expected, Melissa did not only inquire on him, but also filed a missing persons' report when he failed to show up and could not be contacted. Where this lead was detectives visiting her and asking the normal questions that the police might ask.

"So how long has he been gone?" asked the first detective.

His partner asked, "Was there anyone that may have wished him harm?"

To this Melissa replied, "To my knowledge, no one would have cause to hurt him. He was a contractual lawyer, not a criminal lawyer."

The detectives both shook their heads and wrote down what she had said. "You know," Melissa said, "some time ago there was an email sent to me about how Frank was a convicted child molester. I never put too much stock in its being true and dismissed it as a really bad prank."

One of the detectives asked, "Do you still have that email?"

"As a matter of fact, I do," she said. "I kept it just in case there was some continued harassment, so I could use it as evidence."

His partner asked, "May we see it?"

"One moment," Melissa said. She retrieved the email and printed off a copy for the detectives.

"Thank you." They wrapped up their interview and left.

Melissa came over one evening, and we could tell that she had been crying. We invited her in asked what was wrong. As I sat there and listened to Melissa recount the story of the detectives visit, Jill and I looked at each other and then back to Melissa.

"So, they ran his prints to verify if what the email said was true?" I asked her.

Jill turned to her almost as if on cue and asked, "So, what you're saying is, when the prints came back, it showed that he had been convicted of actually molesting a child?"

With new tears forming in her eyes, Melissa said, "Two children to be exact. I think he may have been targeting my children. Oh my god, my kids." Jill held her as she cried.

"Why wasn't he in jail then?" I asked.

Melissa looked at me and said, "He cut some kind of deal or something. I'm not sure, it's all kind of blurry after I heard the news of the conviction and then thinking that my kids could have been his next victims." The tears came again as my wife and I made eye contact, and without even needing to do or say anything, we both knew right then and there, sending that email was a damn good idea.

After Melissa collected herself and we talked a while, she said, "Before I left the police station they asked if I had any interest in perusing the missing persons' report."

"I can guess the answer to that one." Jill said.

"I'm sure you can," Melissa said. "I told them that I didn't care if he was ever found, and if so, there is no need to let me know."

After Melissa left, the house got quiet. With the kids in bed and Melissa and I were in our room, I said, "I wonder if they will ever find him."

Jill looked at me and said, "I hope the worthless bastard is dead and rotting in a ditch somewhere."

I smiled to myself inside and thought, 'dead? Yes. Rotting somewhere? Nothing to rot when it's no more than a pool if goo.' Right then and there I was convinced that what I was doing was a good thing. Regardless of the outcome for me, the more people that I could remove from this world that has the intent to do harm to others, the better for the world.

Now comes the real thought on how to do what I do and not get caught. The only way that I could keep doing what I was doing was to think hard and plan every move fully and precisely. After seeing the way Melissa reacted the news that her fiancé was a convicted sexual predator, and the fact that she neither wanted to know nor cared if he was found, it showed me that I was doing something good. I would find a way to communicate to all persons of ill repute that there would be consequences for actions, and if you do get convicted of a crime, you had better go ahead and take the sentence given to you and not try to wiggle your way out of it. You never know when and where I may be watching from. But always remember, if you do strike a deal or manage to get away with what you have done, don't be shocked if one day you wake up tied to a chair in a dark place wondering where you are.

❖

CHAPTER 7

fter a few months had past, I was almost ready to go crazy. Either I never really noticed how much shit there was going on in the world, or as I suspect, we just don't think about it much. We put it out of our minds or just ignore it until it happens to us or someone we know or care for. Well no more!!! It has happened to someone I care for. Even if that someone was only a friend; she was still someone I cared for. Even if I didn't care for Melissa as a loved one, those kids were enough for me to take the actions that I did and will continue to do till the day I die or get arrested.

As I was planning my next kill, the excitement overtook me. Jill and I had always had a fantastic sex life. Always eager to explore each other's bodies and find new ways to please each other, tonight was no different, except I was full of energy and not knowing why. Maybe it was the thrill of my returning to my vigilante hobby, I hope, or I really was a sick bastard that got off on the kill itself. I was really hoping that it was the former and not the latter.

As always, the sex was awesome. The way she can make my body go into spasms of sheer sexual pleasure with only her tongue and lips as she pleases me orally is really indescribable. If I had to use a word, that word would be

BLISS. I returned the favor by teasing her with my tongue. I found her clit and vigorously massage it with my tongue, until she clamped onto my head with her thighs and nearly broke my neck —my face flooded with her orgasm. We then took turns pleasing each other in whatever position or positions that we felt like trying until we orgasm and roll off the bed sweating and gasping for breath, the room smelling like sex.

As I ramp up the search for my next target, I peruse the sex offender lists and the police blotters and public records for anything of interest. I really have no real problem with drugs, or at least, not with adults doing them. The way I look at it, if you want to put that rotgut shit in your body, go for it. I do, however, have a huge fucking problem with people pushing and selling them to kids. Let the kids grow and make stupid mistakes all on their own. Don't get them hooked before they ever get a chance to live life. That being said, I decided that my next target would be a drug dealer and anyone that is affiliated with him. A monumental task I am sure, but a task I will gladly take on if I find one that is supplying to kids.

I thought about how I should go about finding someone that will fit the description of what I was looking for. I sat back and pondered this for some time. The more I thought about it the more I realized that I had never really been around the drug seen and have no idea how to go about finding out who sells the stuff, let alone who is doing the supplying. Then, like a clap of lightening that comes from nowhere it hit me—little miss hot pants. Yes, yes, yes! The house I always saw her at when she wasn't at her home and always before she went out to party. I made plans the best I could to try to infiltrate the place and carry out my plans.

Not really knowing how to 'infiltrate' a drug house, I took the best course of action that I could. God I love Google and the internet. The amount of shit you can find online is staggering—everything from past arrests to how the busts went down. Yes, I realize that not everything on the internet is true, but I will have to take the good with the bad and try to come out in the middle with a half assed good plan, after about two hundred episodes of everything from Law and Order to NCIS. Not to mention. you would be surprised the shit you can learn from documentaries and so on. Hell, I think I eye guzzled the H and B of HBO in one day.

As far as I am concerned, drug dealers and gang leaders are all the same. While my dislike for gang leaders is rather strong, I really hate drug dealers. There is something about a person that is willing to watch a kid buy drugs from them and then use them in the hopes that they will become addicted and become a regular user for no other reason than to profit off that person's habit.

Anyway, sorry for the rant, sometimes I get carried away. I got on line and perused the public records, from a public venue of course—no reason to give the authorities a trail to follow if I ever make a mistake and they need a way to track me. While butt sex may be something that gay men enjoy, I do not, at this time, see that in my life, but it would probably be ever present if I were to get arrested and sent to prison.

The little experiment that I was putting together turned out to be far easier than I was expecting. In only a few short hours, I located the house where my little she-devil victim was frequenting. A little more time on the computer and I found out who owned it, and after a brief search online, I found a picture of the man. Wouldn't you know it, the same guy I saw my 'I would love you to love me' talking to, just so happens to be the owner of the house and oh my, what a police record he doth have. With that amount of arrests and some of them leading to a very small amount of jail time for drug use and distributing, it is pretty safe to say he is definitely a dealer.

As always, I did my homework. I drove around some of the known flop houses and junky hang outs to get an idea of what I may need to blend into—the fuck up crowd of misfits and habitual users. Not a lot work is needed to dress up and fit in. Basically, you have to not bathe for a while, chew on your lips a bit and have an overwhelming smell that resembles death warmed over. If you look real close, and this will be the hardest one to fake is the look of despair, as if everyone that was addicted knew they were and could do nothing to stop it.

I found some old jeans and an old work shirt and drug them behind my car for a bit on a backcountry road. With the clothing good and soiled I put it and ran five miles and got a good sweat going. To my good fortune I saw some stagnant water in a ditch and dove in. Rolling around in the dirt afterward completed my new look. Then, all I had to do was case the house that I planned to take down. Watching the coming and goings of the inhabitants, I got a fair idea of who was there and when they came and went. After some observations, I settled on starting my infiltration the next week.

I told the wife I was going to be working nights for a while, so that I could work with a particular group of chemists on a project that I was interested in. "Probably take a month or so, but I will finish up as soon as possible."

Jill said, "No problem, I am swamped with patient reports anyway."

I slept Monday afternoon and got ready for the first night of whatever this was.

I drove to within a few blocks of the house and parked my car in an inconspicuous place that I scouted out and walked to the house. As I was walking, I noticed how quiet it was—no wind and very little traffic noise. I wondered to myself if that was normal, or if due to the nature of the neighborhood, it was just a good idea to stay inside at night. I walked up to the house and saw some people hanging around. I inquired as to whom I have to speak with for a fix. There was a look of uneasiness on their faces and no one spoke up too fast. I supposed this was the stranger danger side of the habit, the possibility of them thinking I might be a cop never entered my mind.

Someone went inside, and in a few minutes, a big bruiser of human being came out and asked, "What do you want and how do you know about this place?"

I said to King Kong, "Sam told me that you all could take good care of me." The bruiser's name, I found out to be of all things, was Buddy. I believe this to be a name that he himself made up and not his given name.

Buddy looked at me and asked, "If you know Sam and she gave the address to this place then you need to tell me about her, if you fail to do so in a satisfactory manner I will hurt you." He said it in a way that led me to believe something bad indeed would happen. Having seen her naked as I was ending her life made it easy to describe her.
\

I looked at him and said, "First of all I am not a cop, nor am I affiliated with any law enforcement agency. Second, Sam is a skinny little white girly that make members of a gang bang become celibate. Small butterfly on her left butt cheek, and let's not forget that I do believe she could suck start a Harley Davidson."

I looked at Buddy and asked if that was a satisfactory answer—probably not in the right tone, but it was already out.

Buddy looked at me with the beginnings of a smile on his face and says, "Yep that about describes her to a tee." He then began to laugh and said, "Suck start a Harley, now that is a good one." He also said, "Got to watch out for the place you know?"

I nodded my head and said, "I understand."

Buddy showed me into the house and asked me what my favorite poison is.

"Heroin with a side of really good weed, not that ditch stuff, but the best you got, and yes, I can pay for it."

"Right on," Buddy said. "Oh, by the way have you seen Sam lately? She used to be a regular but hasn't been around for a while."

"No," I said. "Not in at least that long, it's almost like she fell off the earth."

"HMM," Buddy replied.

I got my drugs and paid him and went to a corner and pretended to get all fucked up.

Over the next couple of weeks, I observed that Buddy was just a pusher and that the real boss was upstairs and was seldom seen by anyone.

"Hey man," Buddy says one night. "You want to see the bosses ride?" He spoke this with a smile and what looked like a little hero worship.

"Sure," I said.

"Well come on then." He took me outside and around to the garage where I saw an attached carport. There was a vehicle parked there nice and snug as a bug in a rug with its cover on it.

"Wait till you see this," Buddy says.

"I can't wait," I said.

Buddy pulled back the cover and a beautiful black Dodge Challenger '1969', if I had to make a guess, sat staring back at us. Buddy said, "Isn't she a beauty?"

Loving old muscle cars, I replied, "Yes, it is that indeed."

Buddy went on further to say that it was the boss's pride and joy, and the one reason that he did the whole drug thing.

I looked over at buddy and said, "He does all this for a car?"

"Yep," Buddy replied.

"Well shit, I guess that's one way to go get what you need."

"I know right?" Buddy said.

The whole time I was listening to Buddy talk, I just kept thinking that this guy was poisoning all these people for a car. Now I really want to kill this piece of shit. Don't get me wrong, it was a beautiful car and I couldn't give two shits as to how many adults they sold drugs to. The kids however, that was a whole new story. Adults have a choice to do stupid shit, and often times do. Kids are impressionable, 'cool' is a thing to our youth. If you want to fit in with a certain crowd and that crowd happens do drugs, odds are that the youth will do the drugs to fit in and be part of that crowd.

I decided to get in good with Buddy and tried to be a real player in this thing. To what end you may ask? I needed to get close to the boss, so I could end the chapter that he called his business.

Since starting this little venture, I had read a lot of books about serial killers—from the how and a reasonable why, to the actual crimes themselves. In FBI profile books to psychology studies on the criminally insane, the biggest thing I kept seeing were the patterns in all of them. One person may keep a personal possession of the victims; another may keep a body part. It all seemed to depend on the perp (perpetrator) and what his or her twisted likes were. Others yet, may carve something into the body to leave their mark; others still will taunt the police officials. All of these things always lead to the killer's demise or capture. I had no desire to kill just to kill. The people I choose to eliminate are people that are really just a step above pond scum, so I really need no trophies or any nonsensical crap like that. I don't keep a diary or anything else that could, if discovered, lead the authorities back to me. As I have said a few times before, I have NO desire to go to prison.

Over the next couple of weeks, I worked my way into the good graces of the house and asked Buddy, "Any chance I can work a permanent spot here instead of slaving away at the same old nine to five crap?"

Buddy looked quizzically at me and said, "I can ask, but you will have to have a face to face with the boss and prove yourself to him. It will take some time, and you'll have to do whatever he asks regardless of what the task is. You think you're up to that?"

I looked at Buddy with a smile and said, "If it gets me out of the general population of what we all call work, than yes I can. Oh! Buddy, tell the boss that I am pretty handy in a chemistry lab if that helps."

He looked at me and said, "Will do, not sure if that will make a difference, but I will tell him."

"Thanks, man. Oh yea, where's my goodies?" I said to Buddy.

"Right here boss, enjoy," Buddy said with a smile.

The next night Buddy cornered me, "Hey Jack."

"What's up?" I asked.

"The boss wants to meet you, but he wants to get some info from you first, so he can see what he can use you for, if anything," Buddy replied.

"Ask what you want to man." I said.

"Hang on, I have a list—don't want to miss anything the boss wants to hear," He said. "First of all, where do you work and when can you be here, or do you want to be a fulltime night guy?"

"Night guy please," I said.

"Ok, next question is...", Buddy looked at his paper and appeared to not be able to read his own writing.

I of course, took advantage of this moment and poked at him a bit. "Can't read your own writing?" I laughed.

"Shut up," he said.

"Hey man, it's all good. I have a terrible habit of writing so fast that I can't read half of what I write either," I said.

"Yea, same here," He said and we both got good laugh out of it.

"Ok, ok, back to business," Buddy said. "I think I know what this chicken scratch says now." Buddy said with a smile. "I told him you look like you're in good shape, so he wants to know if you want to help me with security."

"Yea, sure," I said.

"Also, he wants to know how 'handy' you are with the whole chemistry thing."

"Took it in high school and college, actually I majored in chemistry. I just dropped out before I got my degree," I said.

"You have brains and you want to hang out here?" Buddy asked, with a puzzled look on his face.

"Fuck yea I do," I said rather animatedly. "The real world of nine to five sucks ass man. I would rather master-bate with sand paper than go back to that shit."

That drew a laugh out of Buddy. "I can only imagine," He said.

"What?" I asked. "Masturbating with sand paper?"

He said laughing, "Oh, fuck no man. You are a real sick son-of-a-bitch you know that?"

"Yep," I said.

"Alright then," Buddy said. "I'll tell the boss and let you know. Oh Yea, this round is on the man." He said and threw me my party powder.

"Sweet man, tell the boss thanks."

"Yea will do," Buddy said as he headed upstairs.

I went home and took a short nap and spent the weekend with the wife and kids and loved every minute of it.

"So how is the project coming?" Jill asked.

I slipped a second and said, "What project?"

Jill looked at me and said, "The one at work goof ball, do you have more than one?"

"Oh, shit, duh," I said. "I have no idea how people can work more than a few months at a time on night shift, it's scrambling my brain."

Jill looked at me and said, "You remember when I was doing my internship and pulling all those hours at the hospital?"

"How the hell could I forget," I said with a smile. "There were days I thought you might fall asleep standing up when you got home."

"I felt like it some days," she said. "Just keep hammering away and it will be over soon.," she said and came over to give me a hug. "Thanks for taking the weekend off to spend with us. I know you have been working hard, but I love the fact that you put all that aside for a few days knowing that every day you don't work may mean another night that you will have to work. Still, here you are with us," she said to me as we embraced.

Almost as if on cue, the kids said, "Ewe, get a room." We all laughed and exchanged playful banter for a bit till we decided to go grab a bite to eat.

We rented some movies and settled in for the evening. I asked the kids how school was treating them.

As kids will do, they both shrugged their shoulders and said, "good, I guess."

"Ah the days of no cares in the world except for food and friends," I said.

When the evening was over, and the kids were heading to bed, Jill and I sat in bed and watched the late edition of our local news and then went to bed ourselves. Yes, I still slept, rather well actually. This may be because I was completely comfortable with what I was doing, or I was just one crazy ass white boy—jury is still out on that one.

CHAPTER 8

nother few weeks passed and Buddy came up to me and said, "The boss wants to see you."

"Cool," I said. "Anything I need to know?" I asked.

"Nah, just be yourself; he's a real cool dude." He said. We walked upstairs and down a hall to a back-room door. Buddy knocked and announced himself, "JT, got the new guy here to see you." \

Form inside the room I heard someone—the someone I assumed to be JT said, "Yea Buddy, bring him on in."

What I saw as I laid eyes on the dealer was not what I was expecting a dealer to be. In front of me stood a regular looking white guy. By regular, I mean the man would not be able to be picked out of a crowd on the street on any given day in any city you might visit. Oh yeah, anyone out there that had the 'bet you would have thought it was a black guy' shit racing through your head, knock it off. I could give two shits what color of skin a bad guy has.

Anyway, JT motioned me over and offered me a seat. "So, Jack, I hear you want to be in my employ?"

I looked at him and said, "Yes sir I would like that indeed."

"First of all, drop the sir shit, my dad is sir," JT said.

"I can do that," I said with a smile.

"Alright then, down to business," he said. "Why do you think you can be security for me and handle the tough stuff if needed? What makes you qualified, if I may be blunt?"

"Well.," I said, "between the martial arts I took as a kid and my military training as an adult, there aren't too many people that intimidate me or make me back down from them. If there ever comes a time that I feel I can't handle the situation, well, there's always fire arms to solve that problem."

We talked a bit and he asked, "So why this work?"

"Money is easier than the bullshit that I am doing now."

"What type of work are you doing now?"

"Janitorial and sometimes carpentry," I said.

"Exactly what kind of money were you thinking you would make here?" JT asked.

"Make me an offer, I realize that there are dangers in the job and that it is probably a fulltime gig. So, I figure ok pay and a little pick me up to keep me going if I need it—providing that's alright with you, of course."

JT looked at me and said "Perks of the business are the pick me ups, as long as you're not breaking the bank in the process. As for the money, it will not make you rich, but it is lucrative, just ask Buddy."

I turned to Buddy and he nodded his head in agreement.

"Sounds good to me," I said. "I plan on just leaving the crapper cleaning job, so can I start tomorrow?"

JT looked at me and said. "Sounds good to me. The day guy leaves around 7:00 p.m. so I would like you here around 6:45."

"Sounds good to me, and thanks for the job JT."

"No problem man, just don't let me get killed and all will be cool. Oh, one other thing. No downer shit while on duty, that you do on your own time. Only the upper's, we clear?"

I told him yes and thought to myself 'He said don't let me get killed'. I laughed. 'No one is going to kill you but me.'

Buddy's story was one of your normal 'lost in the system' kids and I felt a little sorry for him. I thought about not killing him, but I probably would have to just to keep him from stepping into JT's place after I was done removing him from his place as king fly of the shit pile. Doing my thing every night I continued to observe the routine of all that was going on. One thing that I noticed the moment I began to work was that Buddy started to leave for about an hour or so each night.

"Yo, Buddy," I said.

"What's up Jack?" He replied.

"Dude, where do you go every night? You got a little action on the side you are taking care of now that I am here to help?" I said this with a great big shit-eating grin on my face. One of those 'you been had' looks.

Buddy looked at me and motioned me over to him.

"Sup man?" I said.

"No action on the side, no need. If I feel the need to get frisky, I just need to dangle a bag of whatever the piece of ass I'm after is using, and I am in." Buddy got this, hard to describe really, look on his face. The look was almost like he was embarrassed.

"Dude, what's with the look?" I asked.

Buddy smiled and said, "I love food."

"Ok… so do I." I said.

"Yea, yea I'm sure you do, but have you ever had something that you could not get enough of?" he asked. "I mean something so good you have to have it as if it is the last thing you will ever eat?"

I looked at him and said, "Not yet, but I may have to have whatever it is you are about to tell me about."

Buddy smiled and said, "There is this Mexican food joint a couple blocks away that, and this is no exaggeration, it has the best smothered burrito that you can ever wish to sink your chops into."

I let a little laugh out and said, "Not laughing at you but with you man, really. You're telling me that you leave every night for a burrito?"

"Yep," he said.

"Must be one hell of a burrito?" I said.

"As I said, like nothing you have ever had. If I could put it into words' I would have to say it is like sex on a plate," he said.

Laughing I said, "I'll keep an eye on things while you go get laid each night then. Just bring me back some plate sex from time to time will yea?"

"Hell-yea I will and thanks man," he said.

Unknowingly he just gave me the opportunity to end his life if I need to. Having a pattern, you see, could give me a way to take him out, and in that neighborhood a random drug killing was not an uncommon event—one down one to go. Now all I had to do was work on JT and how to take him out. Then I could go home to be with the family again, with the knowledge that there are a few less people out there that can cause such harm on such a large scale.

Having figured out how to take down the number two, I set my focus on finding a way to get to JT without raising suspicions of what I was planning. This proved harder than I thought. While JT, in his own words, worked hard to attain all that he wanted by running his drug empire, he never left his room. I mean never. He had someone bring his food to him. If he was feeling frisky, someone was brought to him so that he could scratch his itch, and all his laundry was done for him. As for personal hygiene, he had everything that he needed in his little fortress on the 2nd floor. I guess we were used more for security of the house, sort of a first defense and peace keeping. While this may pose a small problem, I thought, it wasn't impossible.

The plan I came up with was to get rid of Buddy while he was on one of his, burrito runs. That still makes me laugh when I think of that Goliath becoming so giddy over a food item—oh well, to each their own. If I took Buddy out on his way back from his food run and left the body where it could be found, most likely, given his background and the neighborhood, it would be played off as just another drug deal gone wrong or a vengeance killing by a rival drug group. That left the JT problem—a problem that I figure I can solve with a little gas and some sleep meds.

The night came, and I waited for Buddy to take off in pursuit of his sexy burrito. I followed him and lay in wait for his return. My new plan came together to advertise what I was doing with my kills—in other words, letting people know that crime may be punishable by law and end in a jail sentence, but my punishment is death, so if you do the crime then do the time, or pay the ultimate price. I tried to make this first kill look like a turf war. I saw Buddy come around the corner of the alley as he did every night and I watched him go by. I treaded lightly as I aimed the Taser at his backside and fire off the prongs. Immediately his body stiffened up and he began to shake, as the volts rush through his body.

I walked up to him with a smile on my face and said, "Damn, now that's gotta hurt."

He looked up at me and said, "Why?"

I replied, "Why the taser? Well, that's simple; you are a big motherfucker and if you knew I was going to kill you, you may have tried to stop me. I know I would have tried to stop me." He lay there stunned and I explain to him the why. "Here is how it is," I said. "I cannot have people selling the shit that you and JT are selling to children and teens. If the idiot adults want to put that shit into their body's so be it. The kids, however, should have always been off limits." With that being said, I pulled out my gun and shot him twice in the chest and once in the head.

I put on a pair of medical gloves and pulled them up over my shirtsleeves and pulled out the knife I had with me. I opened Buddies shirt and carved 'pusher' in his chest. I figured this may give the cops the idea that someone may be targeting drug dealers, for now anyway. So much for letting them think it was local dealers turf issue. Oh well, I think to myself. I was trying to figure out how to communicate the whole, do the crime and I'll get you thing. It seemed like an adequate way of going about it. I would just have to be extra careful from there on out not to leave any clues from my person on or around the bodies of my future victims. I started to walk away and stopped, I turned around and went back to Buddy's corpse and just for the hell of it I reached down and took the burrito from Buddy's hand. 'Guess I won't have to buy one now.' I said, laughing to myself. I strolled back to the house, eating the burrito on the way. 'I'll be damned,' I thought, 'this is one hell of burrito.'

I got back to the house and finished out the night. As not to draw attention to myself, I went upstairs and knocked on JT's door.

"Enter," he said.

"JT," I said, "Have you seen or heard from Buddy?"

He looked at me and said, "No, why?"

"I was walking around the house making sure that everything was kosher and all, but when I came back to where I left him at the entry way he was gone."

JT stood up, and for the first time since I'd been there, showed some concern. His voice a little unsteady, he said, "What do you mean he is not here? Did you check the can?"

"I checked everywhere before I came to you and said anything. Have there been problems in the past with him leaving or maybe there is a rival dealer trying for your turf?" I asked.

JT scoffed and said, "There is always a rival looking to expand, this usually means taking over someone else's turf."

To it I responded, "Yeah, that makes sense. What about leaving for food, or well…hell. Is there anything in the past that he may have done that might explain his absence?"

JT sat back down put his hands on his face and sighed. "Buddy thinks he is being sneaky, but I know he has this little place that he goes for some Mexican food." He laughed and said, "Him and that fucking burrito love affair he has. If he could, I swear he would marry that fucking burrito."

I laughed along with him and said, "That's a real weird thing to have stuck in my head JT, thanks for that." We both laughed for a while and then returned to the silence.

"Ok, ok, let's get serious again," JT said. "If he went after that burrito of his, he usually goes down the block and cuts through the alley and then turns right at the end of the alley. The Mexican food shack is a couple hundred feet down on the right."

"Ok," I said. "Do you want me to head that way and see if he ran into some issues on the way to or from his food shack?"

JT stood up and said, "Yes, but make it quick." JT pulled open his desk drawer and retrieved a pistol and said, "I will hold down the fort until you get back."

I turned around and headed for the door when JT said, "Jack, be careful out there. I have heard rumors that Junior, who is the leader of the next turf, was looking to make a move on us."

I turned back around and said, "Will do boss."

"Oh, Jack, you do have a weapon, right?"

I smiled and said, "Like an American Express card, I don't leave home without it." As I said it I pulled out the gun I shot Buddy with and showed it to JT. "This little baby is my best friend and has kept me out of a lot of trouble." I watched as JT placed his own weapon in his waistband and thought, 'Damn this is too easy.' I raised my gun and fired three times just like I did with Buddy—two in the chest and one in the head.

JT's head snapped back as a pink mist blew out the back of head onto the wall behind him. He crumpled to the floor next to his desk. I walked around and again placed my gloves over my hands and pulled JT's body to a position on the floor, so I could see. I opened his shirt, removed a letter opener from JT's desk and carved 'DRUG DEALER' on his chest. I then took the letter opener and stabbed it into his left eye and walked out. I contemplated for a moment taking JT's hot rod but then thought better of it. I grabbed the keys and headd down the hall, seeing a regular to the place I handed him the keys and told him to enjoy the car—that I wanted something new.

The man looked at me and said, "thanks."

I strolled out of the house and walked down the road toward my car. As I walked, I notice how quiet it was—no people out, no sign that anyone had even been aware of the two killings that had just happened. I could see how no one may have heard me killing JT. However, shooting Buddy should have garnered some attention from someone. Even a curious someone that had heard the shots might have come looking to be sure that it was not a loved one or friend. That reminded me that I might need to get a sound suppressor for my gun.

Contrary to popular belief, a silencer does not make the weapon silent. It does as it says and suppresses the sound. It is quieter than one without a suppressor, but it is not silent. I would have to watch the police blotters for shootings in this area and see what came of the night's events. I was sure that I would set off some alarms with the chest carvings. While it went against my theory of not leaving anything behind for the authorities, I feel an overwhelming need to get my message out. The message being, that crime is no longer just punishable by probation or a jail sentence. Unless of course the sentence fits the crime, and regardless of how much money and influence you have this will not protect you from me. In summary, if you do the crime you will be punished for it, one way or the other.

I got home around three in the morning, having already showered at a local YMCA, and trashed the clothes in a burn barrel that was ablaze under an overpass. That successfully disposed of that little piece of evidence. I went upstairs and crawled into bed next to Jill and said, "Hello my love, all done with that project. Life can go back to normal now."

She rolled over and gave me a kiss and said, " Good, we missed you."

I looked back at her and said, "I missed you all too."

CHAPTER 9

Now that life was back to normal, for the most part anyway, I would wait for what I determine to be an appropriate amount of time between kills—if there is such a thing. I was enjoying the time
with my family and the laid back pace of everyday life. The papers did mention the two homicides that I perpetrated, and that they believe there may be a serial killer out there who seems to be targeting criminals. I thought to myself, 'now that is going to concern a lot of people, YA RIGHT!!' They were excluding the possibility of it being a rival gang, making the murders look like the work of a serial killer. For now, only time would tell whether or not this person would strike again and what, if any, the motive was.

I smiled to myself and tought they would soon see that, indeed, it was a serial killer and the motive will be revealed as vigilante justice—the kind of justice that the law did not condone. I'm sure by the time it was all over, if and when that came around, there would be some law enforcement personnel that would agree with me, even though the could not ever say it publicly.

Jill walked in that particular Saturday morning and said, "Good morning my love."

"Well good morning to you as well darling." I went on to ask her if she had seen the news about that slaughter on the other side of town.

"Hard to miss given all the coverage it is getting."

"I think it is not a real loss given what the two victims were doing," I said.

Jill looked at me and said, "While I don't believe that murder is good, I am not about to shed a tear for people that sell kids drugs or for anyone that harms children in any way."

You see why I love this woman?

"I do hope, if it is a serial killer, that he only takes out the trash."

I looked at her and asked, "Trash?"

"Yes trash, you know the bad guys, drug dealers, child molesters, rapists and so on," she said.

Nodding my head, I said, "That would be nice. I can't say anyone will really miss them I suppose."

Jill replied, "I doubt they will. I certainly will not."

We spent the rest of the day in town where we caught a movie and generally just screwed around untill super time. We decided to go to Dave and Busters and have some food and play the games. Jill and I were still kids at heart and loved playing in the arcades whenever possible. So anywhere that had an arcade or some kind of fun and games, was always on our list of places to go. When we returned home, we showered and got ready for bed. The day was long, and all of us were ready to crash. We all were ready for bed and more than willing—all of us except for Jill.

Apparently, she had had a lot of fun and had plans to carry on the fun into the bedroom. Far be it from me to turn the poor lady down when she was seeking some extracurricular adult activities—especially when she is so good at it. Having the kid's room on the other side of the house when we bought the place turned into a blessing in disguise. Not that we are overly loud in the bedroom, but we are not what you may call quiet either.

We started out in the shower. What was just supposed to be just a shower, turned into foreplay when Jill, who was washing my back, worked her hands around to the front. With a velvet touch and the assistance of the soap she began to clean other parts of my body. The particular part in which I speak reacted swiftly and a low moan escaped my mouth. I was either really dirty, or she was really liking what she had in her hand. She then removed the shower head from its holder and rinsed me off. Turning me around, she ran her hands downward along my chest and abdomen untill she reached my midsection. With a firm grip on me, she took me in her mouth. Over and over again, she took me in and out of her mouth.

Fearing it may lead to an early end of our fun I lifted her away from me and put her up against the wall of the shower. I kissed her passionately as I made my way down toward her breasts. Circling her areoles with my tongue, I felt her body stiffen. As I took her nipple into my mouth, she let out a sigh of pleasure. The sigh grew into heavy breathing as I moved down to her clitoris and begin to lick. I continued to pleasure her and got a small squeal as I thrusted a finger into her. I increased the flicking of my tongue and speed up the in and out motion of my finger until she orgasmed.

When she had finished her first of what I know will be multiple orgasms, I lifted her up, and she put her legs around my waist. Wasting no time, she grabbed me and guided me inside of her. I thrusted in and out of her as she threw her head back in pleasure. With a firm grip on her butt and the water from the shower rushing warmly down our bodies, we went at it till she screamed out.

Still inside, her we walked out of the bathroom and I sat on the bed, laying down and sliding back. Jill straddling me, she moved back and forth on top of me, the motion driving me deeper and deeper into her. Just for some added pleasure and a harder climax, I begin to massage her clitoris. It made her move faster and faster until I felt the wetness of her next orgasm. She slid off of me and on to her back. I reenter her and we continued our escapades. In and out, over and over again, slowly speeding up. we made love untill we both climaxed simultaneously.

Rolling off her—both of us sweating and panting like marathon runners—we lay there.

She laid her head in the crook of my neck and said, "So much for the shower."

We both laughed and after a bit of time we got up and again took a shower.

Monday morning rolled around again—life as normal, (wake up, get ready for work, eat, and get the kids off to the bus.) When all that was done, we both left for our jobs. I satisfied my daily job requirements and spent a little time on the computer looking for my next victim. As alarming as this sounds, the sexual predator lists are enormous. According to a 2012 survey done by the (NCMEC) or 'The National Center for Missing and Exploited Children', there are 747,408 registered sex offenders in the U.S. This is up nearly a quarter from the 2006 tally of 606,818 registered offenders. That number almost makes me physically ill. Just thinking about how many people are out there doing these atrocious things to children is mind-boggling. A sudden feeling of hate filled me, and it just reaffirmed, at least to me, that I was doing the right thing.

According to a 'Rape, Abuse, and Incest National Network' or RAINN statistic, every ninety-eight seconds, an American is sexually assaulted. Every eight minutes, that victim is a child. Meanwhile, only six out of every one thousand perpetrators will end up in jail. Fucking unbelievable, right?! What kind of sick twisted ass monkey do you need to be to rape someone, let alone a child?

Those stats helped me to make up my mind as to who would be my next target. As I perused what I have come to call the 'hot sheets', I ran into a name that I remembered hearing about on the news—not sure when I heard it or why I remember, only that I do. Regardless of the when or why, I decided to do some research on Mr. Rapist, but not at work. I never look up any one in particular on any computer that may be traced back to me. When I needed to research a new target, I always went to an internet cafe and used their computers. Pay to play, so to speak. As it happened, this well-built asshole—note to self:

'bring Taser'—was a less than honorable individual. According to the perp list I was looking at, he was charged with not one or two, but four counts of rape.

Next to child molesters, I put rapists at number two on my 'You are a real fuck-up' list. As it turned out, Mr. Muscles, or Chance, which is his given name, was ultimately convicted of only one of the four rapes. Even after being charged with four rapes, they could only convict him of one. The other three women were so messed up mentally, that they refused to testify. The punk only did two years and was paroled for good behavior. Lord only knows what he has been doing ever since. Not getting caught is what he has been doing.

I found his name on the perp list, and after some time staring at the computer, I found his last known address. Then came the fun part, planning how to end that dip shits life.

Let's take a side bar for a second so I can tell a story of what I wished would happen to Chance when he met a she-devil.

One morning, Chance wakes up with a vague memory of the proceeding night's events to find he is in an unfamiliar surroundings. As he takes in the place, he notices a very beautiful woman. Her skin is a dark tan and she is in excellent physical shape. Add to this the long reddish blond hair and oh la la. 'Ouch,' Chance thinks, 'just my type.'

He strolls over to the young vixen and wonders how he might over power her and have his way with her. 'I am an all-encompassing force of nature,' he thinks to himself. 'No woman can resist me and what I can offer them. Even if they say they don't want it, I know that they really do. They all want me and want I can give to them.' Chance laughs to himself and continues to walk her way.

As he gets closer, the 'she- devil' turns around and says, "Well hello there handsome, aren't you a fine specimen."

Taken off guard, Chance is at a loss, this only lasts a second however. The cockiness quickly takes over again, and Chance says, "Well hello to you, and yes, I am a truly amazing man." She is so beautiful that it nearly takes his breath away. "You are one hot ass chick.," Chance says. "The only thing that could make you hotter is me." Yes, yes, I know, that was corny. I told you he had an, 'I'm all that—Roman God' type complex.

The she-devil looks at him and laughs. This of course makes Chance a little irritated. "So, let me get this straight." The she-devil says. "You on me is the only thing that will make me hotter than I already am, is that correct?" She says this with a whole lot of sarcasm. "What exactly will you 'DO' on me?" She asks.

Without a pause, Chance says, "It's not what I am going to do on you, but to you—is what you should be wondering." With a half-smile, half sneer Chance says, "I am going to fuck you."

"Oh really?" she says. "Will you put it in my vagina or my ass? Or are you a super stud and pleasure me in all my holes?"

This of course starts to turn him on and he says, "Whatever you want, or more to the fact, whatever I want."

Laughing out loud, the she-devil says, "Well then super stud, why don't you just try it."

By then, Chance is both turned on and pissed off, all at the same time, by the sheer boldness of this women and her 'come and get me if you can' attitude.

Chance lunges for her, grabbing her arm and twisting it behind her back and whispers in her ear "How tuff are you now?" He pushes her onto the ground and onto her stomach. "I am going to fuck you until you're dead or my dick falls off you hot little bitch." Chance says in a sadistic tone.

If only poor Chance could see her face, he would have noticed that there was no fear in it but a huge smile instead. She allows him to feel her up and begin to tear her clothes off, all the while saying, "No no, please don't, please don't rape me." This of course makes Chance smile as he feels his erection trying to escape from his pants. He hikes up her skirt and peels off her panties. Pulling down his own pants, he is just about to penetrate her when out of the blue she arches her back and throws him off her like he is a feather in the wind.

When Chance hits the ground, he lays there on his back in utter disbelief. His rock-hard cock standing up in the wind is as confused as the body it is attached to. The she-devil meanders over and stands next to him. Looking down she says in an evil hissing voice—the type of voice that you only hear in your nightmares—so you like to fuck? WELL SO DO I." Taking him by the feet she carries him to a near bye bench and throws him over it.

Quicker than he thought possible she has him bound and immobile. She walks around to the front of him and takes him by the hair; she lifts his head up so that she is looking down at him. In that same creepy ass voice, she says, "WELCOME TO HELL ASSHOLE."

Sweat running off his brow, Chance asks, "What are you going to do to me?"

She laughs and says, "I'm going to fuck you till you die, or my dick falls off. Does that sound familiar Chance?"

Being the self-absorbed asshole that he is he begins to laugh. Seeing this man laugh—and not just any laugh, but one of those laughs that come from way deep in the belly, the kind that some people might mistake you as a mad man—this makes the she-devil look at him.

She asks, "Did I miss something? What exactly do you find so funny stud?"

Chance gets control of himself long enough to speak and says, "Maybe I missed the memo but, don't you have to have a dick in order to fuck me, let alone have it fall off?"

The she-devil still naked looks down and begins to laugh herself and says, "Silly me, I guess that would help to have one of those wouldn't it?"

Chance being the forever smart ass says, "Well duh, you may have a smoking hot body, but you lack a whole lot of smarts."

This makes the she-devil smile and tell Chance "Well here is the memo you missed, when I said welcome to hell I was not joking. Let me prove it to you."

This gives Chance a pause, a little skeptical but always the narcissist he says, "Yea, you just go ahead and prove to me whatever it is that you think."

She looks at him and says, "Please observe your future." Then she points down to her sweet spot. This is not a difficult thing to do as Chance is still taking in all that this beautiful she-devil has to offer with her magnificent body. As he stares at her most sacred spot it begins to move. Not just move but appears to be swelling.

"What the fuck!" Chance says. He continues to stare as the swelling begins to form what looks like a penis. "Oh hell no," he says.

The she-devil begins to gyrate her hips like that of a stripper dance. Meanwhile, Chance just looks on in sheer horror as what started out as a small swelling at her vagina is now a real penis. Not just your normal penis, this is the kind of penis that would make the weathered porn star look at it with contempt. After what seems to be a life time of watching it grow and having her swinging it in his face, Chance's face goes white as he realizes he is truly going to get fucked to death and begins to weep. She makes a bottle of lube appear in her hand and says, "Don't cry, you know you really want this." As she and her impressive piece of man meat disappear behind him, he begins to scream.

Now that is real justice. Bet you thought I was going to go into the gory details, killer I may be but DAM, not even I could stomach that.

CHAPTER 10

Ahh, poor Chance, NOT!!! So anyway, where was I in real life? Oh yea, I was researching Chancy-poo's whereabouts, so I could give him some justice of my own.

So, the computer turned up some past residences, and I looked at the public records for some of the places he was arrested hoping it might lead to some places that he hung out so I might locate him. As it turns out, he was not just arrested for rape. Apparently, he was somewhat of a brawler and was picked up for disturbing the peace, public intoxication, and various degrees of assault. My hope was that he was stupid enough to return to his old haunts and continue on as though nothing had ever happened. Given the limited amount of things I had learned about the asshole so far, I was willing to bet returning to his old stomping grounds was exactly where he would head.

On my lunch hours, I cruised by the different places that Chance was known to be. Wouldn't you know it, after only a week, I spotted him coming out of a gym looking all pumped up, acting as though he was Gods' gift to women—pompous asshole. He walked down the street eyeballing everything with tits and a heartbeat, pausing occasionally to let the women know what they were supposedly missing and how much they really wanted him—even if they don't know it yet. I told you he was an ass.

I continued to observe him until I saw a pattern form in the shape of his comings and goings to the gym. He also went to a smoothie shop on a regular basis for what I am sure was some powdered veggies in a fruity smoothie. However, on his way home he always walked through an industrial area as a short cut to his apartment complex. This was both quiet and perfect; all I had to do was get him there and do my thing. Good thing they were shut down for the day by the time he was walking home—no witnesses, no crime. I would have to check and see if and where there may be cameras. If there were cameras, then I would have to disable them.

To my surprise there were only a few cameras, most of which were aimed at the entrances and exit. If I had to guess I would suppose that this was to monitor who was coming in and going out. Having not yet gone to wireless technology for video surveillance, the disabling of the system would be relatively easy. On the day of my choosing, I would simply find and cut the power to the building. Then, just to be safe, I would wear a mask as I came in from the rear of the complex thru a hole which I would cut in the chain link fence. Entering from the rear would help for two reasons. One would be in case the security system had a back-up power supply and also it would eliminate the chance that there was a camera that I had missed.

I took off work early on the day I chose to remove the target from the world of the living and if I were lucky, send Mr. Chance to the she-devil he so ultimately deserved. Cutting the power was quite easy; the main power box was anchored just outside of the complex and secured with only a padlock. I cut the lock off and pulled the lever the moment I observed Chance walking toward the facility. Having already cut the whole in the fence I hurried over and entered the complex.

I walked around the farthest building on the end, closest to the point at which Chance would exit on his way to his apartment complex. As Chance drew near, I stepped out from the building and walked into his path until he saw me. Being the arrogant ass I knew him to be, the first words out of his mouth were, "What the fuck do you want asshole?"

'So predictable,' I thought to myself. I replied, "For you to die or turn yourself into the authorities and confess to the other rapes that you were not convicted of and do your time, asshole."

Chance just smiled and said, "I have no idea what you are talking about."

"I figured you might say that," I said.

Having planned for this, I took out the taser and filled him full of electricity. I never get tired of watching people spasm uncontrollably as the volts fly through their bodies until they hit the ground. I swear sometimes I can laugh 'til I about pee myself.

With Chance being on the ground I took a few moments to allow him to reflect on what he did and see if he has anything to say.

"So buddy, what say you?" I asked.

Still jerking from the taser, he looked at me and said, "Say what about what? I never raped anyone. Everyone I had sex with wanted to have sex."

"Let me guess, whether they knew it or not, they did want to have sex with you. Right?" I asked.

"No one was ever forced to have sex," he said.

"So those charges were all just women claiming that you raped them, right? 'Cause they forgot how much they really wanted it. Then out of the kindness of their hearts and instead of retracting their statements they just decided to not show up to court so you could go free. Please tell me if I am missing anything," I said.

Chance, being a world-class asshole, looked at me and said, "Those women didn't come to court because they realized that, indeed, they were mistaken and were just too embarrassed to say so."

"I figured you would say as much. So, after you are dead, I am going to write rapist on your chest. So, when they find your body, those other women that were kind enough to let you off the hook can have a little closure." I told him this as I noticed that he was beginning to move around, and so, to avoid him getting even the slightest opportunity to defend himself, I tased him again.

That time I almost fell over laughing so hard. Watching your average person twitch from a taser blast is one thing. Watching a big-ol muscle bound dude twitch is a whole new thing. All his muscles tightened up causing his oversized arms and legs to contract as though he was trying to get into the fetal position. On, off, on, off—I applied and released the power button to the taser until I just couldn't take it any longer as the tears rolled from my eyes.

Once I got control of myself, I told him, "As much as I would like to prolong this, I am sure that the authorities or at least local security is on their way to see about the power outage. I would love to say it's been real, but this is not one of those times."

Chance started to whimper when I took out my pistol. "Sucks not having control of what's going to happen to you, doesn't it?" I shot him in the stomach and then the groin, making sure that his twig and berries were in the direct line of fire. Without hesitation, I got out a piece of a glass bottle which I had broken earlier and wrote 'rapist' on his chest. His screams pierced the evening like the wail of sirens in a quiet   neighborhood. Oh, wait those are real sirens. "Got to go," I said to him. I took the piece of glass and deposited it into his carotid artery.

With the deed being done I quickly made sure that I left nothing behind as the sirens grew louder. I ran around the building and back to the hole I had cut in the fence to make my escape. Before I entered the woods to the rear of the facility, I looked at the whole in the fence and insuring that I didn't snag any piece of me on the jagged edges of the cut fence. Satisfied, I continued to the woods. As I enter the woods, I heard the squeal of tires. The cops came to a stop at the guard shack. Killing the power must have set off some kind of alarm that I had not anticipated. The way I figured it they would have to consult with the guard and then do a sweep of the complex to see if it was just a power outage or if the loss of power was being used to commit a crime. By the time they discover it was indeed the later of the two, I would be clear of the facility and in my car driving away.

It's funny how the disappearance of some people warrants more attention than that of others. As it came to be Chance happened to be somewhat of a semi important person—maybe not important in the terms of everyone knows him but the type of important that people will notice that he is missing.

My second victim, as far as I can tell, hadn't even been reported missing. The lawyer was missed almost immediately. That was not a real shock given the fact. He had a regular job and a girlfriend to come home to at night who noticed him missing as soon as he did not come home or contact her in a reasonable amount of time. Three and four were discovered, of course, due to the fact I was not trying to hide them. Not only was I not trying to hide them, but also, I wanted them to be discovered.

Now that Chance was dead and a third message was carved on a body's chest, there would be a confirmation of a serial killer. Time to watch my P's and Q's—Pints and Quarts— an Old English warning from bartenders to their patrons to watch how much they were consuming so not get overly rude. Sort of like, 'Mind Your Manners.'

Come to find out, Chance was a stunt double in some very popular movies. Having his body found stirred things up. The news was covering it and it made the papers. The news said that the FBI was invited in to assist in the investigation, because there may be a serial killer on the hunt. No real connections had been established between the victims as of yet, however, as it was an ongoing story everyone should stay tuned to hear any new information.

CHAPTER 11

I knew it would only be a matter of time before the authorities would get involved. The second I decided to start sending a message on my victims would be that time. It would probably be my downfall, but I had to get out the message somehow. The message I was aiming for was that, crime will have punishment, if not by the law than by me. Have no doubt, there will be accountability, maybe even for me.

"So, what do have cap (captain)?" asked detective Jamison.

"Oh, you know, the same old shit sandwich in a different wrapper," he says.

"Yum," replied Jamison. "Kind of messy, but I have a very real feeling that we may have a serial killer in the making if the two homicides tie together as it looks like they are going too."

Jamison looking intrigued and thinking back to some of the recent homicides that had come across his desk said, "All in our jurisdiction or we going to have to do this in tangent with other precincts?"

To that the captain replied, "I am going to try to set up a task force to work this with you in the lead, so you all can work on it without the interference of jurisdictional bullshit that slows down the process."

Jamison looked at his captain and asked, "What leads you to think this is a serial, Cap?"

Without hesitation the captain said, "We have three bodies so far, and as you know, after two, he can be classified as a serial offender. Beyond that, the three bodies have similar carvings…"

Jamison interrupted, "Carvings?"

"Let me finish, Jamison," the captain said. "As I was saying, the bodies have carvings on them that look to be what the victims may have been or done." The captain continued by saying, "I say 'may have done' because we are still running the background on them to see if indeed this is the case."

Jamison thought a bit and said, "Does this tie into the body we found in that industrial park last week where the vic (victim) had rapist carved into his chest?"

"Yes, it does, we think they found two bodies a month or so ago that had similar carvings on the chest saying, 'dealer' and 'pusher'. We also know that those two were exactly that. One being the dealer in a crack shack, henceforth the word dealer on his chest, and the other being his pusher with the corresponding name carved into his chest." The captain went on saying, "So far there is no reason to believe that this is racially motivated. All three vics were white males of varying age and backgrounds. The only reason we even have IDs is because the killer took nothing, and other than their wallets being on them, we've positively identified them from their prior's that were in the system."

"So, let me get this straight," Jamison said. "The only thing we have tying these vics together are the carvings on their chests and that they all have priors, correct?"

"That about sums it up for now," the captain said. "Now, you and detective Hart go take a look at the crime scenes, and see what your take is on it all. Then, let me know what you think."

"Sounds good, Cap," Jamison said and walked out to find Hart.

"Hey Hart, get your skinny ass over here we got a case."

"Where are we going and what is it about?" Hart asked.

"Ever had a serial case before?" Jamison asked.

"Are you screwing with me? Because that would be really fucked up of you to yank my chain like that."

Jamison laughed and said, "Not this time stud, three bodies and waiting with no real leads to speak of. Cap wants us to go visit the crime scenes and see what, if anything, we can see—sort of get a feel for things and see what pops in our heads."

Hart looked at Jamison and asked, "What will there be to see at a months old crime scene?"

Jamison replied, "Not so much what there is, but what the surroundings are like and what kind of planning may have been needed to pull off the crime. This may give us some insight on our killer's intelligence and his ability to plan and escape."

"Oh ok, that makes sense. By the way Jamison, careful what pops in that old ass head of yours. You might blow your ears off."

"Oh, ha ha shit stick." They both laughed as they got into their car and drove off.

They drove up to the industrial site first, as it was the most recent crime scene. Meeting with the detectives that first caught the case they went over the happenings of the crime. Detective Hanson began by telling them how the perp (perpetrator) got into the complex, and to his estimation, how it went down.

"We found a hole in the fence around back and scoured the area for clues. We came across the power distribution box which we believe the perp sabotaged in order to kill the power to the facility. That, in turn, set off a silent alarm. We also believe setting off the alarm may have forced our perp to up his timeline and act faster than he may have wanted to when he heard the patrol cars roll in."

Jamison looked at Hanson and asked, "So how smart do you have to be in order to kill the power at one of those boxes and would someone know that it could activate the alarm inside?"

"As for who can kill the power at the box, just about anyone that has any knowledge of them. This knowledge can be found on the net, as well as a very simple understanding of the thing by just opening the box itself. You see the distribution box has several shut off's inside for use by the electricians and linesmen in order to service both the box and the power coming in and going out of the box itself." Hanson said. "Now whether or not the perp could have known that it would or would not activate the alarm is hard to tell. Each alarm has multiple redundancies depending on the customers specs."

"I see," Jamison said. "Hey Hart, you have any questions or thoughts on the matter before we move on?"

Hart looked up, shook his head and said, "No, I'm good so far—all pretty self-explanatory stuff." With that they all followed detective Hanson and moved on.

They walked around the complex and Hanson explained, "We are not sure how the perp lured the vic to the complex, but he must have known that the guy would be there, given the fact that he cut the power in order to gain access to the complex to confront the vic and ultimately kill him."

Hart piped up and asked, "Did the facility have any type of video surveillance that wasn't affected by the power outage?"

To this Hanson answered, "We took a look at the feeds that they did have and asked around, however, all the feeds did in fact go out at the same time that the power was cut."

"Well shit," replied Jamison.

Hanson also added, "Not that it matters now, but they said that they are in the process of getting a power redundancy for the security system as we speak. It is not supposed to be complete until sometime in the next couple weeks."

Jamison asked, "Were there any systems already online and recording at the time of the murder, or maybe some kind of recording device on the guard shack by chance?"

"In a perfect world yes, however, not in this instance unfortunately," Hanson told Jamison.

Hanson took them to the spot where the perp gained entry to the complex and showed them the hole in the fence, then walked them through what he thought may have been how the killer snuck up on the vic. "The way we put it together was that the killer laid in wait somewhere over on this side of the building while he waited for the vic to pass by. After he want past him, I am assuming it was a male given the size of the victim. Also, the M.E. (medical examiner) concluded the two small puncture wounds on the body were left there by the darts of a taser. Those proceeded the gun shots and stabbing.

"Makes sense," remarked Hart.

Jamison chimed in and said, "I would have to agree with you on this being a male perp if the other crimes turn out to be connected. The only thing that I would give you on the remote chance that it's a female perp is that so far none of the facial areas have been affected, and this poor bastard's junk was shot to hell." To this last statement about the groin being all shot up all the detectives gave a noticeable cringe and shivered.

Hart asked Jamison, "Hey boss, was the captain going to invite the feds in like I have heard on the news?"

Jamison looked at Hart and Hanson and said, "Like the captain told us Hart, we are trying to form a task force. He has contacted the Feds and invited them in, but they are waiting on our preliminary report before they commit."

"Oh yea, Hanson, did you want to be part of this task force if it comes to life?"

Hanson looked at them both and said, "Hell yes. I would love to catch this person whether it is a serial or not. I have also always wanted to work with the feds to see how they do their thing."

"Sounds good then, I will have our captain bring you in if your boss will let you go that is."

"Oh, if it turns out to be a high-profile case and the feds get involved and he didn't let me go, he would be kicking himself in the ass for a very long time. I doubt he will have a big problem with it as long as your captain can make the task force come to be," Hanson replied.

"Well if you want to be on board with us, why don't you give your captain a call and join us at the next scene. Tell him what makes us believe this to be a serial murderer. We can give you the file on it on the way there, how does that sound?" Jamison said.

"Sounds good to me."

They made their way over to the other side of town. Hanson read the files on the way, having left his vehicle at the station. They all rode together in order to chat about the information in the case.

"So, what's the good word Hanson?" Hart asked.

Hanson looked up from the files and said, "About what?"

Obviously distracted by the case files, Hart laughed and said, "About joining the task force, that is why you went in and talked to your captain, right?"

Hanson, feeling a little stupid that he had not caught on to what Hart was asking him but so enthralled with what he was reading and wanting to get back to it, said, "Oh yea. He said to go with you and see what I see. If there is something, he will leave it up to me to decide if there may be anything to be had. He will then call your captain and make the decision from there."

Jamison looked over at Hanson and said, "As you can see, the crime has the same chest carvings as the industrial complex killing, however, the perp must be above average intelligence in order to infiltrate a drug house. You know as well as I do that, they don't just trust anyone. So in order to gain access to the boss, this guy had to have gained trust over time and must have scouted out this place well in advance. The key to it all is the how or who he knew to find it."

Both Hart and Hanson nodded their heads in agreement. Hart looked and Jamison and asked, "Do you think the vice squad can drum up some names of people that frequented the house? If so, we can track them down and at least question them. It's a far stretch given that they will all probably be to strung-out to even know their names, but if he has done this before one of the resident druggies may have a record of some crime that may fit his M.O (Modis Operandi)."

"Good idea, Hart," Jamison said.

They pulled up to the house and got out of the car. Taking a look around, the got a feel of the place. The house was now abandoned and the crime scene tape floated like a flag in the wind. As the detectives took in all that there was to see this far after the crime, Hanson asks, "Where is the ally where the other victim was found?"

"Over there and down a block. You want to see the area?" asked Jamison.

Hart added, "I saw in the report that the vic with pusher carved on his chest was known to frequent a Mexican food shack just down the road. I don't know about you two, but I am getting hungry."

The two other detectives nodded their heads and walked toward the ally where the other man was killed. The little food shack was not much more than a little shed, similar to the ones that you might buy at a home improvement store like Lowes, or Home Depot. However, the smell emanating from it was amazing. Just coming near the place made our mouths water.

"Well shit. No wonder this guy always came here to eat. I was only mildly hungry when we decided to come here, but now I feel as though I could eat the north end of a south bound skunk," Jamison said. "For you younger folk, Hart, that's the stinky end."

"Oh, you are a real comedian Jamison, or is it an asshole? Sometimes the lines get blurred." Hart said. Jamison and Hanson both started to laugh.

They all had some food and asked the proprietor of the food shack if he remembered the person that was killed in the alley on the other street a while back.

"Yeah yeah, I remember him. Mostly nice fella, except he was always in a hurry. Always looking around as if he were doing something he wasn't supposed to be doing. I asked him if he was looking for someone, and if he was ok. He just said he wasn't supposed to leave for lunch, but he couldn't get enough of my food. I said thank you and gave his meal for free that day. He always came to eat at the same time each night. You know now that I think of it, the last couple of weeks before he was killed he did seem a little less worried about things. Maybe he had some new help or something at work so he could actually take a real lunch break."

Jamison thanked the guy and they all headed toward the alley where the crime was committed. They turned the corner and walked toward the scene. "Hart, break out the crime scene photos, and lets' walk through the ally and make our own determinations."

"Yea boss, will do."

"Any thoughts, Hanson, from reading the file on the way over here?" Jamison asked.

"What I got from the file was pretty much just basic stuff, not all that dissimilar to any other murder file. The how and where were there, but as with all unsolved murders, the who is still missing." Hanson replied.

"I was thinking the same thing in terms of it looking like any other murder in a back alley of nowhere," Jamison added. "However, we have to look at it through different glasses. We have to look at it from the point of this guy was tracked and followed for the sole purpose of being killed here before he got back to the security of the house."

"But why here, and why before he got back to the house?" Hart asked.

"From what I have read so far in the different reports, both prior arrests and so on this guy was running as the second in command or the dealers right hand man," Jamison said. "If I had to make a guess, I would say this is the guy that our perp had to get by in order to make it to the big boss," Jamison added.

Hanson put his two cents in and said, "So maybe our perp be-friended him, and after gaining his trust, carried out the crime. The owner of the food shack did say that our vic did seem less paranoid and more relaxed as if he were not quite in so much of a hurry or as if someone may be there in his place while he left to eat. Our killer first took out this guy, then went back to the house and took out the other one."

"The file from the M.E said times of death were similar," said Hart.

To this Jamison added, "Ok, so if this went down the way we think then I would have to believe that this guy infiltrated the house, gained the trust of both parties, and when the time was right, he perpetrated the crime. If that is to be believed, then we are dealing with an above average intellect—someone with both the time and means to put off what he is doing to plan and execute this crime."

"I agree," said Hart. "I also think this just got a whole lot hairier than we thought."

Hanson piped in and said, "There is no way at all that this is his first kill—way too clean and carried out. If this is his first, and I truly believe that it is not, then we will be seeing a whole lot more from this guy."

Both Jamison and Hart nodded their heads in agreement. "So, let's get into this and tear it apart. There have to be more bodies, or at least some missing persons." Jamison said.

"I'll let my captain know and see about being transferred to the taskforce so we can get this guy," said Hanson.

"Sounds good to me," replied Jamison. He then looked at Hart and said, "Time to put that big brain of yours to work."

"Will do boss," Hart replied.

CHAPTER 12

Life returned to normal for a while in my house. As I do my diligent follow up of my victims, I found out that, indeed, the cops were taking interest in the three bodies found with carvings on them. The news reports went as follows: "Following the deaths of two drug related persons at a known drug house on the lower east side, and then a new crime that was discovered in an industrial park in a completely different area of town, police detectives are beginning to believe that a person or persons may be targeting these individuals as some kind of revenge killings or ritual killings. As it is early on in the investigation, our sources are only saying that there are no persons of interest at this time and there are no real leads to speak of."

'Hum,' I thought to myself. 'Well I guess I got my message out. I will let them put together the rest for themselves and I am sure that they will. They may not find me, but they will realize that there is a Vigilante out there. In the mean time I will give them something else to look at and ponder over.' I looked over the print outs of the bad guy list, as I have come to call, them and did a little victim shopping. 'So many to choose from, and so little time to do anything about it. Rapist, chimo's, murderers, now there is a new one.'

I read about a man who, on a night of drunkin rage, killed three people when he got mad after the bartender cut him off and asked him to leave the bar. The plea of not guilty due to reasons of temporary insanity was followed by a one year stay in a mental rehabilitation center to deem whether or not he could reenter society. I did a little more probing and found out that after the year the man was released and moved to a different part of town. While this piqued my interest, it wasn't what I was looking for. Everyone gets mad from time to time and does stupid shit. I found nothing else on the man and put him in the maybe category and kept on going through the list of perspective candidates.

After what seemed like an exhaustive search, I found my next target. This particular piece of work had scammed several hundred retired people out of their savings, and they were then forced to go back to work. When accused of theft by deception and fraud, the guy pleaded not guilty and managed to get two years of probation, along with a ban from any and all financial related employment for life. He had invested most of the money and was living off the money made from said investments therefore introducing reasonable doubt in the mind of the court by saying that he was a not for profit entity and the money he was paid was his salary. Got to love what a good lawyer can do. Nevermind the fact that he had ruined hundreds of people's lives causing pain and suffering and the possible loss of all their possessions and forcing them to scrounge for the basics in order to live from day to day for the rest of their lives.

Mr. Lawrence Resnik, graduate of a prominent business school with a MBA in business, started out small and found he had a talent for selling retirement funds to people. At least the selling of the funds was easy, the returns and the ability to be able to capitalize on making money for the funds sold was a totally different story. He had been in trouble with several firms for his trading practices in the past. When what he was selling was not only losing money but was leaving buyers without their initial investment, it made them skeptical about buying from their firm or recommending others to the firm. This led to his subsequent dismissal from multiple firms. He believed that he had the ability to sell ice cubes to Eskimo's—narcissistic much? Lawrence, in all his wisdom, decided that as long as he could doctor the books well enough that it looked as though the plans he was pushing were doing well to the outside world and he could get enough saved to run away, he would do just that.

I figured that I would give him a chance to come clean, confess, and offer himself up to the authorities and I would spare his life. Deep down I probably knew that he would do no such thing but at least I would give him the chance to do it. I mean, he never really inflicted harm on anyone in a physical sense. It would be a real let down not being able to take this piece of scum out of the world on a permanent basis, but knowing that he would be behind bars for the rest of his natural life would have to do I suppose. If I got lucky, he would tell me to go to hell and I could hurt him in a really bad way. Ah the joys of wishing.

"Jamison," the captain said. "Where are we with these homicides?"

"We got some background on all the victims and Hart had some ideas about linking the two by their past crimes in concert with the carvings on the bodies. All persons were convicted of the crimes that they had on their chests, however, they also all received light or reduced sentences."

Hart entered room and said, "Someone just called the hotline and said that there was a woman that used to frequent the crack shack who disappeared a few weeks prior to the killings of the other two residents."

"It's a good link for sure," said the captain. "Let's get on this so-called missing woman and see if we can tie her to any of the missing persons filed in this area over say the last six months. Also, let's focus on the women charged with serious crimes and given a light sentence, or let off all together," He added. Both Hart and Jamison and nodded their heads and got to work.

"Well there is no small amount of bad women to choose from," said Jamison.

"You just aint-a-shittin man," said Hart.

"Lets' focus on large controversial court cased where the public may have been less than happy with the outcome of the case, and then we will print pictures and run over to the neighborhood and show the pictures to the public and see if we can get any hits," said Jamison.

As with any society, there was no lack of controversial issues. Leading to the old saying that you can only please some of the people some of the time, but you will never please all the people all the time. They came up with a folder of women that had both gone missing and had committed crimes. Of those, only a hand full of the women were within reasonable distance of the crack house. This made the job a little easier, but of the twenty or so women that they had to show for their work, they knew this was still going to be a daunting task.

"Alright, Hart and Hanson, let's do this," Jamison said. Jamison and hart got into their car. Hanson got into his, and they set off for the neighborhood for some questions, lacking a partner for Hanson on the task force, He would be alone in his canvas, about three blocks on one side of the house. Hart and Jamison took the three blocks in the other direction and met him at the house. The first day of questions didn't really lead anywhere productive. Some people vaguely remembered a blond but were not positive enough to identify her from the photos. They planned to cavas for a week in order to get the maximum amount of exposure to the community, in hopes that different people might come by and be able to identify this mystery women. They did this in hopes that it may lead their investigation somewhere.

Reporting in to the captain at the end of the week, Jamison explained to the captain what they had come up with so far. "We have narrowed it down to two blonds that have similar appearances, so we are going to get into their backgrounds and see if we can locate them."

The captain looked at the team and said, "Good job. Now let's get after it and see if we can get closer to apprehending this guy."

Hart chimed in and said, "You are going to love one of these gals that have been identified."

The captain looked at Hart and said, "You have my attention, lay it on me."

Hart went on to tell the captain, "Remember that women that was out partying way more than a mother with a young child should and ended up coming home and found her young boy dead?"

The captain had an 'I'm thinking' look on his face and said, "Not ringing a bell yet, keep going."

"Ok, her name was Samantha Jericho. Her case drew all kinds of media attention when she got off on a technicality." Hart went on to say, "Due to the law not being specific on the age at which a minor child is allowed to stay at home alone, her lawyer was able to get the charges reduced to neglect. She was all but set free and clear of all other charges after a stint in the drug and alcohol rehab program."

The captain nodded his head and said, "Isn't she the one that disposed of the body and said he went missing?"

"That's correct, but when they found him and an autopsy was performed, they found cleaning agents in his system and she came clean and confessed to coming home and panicking. This panic mode drove her to take the boys' body and dispose of it, so she claimed."

The captain still nodding said, "If I remember right, due to our state not having a law on the lawful disposal of human remains of family members—a law that has since been changed I might add—she was able to walk away virtually free. I remember very well now."

Hart, Jamison, and Hanson all agreed that it was a real cluster fuck of a case after the verdict came down and all she had to do was rehab. The only real positive thing that came of it was a few scattered laws holding the parents or care givers more responsible for their actions.

The captain looked over at the detectives and said, "Let's look into her first. The crime and a lack of punishment for the crime so far, fall into this guys' M.O."

They all agreed and took to digging into her background and seeing what they could find.

'Holy shit', I thought to myself as I observed Mr. Resnik. "It's a wonder you haven't committed suicide by now you boring bastard." This guy could make a tax auditor think that their job was one of the finest and most rewarding around. As per usual, I did my due diligence and waited to see a pattern in which he was susceptible to me snatching this boring ass. Oh my, I sure hoped this wouldn't take long too establish a pattern, otherwise I would go insane before I got to take the dude.

As I watched him, I entertained thoughts of doing a drive by and putting him out of his misery just for posterity's sake—and that of the world around him. It's then I noticed that, for someone that is banned from his big money world of the past, he sure was dressed awfully nice.

"Well fuck me running, is that a Rolex?" Laughing out loud I said, "You sneaky mo-fo, you are a long way from the poor life the courts thought you would find yourself in when they handed down your sentence." This was a true fact indeed. I snapped a picture of the guy and followed him a while. He visited a few obscure places of no real interest until I really start paying attention to them. Many of the businesses were check cashing establishments. Then, in the afternoon, he started visiting several assisted living facilities, and I knew right then and there he was up to some new type of bullshit aimed at screwing over a whole new group of susceptible people. Well, I am here to tell you right now, that was not going to happen again.

I decided I neither knew or cared about how he pulled off his new set of deceptions. I would ask him after he was under my control and still give him the option to confess and serve his time as I had already told myself I would. Not knowing if he would or would not tell me anything gave me a little solace that one way or another he would be put out of business once and for all—dead or behind bars made no difference to me.

After a few days, I nailed down a place to do the take down. While most of his activities were in the daytime and may very well have still been if it hadn't been late

October and the sun was down earlier—thank god for small blessings—one of his last stops was at a diner that he apparently liked enough to eat at every day I had been watching him. I supposed that tomorrow may be different, and if it were, I would deal with that problem if and when it came up.

As it turns out, this little diner must have some good grub, because low and behold there he was again. I parked next to him and waited for him to finish. As he walked out of the diner, I approached him. "Mr. Resnik?" I asked. He looked up a little skeptical as I would assume most people might when approached in a parking lot after dark.

"Yes, may I help you?" he said.

"As a matter of fact, you may." I pointed at the taser and loosed the darts at him. A smile formed on my face as I watched him hit the deck. As I said before, that never gets old. Having looked around prior to approaching him and not seeing anyone but always aware that someone may come upon us at any time, I quickly got a hold of him and pulled him into the back seat of the car. I bound his arms and legs, closed the door, and drove away.

Lawrence began to rejoin the land of the conscious, but I had already driven out to my little shack of horrors and had him bound to the chair that was bolted to the floor. Remembering that I was going to give him the chance to confess and turn himself in, I placed a mask over my face. This way, if I did let him go, I could not be recognized.

"Hi there, welcome back to the land of the living. That whole taser thing gets a bad rap if you ask me. While I am sure that it is truly no fun for you, I get a whole lot of enjoyment out of watching the spasmodic function of the body of the victim."

"What do you want with me? What did I do to you?" Lawrence asked me with the normal amount of unknown and wonder mixed with fear which I had seen on all my victims before.

I looked at him awestruck, which seems to be my normal response to these people and asked, "Is it just part of the criminal DNA to ask stupid questions when you are all finally caught or punished for your crimes—to ask 'why me, what did I do, or I'm innocent', or are all you fuck ups just that delusional?" Lawrence just looked at me and stayed silent.

"So here is how this is going to go," I said. "Against my better judgment, I am giving you a chance to come clean and turn yourself in to the authorities and face punishment. Oh, and by the way, by facing punishment I mean that you will turn yourself in with all proof need to get a conviction and you will plead guilty to all charges that are placed upon you."

He continued to look at me and said, "Guilty to what? I didn't do anything."

This, in turn, earned him a good solid punch to the face and just because I felt like it—to drive the point home—a solid punch to the groin. After he recovered from his minor assault, I said, "Maybe I did not make myself clear. You know what I said, and I know what you did. If you don't decide to confess, I will kill you in a very unpleasant way." My thoughts expressed, I gave him a minute to digest the info and then asked him what he thought.

Lawrence, obviously a smart man said, "Ok, ok, it started a bunch of years ago."

I stopped him and said, "I know what you were charged with and the shitty punishment you got in court. I want you to tell me the things you are into right now and gather the proof of this or option B will come into play."

To this Lawrence said, "Oh, the new stuff."

"Yes, the new stuff," I said.

Lawrence went on to tell me what he had been doing and to who and where I could find the evidence of his new crimes, stating he would turn himself in if I would merely let him go to face his crimes.

"I can do that," I said to him. "However, I will be watching. If you do not leave here after I retrieve the evidence and go straight to the sheriff's office and turn yourself in, have no doubt, I will kill you within twenty-four hours. I will be keeping an eye on you the whole time and trust me when I say you will be better off in jail."

As much as it grated on my nerves to let that low life return to society, I told myself that while he caused a lot of misery for a lot of people, he did not physically hurt anyone and with his soft features, jail will be harder than death. Lawrence told me where he had all the records of his most recent set of deception and the list of people he stole from—a requirement I stipulated so I could pay all of them back. I hit him with the taser and gave him some chloroform and set off to retrieve the evidence.

CHAPTER 13

In our morning meeting the captain had us group up and discuss the progress of the case. "We have the known victims and a theory that this guy is taking justice into his own hands on people that he feels fell through the loops of what he considers real justice. While I applaud the effort to make change, this is both illegal and immoral in today's civilized society." The captain said.

"Jamison, what do we have on the other victims this vigilante may have removed from society in his unique way?"

Jamison responded by saying, "Well Cap, the one and only other victim thus far is the female that went missing months ago from around the area of the crack house that the two other victims where inhabiting." Jamison looked over at Hanson and said, "This one is yours man, fill the boss in on the particulars if you would bud."

Hanson stood up and said, "Single white female, mid to late twenty's, one known child that supposedly went missing and was later discovered to have perished in the residence of the deceased, after ingesting several household cleaning agents having been repeatedly left at home alone by the mother, so she could go share her female parts with the world. This was the general consensus of all the people I could find that knew her and corresponding police reports on the possible victim. Other than several minor charges for indecent exposure and public intoxication, she pretty much flew under the radar."

"Hart, what do you have to contribute?" asked the captain.

Hart took over where Hanson left off and said, "Samantha Jane Jericho is her name, Sam or JJ for short. We know where she used to reside and have contacted the parents of the presumed deceased who indeed had filed a missing person's report after not hearing from their daughter in some time." He continued by saying, "They say that it is as if she had just vanished off the face of the, earth and nothing or no one has seen her since."

The captain replied, "So we can't assume that our guy did her, but if she ever shows up or her remains surface, we may not be able to tie our killer to her. That being said, lets focus on what and who we know and all aspects of their lives we can unearth."

The detectives acknowledged the captain's orders and got to work. "Hang on a second guys," said the captain. They turned around and listened. "We will be having a FBI profiler on their way to join the task force and give any help he can. Special Agent Cline will be here tomorrow, so show him the respect he deserves. They are not taking over, just helping us in the investigation." The detectives all looked at the captain and gave a nod of understanding.

The detectives and agent Cline gathered in the meeting room which was transformed into the task force headquarters room.

"So, Cline?" asked Jamison. "What exactly do you do or are hoping to contribute to the investigation?"

Cline responded, "Well, once I get up to speed on the case, I will try my best to help you all by giving you a profile of the un-sub (unknown subject). This will, in theory, give us some idea of who we are looking for."

"That sounds good to us," Jamison said.

"So, this, in theory, will give us what exactly?" asked Hart.

"With enough information, we will be able to figure out the un-subs characteristics, decision making processes, social structure, and maybe even intended targets," replied Cline.

"At this point, we could use any help that we can get on the guy. He leaves nothing behind except a carving in the chest of what we are suspecting to be a crime that the victims have perpetrated. So far the killer has been correct on each victim's crime." Jamison said to Cline.

"So, you all are thinking he might be out for something like Vigilante Justice or the equivalence of such?" Cline replied to them all.

The detectives looked at Cline and they all agreed that this was indeed what they were leaning toward. "So now that we have an idea of what we think our un-sub may be doing, the next question is why?" Hart said.

"Why indeed?" asked Cline.

"Well hell, it sounds to me that you will fit in just fine here. On behalf of us all here, I would like to say welcome aboard," Jamison said.

"Thank you, I hope that we can resolve this quickly and put this guy behind bars," replied Cline.

As directed by Mr. Lawrence, I found myself at a self-storage unit in town spinning the padlock combination Lawrence gave me. I found it a little surprising that he told me the truth as the lock disengaged and I was able to unlock and open the door. Not really sure just exactly what I might find, I was surprised to see that Lawrence was a very neat thief. In my opinion, it was maybe not the best place to hide this condemning evidence—for that matter why keep such incriminating evidence at all. However, it had made it very easy for me to gather all I needed. I loaded it all into my car and headed back to the shack where I had Lawrence stowed away for safe keeping. On the way to the shack, I stopped and grabbed a bite to eat, and against my better judgment, grabbed a burger for the thieving asshole I had at the shack. Yeah, yeah, I know, he was supposed to be my victim not a pet. The key word here however is 'mine', therefore I can do as I please. Besides, I forgot to tell you I put a healthy dose of extra strength ex-lax in the special sauce.

As we sat there and ate our food, Mr. Resnik had the presence of mind to ask me why I was doing what I was doing. Not why I was doing it to him, rather, why I was doing what I was doing in general. "You know, Lawrence, I just got tired of people falling through the cracks of the system."

Lawrence nodded his head and said, "Yeah, I can see that."

This took me by surprise. "Really?" I said.

"Well sure I do. I am sure that you probably had someone you know get hurt or be in danger of being harmed in some way and just took the law into your own hands."

To this astonishing statement I replied, "As a matter of fact, that is exactly what happened. Too many people, and excuse the finger pointing, like you have done things and all but walked away without a care in the world. If you did care, it didn't seem to stop you from continuing with your illegal actions."

Lawrence was nodding his head and said to me, "I agree with you. Ever since I started my nefarious activity's, I have always known that it would come to a less than happy ending."

"And yet you still did it?" I asked.

"Yep, too easy to stop. Call it an addiction or whatever you want—having that kind of money and being able to live the life style I had always wanted too."

Now it was me nodding my head. For the first time, something one of my victims had said actually made sense. "You know Lawrence, I can actually see how you got all that money from those people. You truly have a way with words."

Again, he nodded his head, and brought the burger to his mouth.

"STOP!" I said. Again, it was completely out of character from past victims, but what can I say? The guy actually told me the truth instead of the same old boo hoo, why me, what have I done to you bullshit.

He looked up quickly with the burger about an inch away from his face and said, "What?"

"I put enough ex-lax on that thing to give you what I can only figure to be called explosive diarrhea."

To this Lawrence began to laugh. "That's a good one."

"Just wipe off the burger and eat it plain and you should be fine." He did, and we continued our conversation.

"So, normally I would have tortured you and cut your throat and disposed of your body," I told him.

His eyes opened a little wider than before and he asked, "Why are you not doing that now?"

I replied, "To tell you the truth Lawrence, I decided that while you may have caused many people a world of discomfort, you never actually caused anyone any physical harm. So, I decided that as long as you turn yourself in, I will let you live." I told him. "Oh ya, just tell them what you were planning and doing right now. No need to drum up ghosts of the past; that harm has already been done. I kind of like you, so maybe if you confess, they will give you a lighter sentence."

Lawrence looked at me and said, "Thank you, I think."

I began to laugh out loud and said, "You see Lawrence, that's why I like you. I tell you that you could have died, but instead I will let you go to prison. To this you respond with a sort of thank you. While I am mostly sure the cops don't know who I am, I would rather not give them a place to start looking. So, I will cover your face when we leave to turn you in. You understand this don't you Lawrence?"

He vigorously shook his head and said, "No problem man. While prison doesn't sound like a great place to be, it sure in hell is better than death."

To this I said "You do have a point. Lawrence, I don't usually have to say this to my victims, however, they are usually not alive and have no way of talking. But I feel as though I should say that if you don't turn yourself in, I will hunt you down and we will start over. However, the next time there will be no survival option. We clear about this?"

Lawrence still shaking his head said, "I will, I will, I will—turn myself in that is. If I may be frank, I am actually tired of looking over my shoulder and waiting to be apprehended."

"Alright then, here's what I am going to do."

I told him that I would have to knock him out and transport him to the State Police Office, where I would leave him and his evidence for them to find. At that point it would be up to him to keep to our agreement. The reason for putting him under was for the safey of both of us. You can't tell the cops where you were if you don't know. I told him he could tell them that I did this to him and he knows nothing more than the fact that he was abducted and told to turn himself in for prosecution—that the evidence is in the boxes. If he did not turn himself in, the person that abducted him would find him and end his life in a less than desirable way. When they ask where he may have been held he could answer with all honesty that he really did not know.

"Lawrence, when you tell the cop what happened you can tell them that if they haven't figured out from my other victims why I am doing this, it is because actions have consequences. If they won't or can't put these nasty people behind bars and keep them there, then I will take them out of this world so they can not harm anyone else. Sound good to you?" I asked Lawrence.

"How about, if you don't mind, I just start out with that. This way you can get your point across, and I don't have to screw around and just go to jail and get settled in?"

I started laughing and said, "You know Lawrence, I think I will miss you. I don't know anyone that wants to get down to the whole getting into jail thing."

Lawrence looked at me and said, "Well I can't, in all honesty, say that I am in a hurry to go to jail, but I am in even less of a mood to be dead."

"Good point," I said. "Oh yea, if them dumb asses manage to let you go, I will not chase you down. Just keep your nose clean, and you will never see me again."

To this he said, "Really, you mean it?"

"Yes, I really mean it." I said, with a little chuckle in my voice. "So, shall we get to it?" I asked him.

"No better time than the present I suppose," he said to me.

"Ok, the chloroform won't hurt; it will put you to sleep. I will take you to the car, and we will call it a day."

"Let's do it," he says.

I soaked the rag with chloroform and told him to breath deep and it would all be over. He did, and like someone turning out a light, he as out. I loaded him in the car. After I placed him in the back seat, I wiped off all his skin and anywhere that I might have touched him insuring that I had left nothing for the cops to use to find me. I took all the things I had brought to the shack—like the food wrappers and chloroform rag—and put them in the burn barrel and lit it. I covered up the burn barrel to prevent any sparks from escaping and starting the forest on fire, and got in the car for the trip back into town.

The trip didn't take very long and soon I drove past the State Police Office. Seeing that there was no real activity and knowing that there would be a camera somewhere, I pulled in behind the building. With my mask on and assuming a limp in my left leg, I unloaded Lawrence and took him right up to the back door and rang the bell at the prisoner entrance. Yes, yes, I know. That was really stupid and overly risky. But you know, I kind of got a thrill out of it.

I got back to my car and set the evidence boxes on the ground next to him and slowly pulled out of the lot. I looked in my mirror to see if they had come to the door as I pulled away. I just caught a sliver of light on the wall as I lost sight of the door and the back of the building. I circled the building and drove by at the speed limit and saw that two officers were helping Lawrence to his feet while another officer was heading to the boxes of paperwork to see what they were. I just kept driving and headed out of town.

I drove the car to a more, seedy part of town and found a nice dark spot under the elevated train tracks. There I parked the car and went to the trunk and retrieved the small can of gas and oil from the trunk. Why the oil you might ask? Well, let me tell you. Oil burns slower than gas and will help to insure the car will burn good and hot. This will insure the old junker will burn to the ground and any evidence that might link me to the car with it. I was very sure that the entrance I dropped Mr. Resnik off at captured me and my car on video, so I needed to dispose of it promptly.

I put the oil all over the dash and seats then generously doused the car in gasoline. I made a trail of gas from the car to one of the pillars for the elevated train and ran back to the car, throwing the plastic container that held the gas into the car. I went back to the pillar and lit the trail of gas. I watched as it raced to the car and heard the 'WOOMP' as the fumes from the gas meet the fire. I felt the percussion wave sent out from it as it ignited.

I find it very funny watching television as people pour gallons of gasoline on a car then stand there and light it ablaze. That is just not something that you do or even try to do. If you don't already know, it's not the gas that catches fire, not saying that the gas doesn't burn. Initially it's the fumes that catch fire, and when they do, depending on how much accelerant you used, the point at which it ignites can be quite violent. Gallons of gas poured on a thing, including the ground can have a serious percussion sent off of it. So, if you find it necessary to light something ablaze, like a car for example, give it plenty of room to boom. The last thing I would have wanted was to be knocked unconscious by the blast and get caught burning my car by a passing patrol car. That would have been a real stupid way to end things.

I walked away from the car after it looked as though it was thoroughly ablaze and headed off to hail a cab so I could start looking for a new junker car to use. As I walked away, I wondered how ole Lawrence was doing. *Lawrence, what a character*, I just shook my head and laughed to myself as I walked away.

CHAPTER 14

"Sir, Sir, can you hear me?" Lawrence kept hearing a voice as the haze of the chloroform slowly dissipated, and his mind began to return to the real world.

"Sir?" the officer said again.

"What?" Lawrence said in a groggy voice.

"Do you know where you are and how it is that you came to be here?" the officer asked.

"Yes, yes, I know, I am here to report a crime."

"A crime?" the officer repeated.

Lawrence thought to himself that being a smart ass would not get him very far right then but thought to himself, *what are you, a fucking parrot?* Instead, he said, "Yes, a crime."

"Is this crime you are reporting been perpetrated against you or another person?"

To this, Lawrence began to wonder if he would have been better off just letting the man kill him than endure this stupidity. Again, he thought to himself, *I was lying in your parking lot unconscious and you immediately ask if I am the one the crime was committed against.* Keeping his cool Lawrence said, "Both."

"Ok?" said the officer, now sounding a little confused.

Seeing this, Lawrence said, "I have committed a number of crimes; the proof of said crimes is in the boxes on the ground over there." He pointed to the paperwork in the boxes that the officers were sorting through. "Also," he said, "I agreed with the gentleman who abducted me, to turn myself in to you, or face death. As you can imagine I choose the least painful of the two options."

"Just to be clear and so I am sure that I am understanding you correctly, you were brought here to confess to some crimes that you had perpetrated, in lieu of death by a man that had kidnapped you and gave you these options?"

"You hear just fine officer," Lawrence said.

"Ok then. If you will please step inside, we will turn you over to some detectives, and they will take your statement and figure out how to handle it from there."

The officers gathered up the evidence boxes and helped Lawrence inside where he was turned over to the duty officer. They would question him and determine which department should take care of his confession, and what charges he would face. As the two officers turned over all the evidence, they looked at each other and shrugged. "If all the criminals would do that our jobs would be a whole lot easier," one of the officers said.

"Yea it would, or we would be out of a job," said the other officer. Both of them where laughing as they walked away.

I watched the local papers for any info that may have been published on my last victim, Mr. Resnik, and his case. A few days after I dropped him off, I was rewarded with just such an article. The headlines read 'Man charged with fraud and delivered to police by a serial killer is thankful for his life.' That made me begin to laugh out loud and instantly like Lawrence all the more. Man could that guy tell a tale. According to the statement given by Resnik, I was six foot five inches tall and 300 lbs. of pure muscle.

"Thanks Lawrence," I said to myself. Up until then, I had no idea I was such a bad ass. The story went on to say that while he didn't agree with my methods, he believes that as a vigilante serial killer, I may be able to clean up some of the more undesirable characters that are plaguing our society. It also said that while he could see my ability to carry out the crimes of punishing the unpunished, he also saw kindness and compassion in me. This I found a little odd, as he had never seen my face. Guess the eyes really are the looking glass to the soul.

The police had their little say so also saying that there was a task force set up to try to apprehend what, until now, was a suspected serial killer. A spokesman for the police said that this kind of vigilante justice would not be tolerated and that they would catch the suspect in question and bring him to justice. I could not help but laugh and say "Yeah, cause you all did such a good job a keeping all the other criminals behind bars. For that matter, you never even got some of them into jail at all. If they had, I would have had no reason to be doing what I was doing.

Well, I guess they know I am out there now. Not that this worries me even a little at all. There is, as there has always been, a chance of getting caught. Given the size of the city and the vast number of people living in it, the odds of me getting caught are right up there with your average person winning the lottery. Guess I will just keep on keeping on—business as usual some people might say. I suppose it is time to start the hunt again. My so-called good deed was done for the year.

The team was sitting in the conference room turned task force headquarters when the captain came in and said, "Alright boys, we have our first break, sort of."

"Sort of?" Jamison asked

"I didn't stutter, Jamison."

"So, lay it on us, Cap." They all gathered around the table and listened as the captain filled them in on the new lead.

"So, early this morning a middle age, white, male was dropped off unconscious to a local state police building. After he came to, he told the officers that he had been abducted by a vigilante serial killer."

"Whoa, whoa, whoa!" Jamison said.

"Let me finish, stud," said the captain.

"As I was saying, the man, a one Mr. Lawrence Resnik, and just in case you think you know this name it's because you probably do."

Hart spoke up and said, "Isn't that the guy that was defrauding all those people out of their life savings by selling fake retirement plans?"

The captain smiled and said, "The one and only. Very good, Hart, this is indeed the man of the hour. So, Mr. Resnik was dropped off at the station and someone rang the prisoner drop off bell and left several boxes containing evidence of Mr. Resnik's guilt." The captain went on to say, "After being interrogated by the troopers on duty, Mr. Resnik told them that after about a day of being in the custody of said killer he told him—and he quotes 'If I turn myself in, he will let me live."

"Damn!" Hanson blurted out. "Sorry, Cap," he said.

"No problem Hanson, I had the same reaction when I heard that also." The captain continued by saying, "The killer, according to Mr. Resnik, told him that as long as he goes to jail and serves all his time, he will leave him alone. But if he didn't, he would kill him in a rather nasty way, very similar to the way he—now listen carefully you guys—in a very similar way that he took care of his other victims that didn't have a choice of turning themselves in."

Hanson got the captains attention and asked, "Did he mention or make mention to his abductor marking any of his victims or did he mark Mr. Resnik in any way?"

"Good question," said the captain. "Unfortunately, we do not have that good of fortune to connect the cases. What I want you all to do is go and interview Mr. Resnik. Leach out of him any and all information that you can that may be useful to narrow down where our un-sub may be working. Cline, I want you to listen as the other three interview Mr. Resnik and see what you can assess of his character. See if you think you can come up with some other questions that may help in the investigation. Primarily—why our un-sub, if it is him, did not kill Mr. Resnik."

They all gathered their things and headed over to the state police building where Lawrence was being held. As Hart and Jamison were already partners, they rode together while Cline and Hanson took a separate vehicle. When they got to the precinct, they asked the duty officer to see the detective in charge of Mr. Resnik and sat down to wait.

After a short while, the detective in charge of the case came in. They all introduced themselves, and he invited them to the back where Mr. Resnik was waiting in an interview room. "Mr. Resnik?" the detective said. "I want you to meet detectives Jamison, Hart, and Hanson, from the city police and special agent Cline from the FBI. They are working together as a task force to catch the man they believe may have abducted and held you. The detective went on to say, "If you help these members of the task force, the DA (district attorney) will take this into account at your sentencing trial."

The mention of the possible lessening of his sentence made Lawrence smile, while at the same time, had him trying to remember if this killer guy that took him really meant that he would leave him alone as long as he plead guilty and did his given time. The members of the task force thanked the detective and waited till he left to get settled in for the task of gaining any information that Lawrence had to give them.

"So, Mr. Resnik," Jamison started.

"Please, call me Lawrence," Resnik said.

"Ok," said Jamison. "Please start from where you last remember being prior to our un-sub picking you up. Sorry, un-sub is short for unknown subject."

"Well, I was leaving a business that I was scamming on a business insurance program, and I was walking across the parking lot on my way to another business when a man stepped out from around the back of a car. I have met all kinds of people and think that I am a fairly decent judge of character, so meeting a stranger in a lot didn't automatically spook me. However, seeing this guy in a ski mask got me wondering what exactly was about to happen."

He went on saying, "Between the dark of night and the fact that he had a mask on—the mask being what turned on my oh shit alarm—I really didn't get a good look at him, other than he was a rather impressive character."

Hanson then spoke up and asked, "Impressive how?"

Lawrence's reply was, "Looked very fit like someone you wouldn't walk right up to and start cussing at kind of impressive. He carried himself well, you know, the type of person that just exudes self-confidence."

Cline standing in back seemed to absorb all of this as he listened inventively. "God only knows what is going on in his head," Hart said to Jamison, just quiet enough that no one else could hear him. Jamison just nodded his ascent.

The interview went on for around an hour with Lawrence saying, "As for the quote un-quote torture that he may be administering to his other victims, none was really dished out to me. I think the worse that almost happened was that he put some ex-lax on my burger that he brought me after picking up the boxes of evidence I had with me when he dropped me off here."

This time, Jamison spoke up. "Ex-lax?" he asked, with a funny sort of look on his face—half amusement the other half confusion.

"Yes, Ex-lax," Lawrence said. He expounded on this by saying, "However, he never let me eat it with the Ex-lax on it. In fact, he told me to wipe it off and I should be ok to eat it."

All the detectives looked questioning and mildly puzzled at this admission of kindness toward a victim, especially given the gruesomeness of his other alleged crimes.

To this point, SA Cline stood silent in the background. Now he spoke up and asked, "So between abducting you and threatening your life if you did not tell the truth and serve your time, he came back with a burger and before letting you eat it he said he had put Ex-lax on it and that you should remove it as to not suffer the side effects of the medication? Does this sound about right?"

Lawrence looked at Cline and said, "Not sounds about right, rather, it is right. I have no idea why he didn't kill or harm me in any way, and I was not about to ask him why or if he would."

"I see," said Cline. "From what you remember of your time with him, did you see anything that might lead you to believe that your abductor might be joking about the other persons he had supposedly hurt or killed?" Cline went on to say, "By this I mean, in your opinion do you think this man could have been a friend or relative of one of the people that you may have committed a fraud on or any one that you may have taken advantage of? This is very important in determining whether or not we are after the man we are looking for, or if it is just another person out for revenge and you were the person that they were after."

Lawrence sat there for a minute and pondered this for a moment, looked at SA Cline and said, "At no time during my encounter did I feel that this man was not capable of doing the things he said he had supposedly done. You ever been around a person that told you something and everything in you screamed that this person was more than willing and capable of doing the thing or things that he said he would?" He continued by saying, "Surely special agent Cline, in your time with the FBI you have run across several or at least one person that you just saw the potential of evil or the ability to do something completely unhinged and absolutely nut fuck crazy?"

Cline looked back at Lawrence and said, "As a matter of fact I have. I also hope I never have to see that again in another human being."

Hanson broke in and said, "Pardon the interruption Cline, but I would like to ask Mr. Resnik a question if you don't mind?"

"Not at all, feel free to ask whatever," Cline said.

"Thanks," replied the detective. "Lawrence, did you see this, as you put it 'a person that was more willing and capable of doing the thing or things that he said he could', or did you see anything in him that may have led you to believe he may, if his tasks were complete, he may stop the killing?" Hanson went on to say, "Do you at all believe from your time with him that he may be ready to kill again soon or say anything about who he may be targeting next?"

Lawrence looked at him and said, "If he had said anything to that affect, I missed it. I do apologize but given the fact I was facing what could have been my death, all I was worried about was doing exactly what the man asked of me. No more or no less." Lawrence sat there for a minute then said, "However, he said that I never really hurt anyone physically, and that is why he was going to spare my life as long as I turned myself in, and that it is a lot better choice than some of his other victims got. This is for you detectives so listen close. I have no doubt in my mind that if I had done something worse, I would not be here talking to you today."

"Thank you, Mr. Lawrence," Hanson said.

They let the jailer take Lawrence back to his cell and discussed what they may or may not have learned from Lawrence so far. "I want to think about all that we learned from Mr. Resnik today and then maybe interview him again at a later date after we put it all together." Cline said.

"Yeah, I agree. However, this guy, as far as I can see, doesn't seem to be crazy. Well, at least not the type of crazy that might indicate a spree killer. I think he thinks and plans all his kills well in advance and with great for thought," Jamison said.

"I agree. I also believe we will be picking up bodies from this guy for a while—at least until he fucks up and leaves something behind that ties him to a crime. Even then, we will have a hard time tying him to the others with just the carvings on the bodies as evidence," said Cline.

"So, Cline?" asked Hart. "What are you feeling about this guy so far?"

"Well, so far all I can give you that is close to truth is that this guy is very smart and probably well-schooled and extremely organized. He leaves nothing to chance, plans every move in advance. The one thing that we can hope for is that he will have pity on another victim and it will lead to his downfall. We will be earning our money with this guy.

Someone did or tried to do something real bad to this guy or someone he knows and it set him off."

"So, you think that the only way we will catch him is on one of his mercy deeds? Why?" asked Hanson.

To this Cline replied, "This is just based on what I have seen so far. It doesn't take into the fact that he is human and can make mistakes. However, with that being said, the lack of evidence at each scene shows the planning and forethought that is put into each crime. If I had to stagger a guess as to the why he chose the means in which he did to solve the problem, I would have to say that he saw no other choice but to rid the world of the offenders. He obviously doesn't believe that the system can do it correctly."

They all nodded their heads and seemed to agree with Cline for the time. As to what they would do next, was a variable that was yet to be decided. For now, they would have to go back to the precinct and keep examining the evidence—as little as it may be—and hope the guy would screw the pooch and leave something behind for them to catch him with. While this was seemingly more and more unlikely the further things advance in this case, stranger things had happened.

CHAPTER 15

I woke up to the sun shining through the window of our bedroom, and wouldn't you know it, right into my left eye. I turned my head to the other side determined to get some more sleep, only to find I was alone in bed. 'That's weird,' I thought to myself, 'I am almost always up before Jill is. Unless that is, she got called in to her practice for an emergency involving one of her patients.' Against my better judgment, or what I would have thought to be my better judgment, I rolled out of bed. I threw on a pair of sweats and a tee shirt and headed downstairs in search of Jill and a pot of coffee.

I turned the corner from the hall leading into the kitchen and waah-la, there she was. "Good morning," I said to her.

Jill turned and looks at me and in a quiet tone said, "I'll give you the morning part of that statement; the good part is still to be determined."

Seeing the seriousness in her face I asked, "What's the matter? You look as though you are going to be ill."

Jill looked at me and said, "Ill indeed, with a hefty side order of really pissed off!"

'Uh oh,' I thought. Trying to remember what I had done lately to piss off my wife. Concluding that I had not done anything, I walked over to her and asked, "So what's the matter darling?"

Jill looked at me and said, "Human trafficking, that is what's the matter." I walked over to the coffee pot and grabbed a cup of joe.

Small side note here: nyone ever wonder where things like, coffee and vomit get their nick names— 'Joe' for coffee and 'Ralph' for vomit? I mean, was Joe some kind of hyper active wild man with an overabundance of energy that constantly bounced off the wall while never spilling even a drop of his coffee? I am not even sure where to start the guessing process for why the name 'Ralph' was coined for a steamy pile of half-digested food. I am sure that there is a good back story for that one too.

Anyway, back to what I was saying before I got side tracked. I poured my coffee and looked at my wife and said, "Ok, I am listening, tell me what's on your mind."

Jill shook her head and began to speak. "I got up earlier this morning to pee and grab something to drink because I had a dry throat. When I got to the kitchen, I realized I may be a little hungry also."

I smiled and said, "Been there." I let her continue.

"I turned the television on and saw what was happening on Fox News." It's no secret in our house that we like Fox News, especially the *O'Reilly Factor* and *The Five*. Ah shit, there I go again. Getting sidetracked. So sorry, where was I? Oh yeah, Jill was saying she had turned on the television to Fox.

"I saw this news report on the human trafficking. I had no idea that it had gotten to the point that it has." Her eyes were getting a little watery as she continued. "What kind of sick assholes would abduct people in order to sell them to other sick assholes to do God only knows what with? It makes me sick to my stomach. They even take young children for sex slaves also. What kind of twisted pervert do you have to be to harm a child like that?"

I look her in the eyes and said, "You would have to be some kind of twisted and fucked up person in order to harm a child like that, to treat them like so much property."

Jill looked back at me and said, "If I were to ever catch someone like that, doing to children what they do…" She shakes her head and looks me right in the eyes and says, "I WOULD KILL THEM WHERE THEY STAND!!!"

Ok, so in case you haven't caught on yet, I really love this woman. I took her in my arms and told her, "If you find anyone like that, you let me know and I will help you end their evil ways, one asshole at a time."

She tightened her hold on me and began to cry. "I love you so much Jack," she told me.

"I love you too, more than you can ever know."

Just in case you haven't already guessed it, I just found my new targets. Well, maybe not found, but certainly have an idea of who to look for anyway. I go to work and pretend to care about what I am doing. Don't get me wrong, I do love my job, but my hobby just took a strong hold in my life. I realize that calling murder a hobby flies in the face of all those that have an actual hobby, like stamp collecting of wood working, but let's be honest, it is a hobby of sorts. The definition of hobby is, 'A pursuit outside ones' regular occupation'. However, what I call it is neither here nor there.

I finished up some paperwork on a project that I was working on and went to an Internet café. I liked using those places because it would be a lot harder to trace me if I happened to ever show a pattern in my killings. I bought some time, with cash of course, and went over to a computer. I started looking up some information on human trafficking and at once became disgusted and astonished at the sheer amount of human trafficking that there is worldwide.

There are stats from places like, The International Labor Organization, The U.S. Department of Labor, National Center for Missing and Exploited Children, and the Polaris BeFree Textline. All these organizations have staggering statistics on how many people, adults and children alike go missing and are used for both the sex trade and forced labor. I guess slavery isn't gone after all; it just went underground. One of those sites went on to say that globally there are around twenty point nine million victims of human trafficking. Some sixty eight percent are trapped in forced labor—twenty six percent of them are children, while fifty five percent of those listed are women and girls. Now if that don't make your ass pucker, then I have no idea what will.

I read all those statistics on some of the horrific crimes going on out there, and it really made me feel as though what I was doing wasn't as bad as I first thought. By no means do I think that it is even close to legal or right, however, I could be doing a whole lot worse. My mind made up, I started researching people that may be involved in the human trafficking rings in my area.

Ok, this may need some clarification. It's not like there is a website that you can look up that says, "Yes, yes, here we are—a bunch of crazy assholes that love selling innocent people for whatever your heart may desire." It's not that easy. I started with public records looking for arrests associated with abductions, child pornographers and human trafficking. While anyone of these wonderful examples of the human race would do, I wanted to be selective for now as to whom I wanted to remove. I needed it to be someone that was tied to a larger group— a person that, if freed from prison would go back to the group and start up or continue operations.

I focused on the newly freed persons and narrowed my search from there. While doing this search, I found a whole new pond in which to draw from for future kills. I narrowed my search down to a couple of real unlucky scumbags. Targets at hand, I started my reconnaissance of the subjects to see who the lucky person was. I wanted to make sure that when I took down my target, it was near to or in a place that his gang could find him before the authorities did. That would help communicate my message to the gang that those types of sales may no longer be as safe as once thought.

My hope was that I could get some pictures of the group my targets were affiliated with and given the opportunity, could take out as many of the bastards as I could—thus communicating to the other groups that this was not a place in which human trafficking would be tolerated. If at all possible I got the chance to take out more of these rotten assholes, I would surely do that very thing.

My first target was a fine, upstanding member of society. For all you out there that may wonder why I said 'fine and upstanding member of society' as though I like them, well that is what we normal people call sarcasm. This asshat whom I speak of goes by the name of Jon Snow. No, not the guy off of *Game of Thrones* or the nineteenth century doctor that helped in the regulation and administration anesthetics—just a guy that happens to share the name with them. It seemed that Mr. Snow was affiliated with a mob-style gang that had their hands in well…shit, almost everything related to the human trafficking trade. From forced labor, to selling them off as sex slaves, to the rich underbelly of our society, you name it they did it. Just the thought of someone buying a child and using them as a sex doll makes me want to vomit—or Ralph if you are so inclined.

Deciding that this waste of a perfectly good skin sack would be my next target, I decided to forgo scouting the other guy I had in my sights and concentrate all my efforts on Mr. Snow and all the people he was affiliated with. Not yet sure if I wanted to try to infiltrate the group as a buyer of trafficked persons or just stalk and kill at my leisure, I observed Mr. Snow and those he spent time around on a regular basis. Deciding that I would not be able to stomach watching people being sold off as slaves for whatever purpose the buyer had in mind, I went with the kill as I identified a route and hopefully I could take out a majority of the gang. I wanted to leave my mark on their persons as before thus slowing their sales long enough to take them all out or get inside and find some damning information to give to the cops and hope they can put an end to their dealings.

This would turn out to be a whole different style of hunting and killing, as most of the time these scumbags traveled together. Guess they thought there was safety in numbers; now there is a foolish concept. I did have a plan to identify the buyers of the trafficked persons and their handlers and do my best to turn them into the authorities if I could not dispose of them personally.

As I said before, sometimes with the right amount of money and representation a person can get off of almost anything. This belief is why, if given the chance, I would kill as many of these assholes as I could safely kill without getting caught. The one thing I would have to remember was not to reuse the area for anything again for a long time. No reason to give my fan club a place to catch me in the act. My method this time was to shoot from a distance, sneak up leave my mark, then haul ass away from the scene. That was where the recon would come in handy. It would take some time, but if I played my cards right, my prey would show me a pattern of movement that would allow me to kill them in a less populated place, henceforth allowing me to move the bodies to a place that would allow me to get as many of those pricks as I could from this particular collection of pond scum. This all hinged on really good recon, because before I could start killing them, I needed to identify their main base of operations. I really, really, really wanted to get as many of those freaks as I could.

The next few weeks went by mostly boringly, as most of the recon was done. Armed with pictures and a plethora of information for the authorities, I choose my weapon. This time I decide to do my shooting with a crossbow—yes, a crossbow. This may seem like a medieval style of weapon, but as I have said before, no silencer really silences a weapon and I had no real desire to get caught or killed. This is why I chose a crossbow. The only thing that may have posed a problem was the reload process. Having practiced over the last few weeks, I felt that the minimal number of seconds I had whittled the reload process to was acceptable and should be fast enough to do the job.

Mr. Snow, as it turns out, was only a mid-level person in the operation, or so it seemed. He did, however, reveal the identities of a lot of the operations personnel, and in turn, the other people showed me more of the higher up's, and so it began. The way I saw it, I would start with the lower level of the gang and work my way up to the higher ups, if I pulled it off the way I had planned it.

The next night, I went about the task of relieving Mr. Snow of his undeserved place on this earth. As luck should have it, he was with another of the less important persons on the chain of importance in the organization. Maybe gang is a better word to use, as organization is a legit term used by many actual businesses. Having identified what I felt to be the gang's main base of operations and having watched the movements of all the people involved that I could, I located myself two blocks down from the building and waited for Mr. Snow and his companion.

Having observed the aforementioned persons taking the same route multiple times, I felt safe in the fact that it would be the route that he would be taking tonight. Sure as the day is long, and pretty close to the time I had anticipated, they came around the corner. The trick would be to shoot Mr. Snow and then get off the second shot thus killing his companion before he had a chance to realize what had happened and tried to run, or worse try to kill me.

They came into range and I got my first target in my sights. Having my breath under control and my target in the cross hairs, I pulled the trigger. The moment the bolt was loosed I immediately loaded the second bolt, feeling assured that the first target was hit. I re-aimed and loosed the second bolt. Finally, I was given the chance to look and see if I had hit both of my targets and had two confirmed kills or if I had to go run after the wounded and put them out of their misery. I peered down out of my perch and saw both men on the ground. Mr. Snow was not moving, the bolt having obviously hit home and ended it immediately. This, however, was not the case for the other man. While he was not running per say, he was squirming in what may have been the last seconds of his life. Either way, I had to go down and load the bodies and remove them.

I climbed down from where I had made the kills and headed their way. Arriving at the bodies, I observed that the second guy must have been hit a little to the right of the heart, never the less he was still not having a very good night, and I helped his evening get a little worse by thrusting the bolt to the left a bit hoping to hit the heart and ending this guy's useless existence. I got my message carved into their chests and retrieved my ride.

Having loaded the bodies in the back of my new beater, I set off to the planned dump site. The site I chose would act as not only a disposal site but double as a nice place that people could discover the bodies and at the same time be far enough from the kill site as not to attract to much attention. That served two very important purposes. One of them was to keep the other members of the gang semi unaware of what was coming their way. The second was to not give the authorities a place to focus on or watch until I was done with my task. I figured I would leave the last body right on the front door step of the building that I had seen them coming and going from. Until that time came, I was going to dispose of the bodies in different spots of my choosing.

One such site was an area that, at this time of night, was all but completely devoid of people. On the other hand, take this same area after six in the morning and someone would have to literally try not to see the body. The other place while risky, was somewhat of a, haha kind of site. Just like dropping off Lawrence at the cop shop, that place is frequented by law enforcement persons. Yeah, yeah, yeah, it may be a cliché, but cops and others love donuts. The trick to the donut shop drop-off, would be to not be seen. I decided to do a rolling drop off of the last body. While I am sorry for all the innocent people that would have to see the body, the shock of the body would draw the officials to it, and if I was really lucky, someone would call the press. I had no doubt that the cell phone and internet footage would without a doubt shine some light on my deeds.

After dropping off the first body and getting close to the second drop off point, I prepared to give the body a push out the passenger side door of my ultra-cool jalopy. Taking a quick glance and seeing that there was no one around, I gave the body a shove and heard the dull thud of the it making contact with the pavement. There were a few slaps of the extremities as the body rolled a few times before coming to a stop just shy of the intended target. Never slowing down, I reached over and pulled the car door shut and kept driving as though I were just an average joe driving by. Two down and quite a few more to go—time to ditch the car and head home for some shut eye and start planning the next kill.

CHAPTER 16

I woke up the next morning and did the same as any other day—coffee, food, and all that other morning jazz. I sat down and talked with the kids and asked how things were going at school— if there are any events that I needed to take time off work for.

"Hey dad?" my youngest asked.

"What's up bud?" I replied.

"Will you take a day off for the spring concert? I have a solo with my saxophone."

I looked at my boy with a smile and said, "It would be my great pleasure good sir."

He smiled and went back to his breakfast. I looked over at my oldest and said, "So how about you? Solved world hunger or you just sticking to the small stuff these days?"

He looked up at me and said, "World hunger dad, that was so last week." He said it in his best sassy surfer voice. We all laughed and continued on with the morning. The kids headed off to school and the wife and I left for work ourselves.

I arrived at work and did a quick scan of the local news and saw that they have indeed found both bodies and that their task force now believed with little doubt that these recent murders were tied to that of several other crimes that resembled that of a vigilante serial killer on the loose. It also went on to say that the general public at this time has nothing to worry about, this due to the fact that the killer is only targeting criminals. The officials were asking everyone to keep their eyes open and be extra observant for anything out of the ordinary. I scanned several other news reports and saw that all the articles and reports were very similar. 'Hmm,. I thought to myself. It appears as though the rabbit is out of the bag. Good.'

"Jamison!" the captain yelled. "My office, now. And bring the rest of your gang with you."

Jamison hollerd at the rest of the group and they all headed to the captains' office. "Uh oh, he saw the news," Hart said. They all filtered into the captain's office and stood in front of his desk.

"Alright you all, this guy has got to go!" the captain said in a not so cordial voice. "If the commissioner climbs too much further up my ass, I will have to start charging him rent. Do we have any new leads on this guy?" He asked.

Jamison looked over at his team and then at his captain and said, "Not yet cap. The guy is a ghost and leaves nothing behind."

Cline looked at the captains and said, "Sir if I may." The captain nodded his head and listened as Cline said, "The profile I can give you of this guy with the info that we have gathered so far is rather limited." The captain raised an eye and gives Cline a look of 'Tell me something I don't know.' Cline saw the captains face and quickly continued. "However, from what we have ascertained, I can tell you that we are looking for a middle-aged male with what I can only guess is a well above average IQ—most likely ex-military or some kind of a competitive shooter given the two shots that where delivered to the latest victims. He is most likely independently wealthy or has access to enough money and a flexible enough job to both plan and carry out the crimes without drawing attention to himself with an abundance of absences."

Hanson jumped in and said, "Where did you get the idea that he must be wealthy and the stuff about his job?"

Cline replied to Hanson in a educator style of speaking. "Well, just look at it for a second. He has to plan the kills, do the deeds, and if he has a family as I am sure he probably does, he has to spend time with them."

Then the captain jumped in, "Family, where did you come up with that?"

"Well sir, so far as I can ascertain from what I have seen. All the crimes have come at night or in the evenings. This leads me to believe that not only is he using the dark of night and evening for cover, but also because he wants to get done and return home with nothing more than a 'had to work late' excuse. This awards him with a great alibi. Also, given the fact that according to the markings he is leaving on his victims, they all have to do with harming someone in an intimate way."

Cline then turned to Hanson and said, "To finish my explanation about the work and money issues. He is either wealthy, thus he has no need to work and goes about his business at his leisure, or he has to make at least a minimal appearance at work prior to carrying out his deeds. The job must pay well enough to afford his weapons and be lenient enough that as long as the assigned work is getting done, he is left alone."

"Ok, all that sounds good and all but how do we use that to help us find our man?" the captain asked.

"Unfortunately, it only gives us a base line to work from, but not really a person to look for per say." Cline replied.

Hart jumped in and said, "So essentially we have a whole lot of nothing then."

"Yes and no." Cline replied.

Like a church choir hitting a verse just right, they all said, "and the yes is?"

This got a laugh out of Cline and the others. "Well, the yes is that we have a slight idea of his choice of targets. My hope is that like the two drug dealers, our guy will take on something involving more people—a gang or organized crime type of business. Something that will require him to work on the group a while awhile thus giving us time to identify some of the victims and tie them to a specific organization or group. Then, we locate the group, try to surveil them and hope our guy strikes and we can take him down."

The rest of the group nodded their heads and the captain said, "Well done Cline, it may not be much, but it is more than we have had so far."

Jamison, always being the wise ass, said, "Well shit Cline, guess you feds are good for something after all."

The rest of the group laughed, and in return so did Cline. "We do what we can," Cline said.

"Alright you guys, the party is over. Let's get to the crime scenes and see what we can get out of them. I've asked the precincts that caught the cases not to touch anything after the medical examiner is through until we can get there and see what we can ascertain from the sites. However, given the public area in which the one victim was left, we need to get down there ASAP." He went on to say, "Hanson and Cline, you two go to the scene over by the bakery; Jamison and Hart, I want you two to go over to the shipping district where they found the other body. Let's get this guy."

On the way over to the crime scenes, Jamison and Hart started talking about what they thought about the case thus far. "So, what do you think about Clines analysis this morning?" Hart asked.

"I'll give it to the Cline man, for having only read the case files and questioned Lawrence that one time. Coming up with all that really blows my mind," Jamison said.

"Yeah, that profiling stuff is one hell of a deal. Like, how in the hell did he just out of the blue come up with all that shit about his employment and stuff?" Hart asked.

"Hell if I know. I just hope that he can keep it up long enough to catch the guy," said Jamison. "So, what do you think of the guy?"

"Who, Cline?" asked Jamison.

"No, our un-sub," said Hart.

"What about him?" asked Jamison.

"You know, are you for or against him?" Hart asked.

"Well as a cop I have to be against his actions due to the fact he is breaking the law. But as a person I can't help but thinking at least someone is getting rid of these douche bags. I mean, we as cops can only do so much, and it really pisses me off when we bust our asses to build a case to try to put someone away, only to get the whole case thrown out and the criminal set free on a technicality."

"I couldn't agree more," said Hart. "While I agree with you that what he is doing is against the law and for that we are duty bound to put him behind bars. It is mildly comforting that some of these dirty ass scumbags are getting what they deserve."

Jamison and Hart arrived at the shipping district to find the medical examiners van was still there. "Oh good I was hoping to get a word in with M.E before she left the scene," Jamison said. The detectives showed the patrol officers guarding the scene their credentials and were allowed onto the scene.

"You want me to look around and get a feel for the crime scene while you go talk to the M.E?" Hart asked.

"Yea sure, I'll get whatever I can from the M.E and get back with you when I'm done. However, I think that we are looking a body dump." Jamison walked up to where the body was being examined and asked the medical examiner what she thought.

"Detective Jamison, long time no see.", Dr. Moore said.

"Yes, it has, how have you been doc?", Jamison asked.

"Well you know, same old boring life as always. The dead really don't carry on too many interesting conversations," she asked.

"So, anything interesting to pass on? I am sure that this is another of our vigilantes kills. I am just hoping that there may be something to help us find the guy," Jamison asked.

The doctor looks up at Jamison and said, "Well as much as I would love to give you some good news, I just don't have anything out of the ordinary. The guy is clean and to the point. Very efficient, the carvings are descriptive and as you can see, right to the point."

Jamison shook his head and said, "Well there is always hope that he will screw up sometime. Do you see any patterns in the weapon used to carve the crime into the chest, does it look like he is using a different blade each time, anything?"

"Looks to me as though it is the same blade; the problem is that it is very sharp. In order to narrow down the type of blade we will need a little more. These wounds could have been made by anything from a scalpel to one of those utility knives people use to clean with," Dr. Moore said.

"Well thanks for the info doc, have you been to the other scene yet?" Jamison asked.

"No, I sent the assistant medical examiner over there. I will check in with him when I am done here." Jamison turned to go and said, "See ya later doc."

Dr. Moore looked at Jamison, nodded her head and got back to the body.

Jamison found Hart and asked what he found out. "Well, not a whole hell of a lot to tell you the truth. Looks like your basic dump job. He is definitely putting them in places that people can find them. My guess is that, this is so he can communicate what he is doing. After hearing Cline say what he did about our un-sub being of above average intelligence, I believe that he is only communicating what he is doing, as opposed to taunting us."

Jamison told Hart what the medical examiner told him, and they walked the scene together taking pictures and just getting a basic layout of the place. Having gone through the crime scene they got in their car and decided to go see Cline and Hanson at their scene.

"Well, I hope those two had better luck than we had," Hart said.

"Not holding out too much hope for that. These scenes look like nothing more than dump sites," Jamison added.

They pulled up outside the second crime scene and made contact with Hanson and Cline. "So what new and exciting info do you have to pass on from your crime scene?" Jamison said in a slightly sarcastic tone.

"Well, we have a whole lot of nothing. Strictly a dump site, doc has really nothing to say that is unique of any other dead body except for the carvings on the body that is," replied Hanson.

Cline stepped forward and said, "This guy is very good, all of his scenes thus far seem to be lacking any forensic evidence at first glance. We will, however, have to wait 'til the crime scene techs have their way with the place so I can confirm that, but I am not real optimistic that they will find anything."

"Yeah, we found the same amount of nothing at our scene also. Even the weapon used to carve the words into the bodies seemed to be one of your everyday unimportant items." Jamison went on to say, "We are going to have to really get into these two victims lives and see if we can tie them to something or someone so we can get some kind of lead."

The detectives talked a while longer before deciding to return to headquarters and continue the discussion there. Back at the precinct they all gathered in the meeting room to resume the discussion.

"So, other than a fat lot of nothing forensically, what do we have and where should we go from here?" Jamison asked.

Hart spoke up and said, "I think we should focus less on who this guy is and focus more on the victims and what they have or have not done. If they were convicted, what was the sentence and was it appropriate for the crime. Then, if we can locate any family members, we need to interview them to see if any of them seem to be the type that might be able to pull of the kind of murders that we are seeing."

Nods were seen all around except for Cline, he had his 'I'm thinking' look on his face and finally said, "I agree on the conviction thing, however, I believe we should focus on the punishment angle. This could be our guys trigger. If people were getting off or had very small to no sentence handed down by the court it can very easily be what set this guy off. In our un-subs eyes, if the sentence did not fit the severity of the crime, then that may be how he is finding his targets."

Jamison said, "Well shit, doc, that's a damn fine idea. Guess I will have to rethink my opinion of all you smart guys,."

Laughing Cline said, "Thank you, I think." He also went on to say, "This will not mean a whole lot right now, but it may in the future when and if we catch this guy. I am willing to bet that someone near him has at some point been harmed or had a very near miss at ending up a victim."

Hart looked at Cline and said, "Now we just have to catch the guy."

"Indeed, that will be the hard part," replies Cline.

After looking as deep as they could into the past murders they believe to be linked to their un-sub, all the detectives agreed that the crimes perpetrated by the victims so far had indeed been grossly under punished.

"Well shit, it's a wonder that we are not just a country of complete lawlessness," Jamison commented.

"Yeah, it's almost as if we don't even have any consequences to the actions of perpetrators. This is the part of the job that I have grown to hate," Hanson said.

"It is a sore point when you bust your ass on a case only to watch the bastards walk away with nothing more than a slap on the wrist," Hart added.

Then Cline stepped in and said, "The most puzzling part of this case is that of Mr. Lawrence Resnik. I haven't decided if our in-sub intentionally sought him out or if after meeting him and realizing that while the crime was not a good thing, it wasn't worth killing him over. This makes me believe that our un-sub has a real reason for doing these crimes and is just not acting out or is psychology disturbed. I do however feel that our un-sub thinks or believes this is the only way that these people will never see justice. This will make him a rather hard person to apprehend."

"Why hard to apprehend?" asked Hart.

"Hard because he will plan each and every murder individually. Our un-sub will take every precaution to not get caught and is in no hurry, nor will he be sporadic in finding his victims. When he kills, it will be when, who, and where, all according to a preplanned schedule."

The other detectives looked at him, Cline could see that they were seeing the same thing that he was seeing. It was going to be a long difficult pursuit. As to how many people he killed and how long it would take to apprehend the guy was anyone's guess.

Hanson spoke up and said, "If I had to take a guess as to where to start looking, I would have to suggest that we stick to the last set of kills given that they have ties to a larger group, and he may be trying to take out the whole group. The step after that would be trying to find out how he is choosing his victims."

Cline looked at Hanson and said, "I was thinking the same thing, however, I have been drawing a blank as to the how. I have several ideas but nothing that I think we can advance the case with anyway, at least I think, let me run a few by you all."

They spent the rest of the day bouncing ideas off of each other about the way the killer went about selecting his victims. Having realized that the guy killed only those that had received a sentence not worthy of their crimes, in other words they all but got off, only made the task of catching or even figuring out who this guy was nominally easier.

Hanson said, "Hey you all, I pulled up the stats on persons paroled and those on probation, and as much as you all will not want to hear this, there are approximately 840,000 on parole and a blistering 3.7 million on probation at any given time."

Jamison looked at Hanson and said, "Your right, that really fucking sucks. Did you think that maybe I was feeling too good about the possibility of finding this creep or what?" The other detectives in the room, including Cline began to laugh out loud.

Cops have a sense of humor often reserved for those in the professions that directly expose them to the gruesome parts of society—for example, cops, paramedics, EMTs, ER doctors and nurses and all others exposed to the 'nasty' in life. This form of humor is called 'gallows humor'. Often times, it is a way for the people in these occupations to cope with what they see and deal with on a daily basis. As you can imagine, some individuals cannot cope with the job and have to seek a less stressful and not so gruesome line of an occupation. As the old saying goes—it's not for everyone".

CHAPTER 17

The detectives and other law enforcement officials were looking for me and trying to put together a case for what I can only surmise to be my utter annihilation. Ok, so maybe not my annihilation, but you have to admit it is a really cool word. Anyway, as they were trying to 'capture' me, I had a personal tragedy of my own, my father died. While you may be asking yourself what the hell that has to do with vigilante justice? It doesn't, however, it is my book and it has to do with me. I was thinking of putting some smartass comment in right there, but I figure I have told enough people in this book so far to fuck off, eat me, and various other colorful words, so I will not this time.

Now I also know that there will be the element of you out there that is like, "oh, fuck the pussies that can't get the haha out of it, and read it as just a book". To those people I will say, "Keep your fucking panty hose on!!!" It's only this once. There will be plenty of profanity and other nastiness down the road. After all, I do have critics to please you know. How would it look if I never wrote anything for them to complain about? If I were to do that than they would really be butt hurt.

Oops, there I go again, on a rant, LOL. Anyway, as I was saying, the passing of my father, while certainly painful and sad, came with a short reprieve from my so-called hobby. As I had said earlier, my father was the owner of the chemical engineering company that I was working for. After college and my time in the military, I had insisted on working my way up the food chain in the company. As with the military, I believed that trust and respect was earned and never given. So, my thinking on this matter was that if I were to work my way through the ranks of the company, I would not be considered the owners boy with the silver spoon in his mouth. This being how I got the company. That and I was the strongest seamen of the other million or so when my mother and father were bumping uglies.

For the most part that was correct—not the sperm part, I know I was a bad ass sperm daddy. "OOH RAH devil sperm, getting me some of that egg". Anyway, as I was saying, again, for the most part the respect was earned, and I performed as expected. Knowing my dad would never let the company fall into private, non-family owned hands, part of my getting to work my way up the chain agreement was that if he were to die I would get full control of the company and the 80 percent holdings of the chemical company that we owned that supplied most of the chemicals we used in our work. While I was paid well for doing what I already did, I became a millionaire overnight.

Don't get me wrong, I would give anything to have my father back, buuuut, I would not turn down the money that came along with the new title. I mean shit, giving me the reins of this kind of money with my side occupation was like giving a sex addict a case of condoms, box of Viagra and telling him to have fun as you drop him off at a whore house. For once, I will be the P.C. dude. (Sorry ladies no offense it just seemed like a more fitting word for the book, keep up the good work.)

The family and I went about the arduous tasks involved in the death of a loved one and attended the funeral. We also attended the after funeral gathering accustom a man with as many ties to the community as my father had. The whole thing was a rather painful and exhausting series of events. After we wrapped all that up, I took a few days off to recoup and reorganize my thoughts and priorities as to how my life would now run from day to day. The next several weeks after that was spent at board meetings getting to know the board members and other important members of the company that I was now in charge of. My first duty as CEO and leader was to appoint an individual to be my personal assistant. This person would have to have intimate knowledge of the company both current and as far as I was concerned as far back as I could reach into my dads' past. I was looking for a person with this kind of knowledge so that I would know how my father had operated things. I believed that knowing how my father had built this company up to the size it was no accident. Having as much knowledge of past events and decisions of the companies' performance and decision making was how I would proceed.

Having found an assistant in the form of an old family friend that had been by my fathers' side since almost the beginning of the companies' inception, I sat back and got used to the day to day life of a CEO. BOOOOORING, no wonder these people get paid so much each year, it's not because they are just that good at their jobs. Well, it's not just that; it's because the only way to keep someone from going completely fucking insane is obviously to pay them. By the end of the month, I felt like I was going to pull my fucking hair out one by one with a pair of tweezers.

WTF, as the younger generation now says, or WHAT THE FUCK, as us old timers would say, was the first thing out of Jamison's mouth as he stormed into the room.

"What the fuck what?" asked Hart.

"Where in the hot smoking hell did this guy go, is what the fuck," Jamison replied.

"What's the matter boss, pissed off cause the guy won't walk in here and turn himself in?" Hanson asked, trying hard not to smile.

"Is it even possible for you to not make some kind of wise crack?" Jamison asked.

"Not to my knowledge boss, but what's really up?" replied Hanson.

"It's like this guy has just disappeared off the face of the fucking earth. He's just gone. One minute he is here and the next minute he is not. Poof, fuck off and good buy?" said Jamison.

Understanding Jamison's frustrations from past cases not going as smoothly as he had wished they would, or smoldering out all together, Hanson said, "No worries boss, we'll get him. Maybe he has just took a bit of time to get this very type of reaction out of us."

"It's only been a month. Maybe we got lucky and the guy got into an accident and is dead," Hart said.

"Yeah, and maybe my dick just grew six inches and I was discovered by a talent agent for a porn movie." replies Jamison. Everyone in the room laughed and things began to calm down a bit.

Cline came into the room, seeing that everyone is laughing asked, "What did I miss?"

Always on the ball, Hanson replied, "Jamison just got an audition for a porn film." The three detectives began to laugh again.

Cline shook his head and said, "Never mind, some things are not worth knowing—especially images of Jamison pumping some little hottie with some kind of horrible music in the background." That sent the others into uncontrollable laughter. Even Jamison joined in on the laughter, finally letting the grumpy go. After a few minutes, the crew settled down and got back to business.

"So, what we have is nothing basically, right?" asked Cline.

"Not just nothing, but a whole lot of nothing to be precise," replied Hanson.

Jamison looked at Cline and asked, "Have you tracked down the leadership or other players in that gang that we..." Jamison used his hand and makes air quotes. "thought our guy might have been after?"

"We know who they are and all about what they supposedly do, just no hard evidence yet to bring them in on." Cline went on to say, "Unlike our un-sub, we have to convict them and not just kill them."

Hanson turned to everyone and said, "Sometimes the latter seems like it would be the easier of the two options." They all shook their heads in agreement. "However, that would make us no better than the guy you all are supposed to be looking for."

They all turned their heads and saw the captain standing in the doorway with a look of, 'What am I paying you all for' on his face. "Captain," Jamison said.

"In the flesh," replied the captain.

"We were…" They all had 'just got busted' looks on their faces as they tried to figure out something to say.

"Stop tripping over your dicks. I know that the case has hit a stumbling block," the captain said. "I was just checking in to see if any new leads have surfaced by some strange twist of fate. But judging by the laughter and what not I am guessing the answer to be a big fat no."

Jamison looked at the captain and said, "Big fat no is an understatement, Cap. I was talking to the guys prior to the Hanson Show and was stating that it seems as if the guy had just dropped off the face of the earth."

Cline looked over at Jamison and the captain and said, "While it is unusual for a killer to stop the way that our guy has, it is not impossible. Any number of things could have or can happen that would have stopped our guy for the time being. Simply put, you have everything from auto accidents to deaths in the family that could have given this guy a pause in his actions."

The captain looked at them all and said, "Cline makes a good point. While this all seems to be a little overwhelming due to a lack of both activity and evidence, let's just hang in there and as much as it pains me to say so. We may have to wait for him to act again and continue from there. At least we have some solace in the fact he is targeting bad guys and not innocent civilians."

With all the matters settled after my dad's death and a firm, or at least a semi-firm grasp on the ins and outs of the day to day workings of the corporation at hand, I tool some time to breathe. As me and Jill sat on the couch and watched some television, I began to think about stopping what I was doing on the side and just live life. The nightly news came on and wouldn't you know, the lead story was about a string of prostitution rings had been busted by a combined effort of local, state, and federal law enforcement officials. The pictures that they showed were of the police leading the girls away in busses sent for them, to transport them to the hospitals to be evaluated and then to try to determine who they were. The pictures set both myself and my wife back and took our breath away.

"Oh my God, Jack They're nothing more than little girls and young women. This is an atrocity."

'Well shit.' I thought, 'so much for life as a normal person.' I could not in all good conscience sit there and just keep pretending that this sort of thing wasn't going on all over this country. That kind of modern-day slavery was in our country again. I say this but wonder if it had ever really been abolished. Instead, it just went underground and out of sight of your average everyday citizen.

I looked over at my wife and said, "You know, if I had the means in which to track down and kill each and every one of those people that did atrocious things to others, I would do it in a heartbeat. If the cops can't handle it than maybe someone else should." This earned me a look form my wife that I wasn't real sure was good or bad, at least not until she spoke.

"You would really end another person's life if that person had done the things that we just seen on the news?" Jill asked me.

Fuck it, go big or go home I thought to myself. "Your damn right I would, without hesitation or remorse. I know that you are a doctor and swear an oath to do no harm..." I was saying as Jill interrupted me.

"Do no harm to people, not animals. As far as I am concerned these people are no more than modern day cave men—one step up the evolutionary chain from a cross between shit and a snail."

That garnered a laugh from me and I said, "Well darling, I would have to say that you are right. The very thought of these animals doing this to young girls and women, or for that matter any living human being absolutely disgusts me."

As you may very well imagine the sex that night was absolutely fantastic. Not that it ever really wasn't, but it seems better when we have a common goal or are passionate about the same thing at the same time. Whatever the case is, it seems to activate our inner animals and nature takes over to produce what I can only describe as purely pornographic in both content, sound and sweaty motion. I love it!

We woke up the next morning and got the kids off to school. Deciding that being CEO of a corporation has earned me a morning roll in the hay, combined with the fact that it was Jill's day off and away we went again. Maybe I should say a roll on the couch, some naked lusting up against the kitchen counter followed by a little penetration on the kitchen table—have to remember to clean that before dinner. Then we moved up to the bed room to finish off or finish again. Ah hell, who's counting anyway?

As we lay in bed recovering from our sexual escapades, I asked Jill, "Were you serious about what you were saying about killing bad people?"

She looked at me and said, "As a heart attack!! Show me a molester of children, a rapist of women, or a person that doesn't deserve to walk the planet do to their complete disregard for human life. I will take the appropriate measures to stop that person from harming another person regardless of what the court system has said about their punishment being adequate for the crime committed. You and I both know that with the right representation and/or amount of money, a person can indeed get away with anything. If that is the case, then I would have no problem putting an end to their worthless lives. I see from day to day the devastation that we as a people do to each other. Oftentimes it is not by accident but of our own free will."

Have I told you all out there in book land how much I love this woman? Yeah, yeah, yeah, I know I have and don't care if you want to hear it again or not. This is my book and I will say it again and again and again. DAMN, I LOVE THIS WOMAN!!!

I thought long and hard about the conversation I wanted to have with Jill and decided to test the waters to see if she was really ready for the truth behind what I was doing— if she was indeed willing to try her hand at what she said she could do. My plan was simple; I was already hunting the traffickers, so seeing how passionate she was about that particular type of crime, I grabbed the other file that I had earlier put away after finding out how big the group that I was currently hunting was. I would get into this new victims life to see how hard it might be to track down and capture him.

Having already looked into his background, I found that he was not only a viewer of, but a distributor of child pornographic films. This helped me to decide that this particular type of scum-bag should be removed from our earth. While he had never really hurt any of these children, he had made it profitable and kept the child porn system needing more children in order to film, therein contributing to the capture and sexual exploitation of children.

I got back to work early and planned to schedule all appointments and tasks in the morning and early afternoon. By doing that, it allowed me to have a fair amount of time each day to do my other hobby. I carried on like this for two weeks and kept showing Jill news reports of other human trafficking and child exploitation, thus keeping the idea of taking out the bad guys fresh in her mind. The level of hatred in her toward those that would do this to others was actually quite astonishing to be truthful.

I walked into the kitchen one night and said, "So I found a bad guy for you."

She turned to me and said, "What do you mean?"

I replied, "You know, one of those people that you would rather let burn to death than piss on to help."

I began to feel more than a little wary about the situation, wondering if I had made a mistake thinking that Jill was serious and all that talk was just that—talk. What looked like a shimmer of light began to form in her eyes as I saw that she realized what I was talking about. I began to feel a little better.

"Oh, those ass hats that think children and women are nothing more than life support systems for a vagina. Those people?" Jill said. She then went on to say, "Are we going to kill him?"

Alright, this I will admit took me a bit by surprise. I mean, this beautiful woman, the mother of my children, and a caring daughter and sister to those in her family just asked me if we were going to kill someone. "Well you know, I got to thinking about what you said the other night and it really started to piss me off. The more I thought about it the angrier I got. I did some research on convicted child porn distributors and human traffickers to see what kind of sentence something like that had attached to it."

Jill, still involved in the evening to dos looked at me as she switched between the dishwasher and putting away leftovers and said, "So what did you find? Are they getting what they deserve or are they just doing a few years and now walking around our streets looking for their next victim?"

"I wish I could say that they are getting all that there is coming to them, but the truth of the matter is that most of them are part of some bigger group and usually turn state's evidence in order to get a reduced sentence. Sadly, they are running around our towns and cities free as a bird doing as they please," I told her.

You have heard that old saying, 'if looks can kill'. If there is any truth to that, then my wife was ready to let loose a fifty-megaton nuclear blast from her eyeballs. "That is complete bullshit!!" she said, her voice not exactly quiet in tone.

CHAPTER 18

The way I see it, if we are going to be a modern-day version of Bonnie and Clyde, I had better ease her into this and make every preparation to protect the kid's futures in case something went wrong. There is no reason for them to get involved in our misdeeds, regardless of whether or not we feel justified in what are doing. I will still teach them about God, right, and wrong, dignity and respect toward others. Now some of you asshats are out there saying "Oh you fucking hypocrite. How can you teach your kids one thing while doing the other?"

Very easy question to answer actually, I am not them. I choose to do these things and will not drag them into it. If for some reason they find out, then I will let them make their own decision as to how they feel about it. If they hate us, well so be it. If not and they want to make a family business out of it. I would have to think about that one. For now, I will leave them out of it. While I know I probably shouldn't bring my wife into this, I am getting real tired of lying to her about going on trips that I am not going on just to perform my killings.

Oh my gosh, a killer with a conscious. Yes, I do have one, I am not a psychopath, at least not in the terms of just kill, kill, kill. I do have an idea of what I am wanting to accomplish. It may be illegal and immoral, but I do have an agenda.

Still not believing that my wife was all that capable of doing what I was thinking, we tracked the new douche bag to a house that was not exactly what I would have expected. Our next target lived in a little ranch style house snuggled into a group of similar houses on a couple blocks of well-groomed and manicured lawns and shrubbery. You know what they say, if you have to hide, there is no better place to do so than in plain sight.

My wife looked over at me and said, "This guy's neighbors would shit a herd of cows if they knew what this guy did for a living."

"That they would, wait, a herd of cows?" I asked laughing a bit at her use of the bovine comparative.

"Going for the shock value my love," she said.

"Consider me well informed, and just so you know, I plan on using that someday," I told her.

Watching the house for a few hours and seeing our guy come home for the evening and laying eyes on him for the first time in person, we started the car and headed home. On the way back to the house, I asked Jill how exactly we should go about doing it.

"Well, I think what we talked about before sounds real good. Observe, see pattern of movement and make plan for takedown."

I looked over at her and said, "That's all good, but how do you want to kill him?" I made sure she fully understood what exactly it was that we were about to do.

"Oh that," she said. "You do know that I am a medical doctor, right?" she asked.

"Yes, I still remember," I replied, laughing, still mostly amazed at the ease of which she is falling into her role as my accomplice. "What do you have in mind then, Dr. Doom?"

She laughed and slapped my arm. "Don't forget who you sleep with. Oh yeah, that person would be Dr. Doom," she said with a smile. "But in all seriousness, I think we should go in and cut his throat."

"Ok, that is a way to do it indeed."

"Maybe remove his manhood and place them in his throat, it's the least that we could do for all that nasty bullshit that asshole has done to God only knows how many children."

To that I replied, "Can't say that I disagree with you. I say we also carve the name of his crime into his chest. No reason to lead people to believe that this is just a random act of kindness once the neighbors find out who he really is."

Jill looked over at me and said, "Good idea, kind of like that one guy that is going around and killing those people. We could be his copycat."

Choosing my words carefully, I said, "Yeah, copycat."

"So, all the things that we have discussed about killing this guy sound great. Now how do you want to go about getting to him or would you rather do him in his house?" I asked.

Jill seemed to be thinking on the matter when she said, "I say that we keep watching him for awhile and see if anything changes or not. I say that one of us should watch him at night and see how quiet this neighborhood is. If it looks like we can just break into his house and take care of business, then that is what we do. Let someone else discover the body."

I was sitting in the seat next to her in stunned silence. The way she just described the take down was almost exactly how I would have done it. The only real thing different was the breaking into the house thing. I will admit that would be something new for me. It gave me a small sense of misgiving, but with Jill and I both thinking about it together I saw no real reason to believe that we couldn't pull it off.

We agreed that we would split shifts, one person watching in the evening to just after midnight, while the other would watch from midnight till just before sun up. If it appeared that our guy stuck to the same schedule for a week that we would go into the next stage of planning. If nothing changed in his day to day schedule, then we would move forward. Jill and I discussed her work hours and agreed that it would be better that she kept working but spent less time at work. We used the very reasonable excuse that due to my fathers' death and the added responsibilities of the new job as CEO, she needed to be at home more, given the fact that my work hours vary so much.

There was a little hesitation at her work given the amount of work that she does there. As a partner in the practice, however, she had leeway as long as her end of the bills were satisfied, and her part of the partnership was profitable. They came to an agreement that suited all their needs; she would hire a P.A. (Physicians Assistant) to fill in for her on a permanent basis, as well as, work on an as needed basis given a small amount of notice if possible.

As for my job, well that was easy. You see, being the Owner/CEO has its benefits. One of these benefits was that, unless I was needed, I just worked from home. The company was running well enough and had been established for enough time that there was not a whole lot of day to day workings for me to be involved in. As I had said before, I did make sure that if I had to go into the office to tend to matters, or to attend a meeting. I tried to schedule it for the mornings or no later than just after lunch. Sometimes there were appointments that didn't fit into that schedule, but for the most part everything worked out rather well and our plans to rid the world of the bad guys was under way.

As my wife had proposed, she took the first shift and just after midnight I showed up to relieve her.

"So, what's the what?" I asked her.

"He came in around ten this evening, and the lights went out around ten thirty, so essentially a whole lot of nothing." she said.

"Well at least he didn't have any young kids with him or anything," I replied.

"He would have already been dead if I had even the slightest thought that he had a child with him, period. I don't care if it was his little nephew or niece." She said this in a way that made me believe that she was for real.

I looked over at her and said, "Jill, we will get this guy. You have my word on that. Do not do anything that can expose you to getting caught or seen. If this shit bag has kids with him, you call me and then wait. Our kids are old enough to watch themselves for a few hours while we take care of some business. Will you please do this one thing for me?"

She replied, "Yes, I will. You had better get your ass here as fast as you can after I call you. I only have so much patience when I think a child is being harmed. Do you understand that?"

"Yes, I do my love."

The next few days went by about the same. I had one meeting to attend and Jill went into work to see patients. The next day I told Jill that I had nothing to do, so I was going to follow our target around and see if he was working somewhere legit or if his child porn business was all that there was for him. If indeed his porn business was all that there was, I wanted to see if he was doing it solely out of his home or was there someplace else that he was doing his nasty bit of business from. The way I figured it, if there was a place that he was doing his thing, I would want to take it down also. I would let the cops do that. After all, I still had to finish up with those assholes in the human trafficking ring. Surely you didn't think that I had forgotten about those ass-hats did you? If you did then that's where you would be wrong, I never forget an asshole.

Jill and I decided that Thursday night would be the night to do our thing. Why Thursday you ask? Even if you weren't wondering, I am going to tell you anyway, so just hang in there. The thinking behind Thursday night was that he was more likely to be home on a Thursday than during the weekend. Even if he wasn't out looking for kids to exploit on the weekend, he may want to go out and do what people like him do on weekend nights—you know, like beating kittens to death, or killing baby seals or maybe even gutting clowns. It would have to be something like that; I say this because no one in their right mind could possibly do the thing that he does to children and still be a normal human being. Even if all he did was sell the shit, it was still providing a means for which the movie makers could film their nasty shit.

"Jill? What exactly do you have in mind for tonight?" I asked her.

"I say we wait for the ass-hat to get home, wait for all activity to cease, wait a small amount of time, then go around back and gain entry to the place. I am sticking to the plan that we made plus one added bonus," she said.

I looked at her and with some curiosity I said, "Bonus? Oh, do tell."

She did. "We are always getting sample drugs from the pharmaceutical companies to try out and send back our opinion on it. The latest version of the old favorite, Ketamine, which is a very powerful tranquilizer with a variety of uses from animal tranquilizers to the treatment of some forms of psychological disorders, they sent us the new samples of this and want our opinion of how it works."

I nodded my head and said, "Sounds fun. How are we going to get it into him then? I have my doubts that he will swallow a pill while we are intending to kill him."

"Is it possible for you to not be a smart ass? Never mind, don't answer that; I already know the answer that you will be giving me. The drug comes in two forms, oral and injectable. I chose to bring the injectable form for the very reason that I to do not believe that he would be in any hurry to allow us to give him an oral medication as we are preparing to kill him."

I just smiled and we continued to go over the plan. It is really amazing what you can find out on the internet. Come to find out, plans filed with the local zoning and planning commissions, like blueprints for homes, can be obtained by a simple inquiry and a small fee—public information and all. These inquiries I did by using a false identity and had them sent to a P.O. Box that was paid in cash and promptly closed after I received the info that I needed.

We went over the plan for entry and take down, and after the approximate amount of time waiting for the guy to call it a night, we got out of the car and circled the block and came to the house from the back. Jill and I carefully inspected the area and the surrounding houses to determine whether or not there were any people still awake or outside for some reason or another. Feeling that it was safe to proceed, we made our way to the rear of the house. Over the last two weeks, we had studied and practiced on several styles of locking mechanisms for residential homes, this being our first attempt at breaking and entering and all.

When we got to the door, we saw that indeed it was one of the most common types of door latches and locks used by your average homeowner. It was a very good thing for us. While we had tried learning how to pick locks, there were so many to choose from that we had decided to pick the top five most used and concentrate on them the most. The only other fear that had been settling in the back of our heads was that our guy may have an electronic locking system. Yes, the thought that there may be a security system didn't escape our minds either.

What were you thinking? I am a professional, if I was a blond in a creepy forest and there was an axe murder after me, I wouldn't run deeper into the forest and trip over the first obstacle that was in the path. Fuck no. I would run my ass off till I reached help. No looking back to see if the bad guy was still there or not, who really gives a fuck? The only thing that I would care about at the time is whether or not a particular part of my body was about to be removed. I sure as shit wouldn't want to see it coming. Example: "Oh no, there is a bad guy after me, I should run. Phew, been running for thirty seconds, I bet the bad guy has forgotten about me. I think I should be able to turn around and see if said bad guy is still there. OMG, indeed he is and oh no there goes my head." Anyway……

There is a fifty-fifty chance that there was a security system. That was the one thing that we were just going to have to take a chance on. My bet was that there was no reason to have a security system on his personal house. After following this douche bag around for the past couple of weeks, we had determined that he indeed worked from a specific place and not out of his home. Now whether or not he had copies of what he sold in the house was totally unknown to us—not only unknown, but unconcerning also. If we happened to find something in the house, we would just make sure as is in plain sight, this way when the body was discovered, it wouldn't take too much effort to locate the child porn and give suspicion to what this ass bag was involved in. After the murder was committed, we intended to make an anonymous call to disclose the location of the filming and distribution site, and with some luck, we could take a few other perverts off the streets. Have no doubt however, if those pervs didn't get the punishment that they deserve they would be seeing us. Hmm…Us. Damn that sounds good.

We gained access to the house and quickly we realized that we ended up on the fifty percent side that was in our favor of not getting caught by activating an alarm. Yay for us. We slowly made our way through the house, sticking close to the blueprints and heading toward the two rooms that we figured would be the bedrooms. We came to the first of the two rooms and slowly turned the knob and opened the door.

I whispered to Jill and said, "Are you seeing what I am seeing?"

To that she said, "I would have to be blind not to see this."

Before our eyes was a library of nothing but filth. I don't use that word loosely in describing what we were seeing. If we ever had a doubt as to whether or not this perverted shit was doing nothing more than distributing the movies, this room removed all doubts.

"I think this guy is way past the common definition screwed up. This guy has gone way over the deep end" Jill said.

"I really have no words. Well never mind this right now, let's go get this sick-o." I said to her. We left the room of child horrors and headed down to the second room. On the plans, we had seen that the bathroom connected to the second room and it would be possible to gain entry to our psycho's room.

"What do you want to do?" I asked Jill.

Whispering, she said, "Let's try the main door first, and if we can let's just jump him. I will have the Ketamine ready. You try to subdue him and if needed I will fill him full of this shit." I nodded my head and we moved on with the plan.

The door cracked open and I crept in first. The room was dark and silent as one would expect. However, there was no sound at all, no snoring, heavy night time breathing—nothing at all. Jill followed me into the room, and I turned and looked at her to give her a shrug of my shoulders, indicating that I'm not sure if he is here or not. I also indicated that I was heading over to the bed to see if he is in it. Before I could take my eyes off Jill, her face lit up, not in the way that people do when they are happy, but the way it does when there is an actual light that all the sudden hits their face. There is a look of terror right before she says, "JACK, LOOK OUT!!!"

CHAPTER 19

"LOOK OUT, JACK!!!" Jill screamed.

Thankful for my reflexes and the forewarning of my wife I ducked just as what I later realized was the handle end of a toilet plunger went flying by my head.

"What the fuck are you doing in my house assholes?" the man said, as he wound up for another swing with his improvised bat. The man swung and again I ducked. This time, however, I came up and sent a fist as hard as I could, given the awkward position I was in after ducking that last swing, and managed to connect rather forcefully with his stomach. That slowed him down enough for me to take him to the ground. The guy was not what you would call a real big dude, but with his fight or flight kicking in from seeing someone unwanted or unexpected in his house, the dude was tough and agile. Regardless of what kind of bad guy he was, one thing was for certain; he was going down.

As I wrestled him to the ground I said to Jill, "Hit him with the juice, but only half, I don't want him out, just slowed down."

She ran over and jabbed him with the night night medicine. Surprisingly, I quickly felt the fight leaving him.

"Are you all right?" Jill asked.

"All good here." I reply.

"That was a tough little shit," I admitted to her.

"He did look as though he wanted nothing to do with us and our being in his house," she replied. We both began to laugh as we sat and recovered our breath.

"Hey, Albert, wake your sorry ass up. I don't have all night you know," I said to him.

Jill walked over to him and slapped him hard in the face. *WHACK*, I heard. This apparently had the desired effect that Jill was looking for as Albert began to move around.

"How much of that shit did you give him?" I asked her.

"Well I thought it was only half the dose, but some extra could have escaped me when he was moving around. I can't be for sure 'cause what I didn't get in him was sprayed on the floor as we were restraining him."

He was fully restrained and seemingly submissive, whether due to the drugs or Albert realizing that he had indeed been captured and had no way to escape, we will never know. In our case, we didn't care either.

"Albert, Albert, you with us you retard?" I said to him as he appeared to again look as though he was wanting to go back to the hazy realm of drug induced la-la land.

"What!!" he all the sudden yelled out.

"Guess that is a yes," Jill said with a smile on her face. Then she gave another *SMACK*. "Let's get one thing straight asshole; you are not in charge here. We are not children with weak wills and an inability to protect ourselves. This is your last day on this planet. Are we clear on this, or do you have some really stupid questions you would like to throw our way?"

Both Albert and I looked at her with a 'Yes ma'am no ma'am' look on our faces. Jill looked at me and said, "What?"

I looked back at her and said, "Nothing at all, darling; couldn't have handled it better myself."

She smiled at me and said, "I just really hate it when someone hurts a child, especially the way this ass-hat does. Making kids, of any age have sex with each other or adults having sex with kids and then selling the taped version of it to others to view, that makes me want to vomit."

Nodding my head in acknowledgement, I looked at her and said, "I am right there with you. You want to do the honors, or you want to drag it out a little?"

She thought on it a bit and said, "Well, we don't have too much time to work with here. Let's see if numb nuts here has anything to say for himself."

I turned to Albert and said, "Hey numb nuts, you have anything to say for yourself?"

He made a series of grunts and then I realized that I had duct taped his mouth shut and would have a hard time hearing him without removing the tape first. "Oops," I said, "my bad." I grabbed one of the edges of the tape and jerk the whole mess off along with what appeared to be some skin from his lips also.

I saw Jill cringe and say, "Ouch, that had to hurt." Albert, no sooner than the tape is removed starts screaming.

"Shut the fuck up!" I said to him and placed my palm over his mouth. I used my palm to keep from giving him a chance to bite me. Jill saw Albert attempting to bite at my hand grabbed hold of his sack, and by sack I do mean his manhood—twig and berries, cock and balls, or whatever you may call your private area fellas. I'll give you all a second to do the whole, "Ohhhhh" thing; I know I did.

That of course did exactly as one would expect— shut him right the hell up. I took my hand away from his mouth and before I could say anything Jill said, "Do you understand the word 'shut up' now?" Albert, clearly in pain nodded his head. "If you keep your mouth shut, then there will be a whole lot less pain, nod if you understand," she said. Albert nodded his head and with that part behind us we got him up and secured him to a chair.

"So, as you may well be aware of, you are not making it out of this," I said. "However, if you cooperate, we can make it a lot less painful, nod if you understand." He nodded. Jill started with the questions.

"You may not think that what you are doing is wrong. I have no idea how you can even come close to thinking that it is at all right, but somehow you have. This belief and the fact that you got off with a less than proper punishment is why we are here." She went on to say, "We correct what our illustrious justice system gets wrong."

I stood there while she said her peace and when she finished, I added, "What I want to know more than anything else is how they get the children for your sick ass videos? If I were able to obtain this kind of information, then I may be able to talk my partner out of cutting you into little bitty bits. You get one chance and only one chance, so make sure that you think really hard before you open your mouth. Please nod if you understand." He nodded, and Jill and I stood back and waited.

I looked over at Jill and asked her, "Does it look to you as though he is thinking up a story? I know if I were faced with certain death, my ass would have spewed out the info I was asked to give as soon as possible, how about you?"

Jill looked over at me and said, "Indeed I would. There is nothing short of the earth spinning off its axis and throwing us all into space that would keep my mouth shut. As that old saying goes, 'I would be squealing like a pig'."

Albert looked at us as though he was seeing a pair of crazies. That may be exactly what he was looking at, but as near as I can see, if we are the crazies and he was the one whose life was on the line, then what he was thinking means exactly shit. Albert sat there a little longer and still said nothing. I looked around and saw an iron hanging from the closet door. I took it down and walked toward Albert. His eyes begin to widen, and I thought for a second that he would begin to talk, but he didn't.

"Will you please plug this in?" I said to Jill and she did. I gave the iron a bit of time to warm up. I spat on the iron, and when the spit sizzled and evaporated the moment it hit the hot iron, I gave Albert a chance to start speaking.

"You know, I think this guy believes that we will not do it. Are you getting that same feeling?" Jill asked me.

I turned to her and said, "I believe that you are right, he must think he is in some elite club of people that are beyond all of us simple folks."

I finished speaking, and before Albert could utter a word, I put the hot Iron on his hand. The burning of flesh immediately stunk up the place. Knowing that Albert, after realizing what just happened, would surely scream, I looked at Jill and she immediately put a plastic sack over Albert's head. The funny thing about screaming, well, really about anything that involves using air to make sound is that you need one key ingredient, air. The scream lasted only a fraction of a second as his brain in all its wisdom realized that there may be a bigger problem than the burning sensation coming from his hand. In-deed there was, it was called a lack of oxygen. I removed the iron from his hand. Jill gave him a second or so before removing the plastic bag.

"So, Albert, are you ready to talk now?" Jill asked. He just looked up at us and said nothing.

"What a fucking idiot," I said, then slammed the pointed end of the still hot iron through his hand.

Jill looked at me and somehow read my mind and said, "This guy isn't going to say a word, is he?"

"It doesn't seem as though he is."

She looked back at Albert and said, "You are indeed a stupid son-of-a-bitch. I hope that they have a special place in hell reserved just for you and the people that hurt children." Jill took the plastic bag and placed it over his head. I grabbed him in order to keep him from flailing too much as his brain realized that there would be no more incoming air. The gasping and body convulsions lasted only a bit, and then he was still.

I walked to Jill's side of the body and said, "It's over, he's gone. No one but his assholes friends will miss him. We have also saved god only knows how many children from being exploited by this crew." I took her hands and slowly helpd her let loose of the bag that was around Alberts neck.

She looked at me with a tear in her eyes and said, "My whole career has been all about saving lives, not taking them."

I looked her square in the eyes and said, "Don't you dare shed a tear for this scum. He has and would have, if not for us, kept hurting kids till the day he died. What we did was save lives, we may have had to take one in order to save many others, but we have saved some."

Jill looked at me, wiped the tears from her eyes and said, "The tears are not for what I just did; they are for all the kids that we couldn't save from this guy and his asshole group of friends."

Understanding where she was coming from and realizing that this took a little longer than expected I said, "I feel the same way. However, I think we should talk about this some other time and finish up here and get the fuck out of dodge before the sun comes and makes it a whole lot harder to leave."

Jill nodded her head and we started to finish up. We tipped Albert over on to his back, still in the chair secured. I took out my knife and cut open his shirt. Jill held the shirt open while I carved the words 'child pornographer' onto his chest. We looked around and verified that we didn't leave anything behind and made sure that our gloves were still on assuring that we were leaving no finger prints. We had on long sleeves and masks to assure that there would be little if any trace amounts of body hair. We worked our way to the back door and looked around outside. Feeling comfortable that there was no one around and seeing no lights on in neighboring houses, we walked away.

We got to our car and climbed in. We took our personal car due to the fact, I hadn't yet told my wife that this was not the first time I had done this. Later, after I told her the rest of what I had done, I would tell her I have an old beater of a vehicle for the purpose of pulling off these crimes in case I happen to have blood on me. That way I would not bring any of that evidence into any of our personal property. With a quick glance at both of us I felt comfortable that there was nothing that could tie us to Albert should we become persons of interest in an investigation.

We drove for a bit in silence and as we passed a shopping center, Jill asked me to pull in. I did and parked the car. Fearing that she was about to freak out, I turned to her so that I might help her to calm down. Was I ever wrong! Jill grabbed the back of my neck and kissed me hard on the lips—with passion the likes of when we were teenagers. I actually think she drew blood from a split lip she gave me as she jumped me. I say jumped me because that is essentially what she did.

She moved from my lips to my neck with her lips while her hands where undoing my jeans. I wiggled out of my pants with her assistance and she took me into her mouth—all of me. She moved her head up and down, over and over again. She brought me to the limit of losing my sanity and stopped. She got back into her seat and removed her bottoms and then came over to my seat. She eased me inside her and began to ride me. Harder and harder she thrust herself onto me. I lay back gasping in delight; her moaning nearly brought me to a climax. She lay on my chest and I took over the work, thrusting in and out of her repeatedly. We were both moaning and thrusting and riding each other until we both came to a climax.

We lay there sweating; she was still on top of me. "That was unbelievable," I said. "Where in the hell did that come from?" I asked her.

"It's a well-known fact that intense events can trigger a strong sexual urge in people. It's sort of a coping mechanism you can say," she said.

I looked at her and said, "Shit I thought you was going to freak out on me, that maybe it just finally caught up with you and you may not know how to handle it."

She looked at me and began to laugh. "Freak out over the death of that two-bit piece of trash, ha, never. I just couldn't wait to get home. Shit I thought with these leather seats that I was going to slip onto the floor I was so wet. So I took things into my own hands, and mouth." She spoke with a smile on her face that I knew all too well. She was going to be alright.

We got ourselves dressed again and headed for the house. On the way home, I decide that then was as good of time as any to come clean about the other people that I had killed. "Jill, I have to tell you something."

She looked over at me and said, "Spill it."

So, I did. "This was not my first time killing someone." I looked over at her and waited for a response.

"Ok," she said.

"Ok? That's it, ok?" I said back, not in a loud voice or anything like that, just a conversational tone as if we were talking about what to get for dinner that night.

"Let me guess. You are the guy that the cops are looking for that has been taking out all those people and carving their crimes on their chests?" she said with what I can only interpret as a smartass type of smirk on her face. I guess the dumbfounded look on my face was too much for her to handle and she began to laugh, subtly at first, Then it turned into a full-on belly laugh, complete with tear and a snort or two for good measure. Her laugh was so sincere that I couldn't help but join in. We continued to laugh all the way home, which I can tell you was no easy feat with tears in your eyes and a pain in your face from smiling so hard that you're not sure if you will just end up looking like the character from *Batman* named Joker. We pulled into the drive and sat there for a few minutes collecting ourselves.

"I am sure you may be wondering how'd I know?" Jill asked.

"Well it has passed through my mind a half a million times on the way home, yes," I said.

"I didn't, well not until you came up with the idea for carving the names into their chests. Even then I wasn't sure, but the way we killed him, and you showed no emotion at all got me thinking. I wasn't sure what I was thinking until you said that this was not your first time." I nodded my head and she went on. "It all came together sort of all at once. When that thing with Melissa happened, you had so much passion in you for making sure that those kids were not harmed. Then all the sudden Melissa's fiancé came up missing—the extra trips you were taking. No, I never suspected that you were cheating on me. I wasn't sure what you were up to, but cheating was never in the list of maybes. You're smarter than that."

I looked at her and said, "So you suspected that I was up to something but didn't know what and you never asked?"

She looked over at me and said, "Never had a reason to, you wouldn't do anything if you didn't have a reason for doing it. I mean anything, that includes killing. I also know that if you were up to something that you are smart enough to clean up after yourself and not put our family into jeopardy. This all sounding about right?"

"Yes, yes it does. I never really meant to get in this deep, but when I found out what Frank had done to those kids, I couldn't handle the fact that he may be in the same house as Melissa's children and possibly do those terrible things to them. I just could let it happen."

She looked over at me with nothing but love in her face and said, "That's why I love you so much and have no negative thoughts about what you have done. As for what we have done, it is what it is. You would give your life for another if it were called for. Why then would I think that you were not capable of taking a life if it meant saving others?"

I just shook my head, leaned over and kissed her hard. "I love you so much, more than I can put into words."

"I know you do, as well you should. I am lovable." She said the last bit with a smile.

"Let's go inside and go to bed. Unless that is, you're up for more teenage hi-jinx"

"Maybe no more teenager stuff, but some slow love making sounds right up my alley," she said.

CHAPTER 20

"Jamison," the captain said in a tone that meant this is no time for playing around because we have some business to take care of.

"Yes sir," Jamison said.

"We have another one. It looks like our fella strikes again," the captain said. "Go grab the rest of the gang and meet me in the war room."

The war room, as it had come to be known, was the converted meeting room we had all been working out of on this case. It received its name due to the fact that we realized that this case was going to be like a long drawn out war. He made a move and we followed and tried to defeat him, only to find that our un-sub had moved on to plan another attack elsewhere.

"I am on it captain," Jamison said.

They all gathered in the war room and the captain said, "Listen up, our un-sub has struck again, or at least it looks as though it is him anyway. Ex-con that, if you were to look, got off real easy given the fact that he was accused of position with intent to distribute child pornography."

We all looked at each other and with that look that said, 'No real loss to society there'. It was just a look of course; we are still cops and still have to uphold the law. That doesn't mean that we cannot think it.

The captain must have picked up on the look and said, "Yeah, yeah, I know. However, just because this guy is taking out the trash that we could not does not make it right. I do feel the same way sometimes when bad things happen to bad people. This however, does not make it legal—even if the offending party has hurt children. Lord knows that I have had bad thoughts aimed at some of the people that we arrest. The difference between police and criminals is that we do not act on these thought and feelings."

Cline looked at the captain and said, "Well said sir, and no that is not an ass kissing remark either Hanson."

They all laughed and then got back to business. "So, our victim was found in his own home and in a quiet neighborhood. As of right now, the usual remarks of, 'he always kept to himself, and 'always a nice guy' were all we were getting out of the neighbors in the area." The captain went on to say, "I want you all to go down there and tear this guy's life apart. Find me something that we can use to nail this vigilante that we have running around before he becomes some kind of folk hero and people begin to believe that it is ok to take the law into their own hands."

When we got to the crime scene, we discovered that Dr. Moore was still there with the crime scene techs doing their thing. We all stood back and discussed the scene while we waited for the crime scene people to gather and process the scene.

"So, this is a little unusual for our guy," Hanson said.

"Ya, I wonder what made him decide to come to a residential neighborhood to get his guy this time. Do you suppose that he is getting sloppy, or was this just a target of opportunity?" remarked Hart.

Just then Dr. Moore came out of the front door and said, "Gentlemen, so nice to see you under such alarming circumstances. We will have to all get together sometime and bullshit in a more hospitable meeting place."

Jamison, being the team leader, was the first to ask his questions. "So, anything new this time or just the same-ole, same-ole? I guess what I am asking is, are there any leads or evidence that might help us in any way at all?"

Dr. Moore shook her head and said, "Unfortunately, as of right now, no. The carving on the chest that indicates what the vic (victim) has done is the only similarity thus far to the previous vics. However, it does appear as though this one was strangled to death and that there was some kind of struggle prior to subduing the vic. We also have some kind fluid on the ground near the body. It is not water and is in a very small spot with no evidence of a cup or any container that would hold fluid that could have spilled. The crime scene techs have obtained a sample of the fluid for analysis."

Cline stepped in and asked, "Doctor, is there anything that you can see on the body that would indicate that our un-sub has escalated to a more vicious style of killing or mutilating the body in any manner at all?"

The doctor looked at Cline and with a little bit of what seemed to be possible infatuation said, "S.A. Cline, it is so nice to see you again. You will really have to pick better friends to hang out with. These three will surely corrupt all that education you obtained prior to joining the FBI. As for your question, no, there is not at this time anything that indicates that there is an escalation in violence on the victim. If anything, it looks like this guy went out rather unscathed minus the burns and puncture wound on his hand."

The other three detectives looked at Cline and tried to suppress smirks. Cline raised an eyebrow at them and sad, "Thank you, Dr. Moore; I will keep in mind the company that I keep from here on out. I will agree with you however on the fact that I have felt as though my cognitive thinking processes are retarding a bit since I have been assigned with this gangly crew. Thank you for the info. Any of you other heathens have anything else to ask the good doctor?"

As if on cue Hanson blurted out, "Hey Doc, can I get your digits for our very special agent Cline please—you know, just in case he has something for you after hours. Something to ask you that is."

Clines face turned red, and Dr. Moore laughed and kept walking away. After the doctor as out of ear shot, Cline looked over at the other detectives and said, "Oh, you all are so funny."

Jamison turned to him and said, "Don't worry about those jokers. The doc is a real good woman, and if you can land that one, more power to you. She does seem to have her eye on you, and that is not something we ever see. She has high standards, not the type of woman that will fall for the shallow guys. If she takes a liking to you, it wouldn't hurt to look into asking her for a coffee, or whatever poses as a date these days."

The detectives split up and looked over the scene, gathering any info that they can and waited for the results of the crime scene techs. Hart called over to Jamison and said, "Looks like this is where they gained entry to the residence. If I had to hazard a guess, I would say this is the first time our un-sub attempted a B&E, (breaking and entering) given the amount of scratch marks on the door handle."

They continued thru the house retracing the killers' steps until they came to the two doors. Jamison asked Hart, "What do you make of this?"

"Of what?" Hart responded.

"There is a bathroom door and then right next to it is the bedroom door. However, the bathroom door is shut, and the bedroom door is where they decided to gain entry to the guy's room. If I were breaking in and trying to get someone you would think that going thru the bathroom to get to the bedroom would make more sense."

Cline turned to Jamison and Hart and said, "While this is true that your average person may do that very thing, please don't take this personal, any of you, but I think this guy is well above the grading curve in terms of IQ. I am......."

"HEY!" Hanson yelled. "All of you get your asses down here."

The other three detectives turned and headed toward where Hanson was vigorously waving from a door down the hall. 'What in the name of burning hell,' was basically the response that was on the faces of the other detectives as they rounded the corner of the room containing the deceased's library of kiddy porn and all other manner of perverted pornographic literature and toys. Not just pornographic, but from a quick glance, they couldn't see anything that would have been considered legal pornography. Every single piece of what was in that room was centered around young children and the men and women that took advantage of them.

As if on cue, Hanson said, "Don't know about you all, but I couldn't give two monkey balls and a side of deer dick if we ever catch the guy that did this to someone that is into doing or watching this kind of shit happen to kids."

They all nodded their heads and walked out of the room.. "Bag and tag all that shit, and get it fingerprinted. If we are lucky, we can get some hits on them and maybe make some arrests or trace them to the group of assholes that is in charge of this," Jamison told one of the patrol officers to have the crime scene unit They headed back to the room where the crime was committed and started over on piecing together how it went down.

Cline continued what he was saying before Hanson had them come to the room of doom and perversion. "I am pretty sure that our un-sub has everything planned down to the second including alternate scenarios and escape routes prior to ever doing a job. It is not uncommon for a psychopath to be at almost the same level as a genius. The real difference is that he or she uses their superior intellect to do real bad things. These things may make perfect sense to our un-sub but be unthinkable to your average person."

They all looked at Cline as though he had something stuck in his eye. "What?" Cline asked.

In response Hart said, "So we could be dealing with someone that is both smarter that all of us combined and has the ability to do this without hesitation, and plans his every move so methodically that the odds of us catching him will be extremely hard if not impossible? Is that about the gist of it?"

"There have only been a handful of serial killers that never got caught. Jack the Ripper is one of those people. For the most part everyone makes mistakes and we will eventually catch him," Cline replied.

"Well, as long as this guy keeps killing people, we will keep looking for him. As you said Cline, everyone makes a mistake at some point," replied Jamison.

"Hart!" Jamison said a little louder that he had expected to.

"I can still hear man. At least until you yelled my name no more than foot away from me." Hart said with a smile on his face.

"Suck it up buttercup. If you would quit being so damn sneaky, I could hear you approach than I wouldn't have had to yell."

"I know; this case is getting to you, old man. So I won't hold it against you." Hart said.

This has Jamison turned around in a second and the other two detectives watched as Jamison swept Harts feet out from under him and had him on his face and cuffed in what seems like a matter of seconds. Cline and Hanson both burst out laughing as Jamison said to Hart, "Old man just handed you your ass you young punk."

Jamison stuck his finger in his mouth and feeling that it was adequately covered in saliva stuck it into Harts ear and wiggled it around. "Wet Willy," Jamison said as he began to take off the cuffs.

Hanson yelled out, "STOP, STOP, I think I just wet myself."

With Hart released they all at on the floor and laughed so hard it brought them all to tears. All the sudden hart said, "No one move an inch."

They all said, "oh yeah, funny, funny." They looked at Hart and suddenly stopped laughing as they saw that Hart was deadly serious.

"What you got kid?" Jamison asked.

"Good move by the way, however, as I was down on the floor receiving my come-up-ins, I thought I saw what looked like two different footprints at the threshold of the door. How crime scene or we didn't see that or mess it up as they did their walk through is beyond me."

Hart pointed out the shallow one, and next to that was an even shallower one—two very clear sets of shoe prints. Hanson and Jamison being the two more seasoned of the four cops slowly walked over and took a look.

"Well fuck me running sideways in a head wind." Hanson said.

Jamison just looked at Hanson and shook his head. "There is no way this is from our vic and our un-sub only, not to mention that this second print is quite a bit smaller than the other one."

"Do you suppose our guy has an accomplice or is someone doing this as a copycat killing in order to avenge a wrong that was done to them by this guy?" Hanson asked.

The detectives looked at each other and seemed to contemplate this. "Have we missed something here, you all. Was there something at the other crime scenes that we looked over?" Jamison asked.

Cline walked over to Jamison and said, "I don't believe you all missed anything as of yet. Let's not forget that this place was a den of inequity—a place that no child would or should be. We may very well be seeing a more focused approached to the killings. I think something lit this guy up, and now his anger is more focused. This can hurt us or help us depending on how you look at it."

Jamison looked at Cline, having a somewhat mystified look on his face and said, "Dude, in English please."

Cline began to laugh as he said, "My bad, our killer or killers have a real purpose now in which to focus their tradecraft. He is going to start going after crimes perpetrated against women and children. As for the second set of foot prints, I would lean toward a spouse. If not a spouse that a close female friend and relative that he trusts completely that may or may not have had a crime perpetrated against her. I am willing to bet that he is no longer working alone."

"Hanson, Hart, I have Clines take on things. Given what we now suspect and what we know from the evidence, walk me through how you think all this went down, starting from the point at which the perps gained entrance to the residence."

Hart started, "The way I see it is, after gaining access to the residence our perps made their way through the house but in a way that suggests that they had some kind of knowledge of the layout of the place. I say this cause the crime scene techs never indicated that they either found evidence of anyone in or near any other place in the house except a virtually straight path from the rear door to the hallway and directly to the rooms."

Hanson stepped in and said, "I agree with Hart on the fact that it seems as though our un-sub or un-subs now may have gained some intimate knowledge of the place prior to gaining entrance. After that, I am thinking that while looking for or vics room, they walked into our vics porn library and realizing that was not the room they were looking for proceeded to the last room in the hall."

Jamison looked over to Cline and asked, "Cline, do you think seeing that room filled with all that nasty shit as it was may have made them a little hasty in choosing to go into the room itself instead of the bathroom first?"

To this Cline responded, "Maybe, but as Dr. Moore had mentioned earlier, she saw no real escalation in violence on the body. I believe that our un-subs just figured that the direct approach was going to be the best."

"Hanson, please continue," said Jamison.

Hanson nodded and continued with his description. "Cline could be right about the direct approach to the vics room, especially given the fact that there may have been two of them, the whole safety in numbers thing and all. But given the evident scuffle in the bathroom entry way and the room itself, I would have to deduce that they either heard the vic in the bathroom and thought to surprise him or the dude was pissing in the dark and as our killers made their way into the room. If our vic was on his way out of the can and saw them, anyone would probably freak out that someone is in their house, then the real shit hit the fan."

Jamison nodded his head in agreement and asked if anyone had anything else to add. Hart stepped forward and said, "The doc mentioned a foreign substance on the floor that has yet to be identified. The altercation that took place seems as though it were not long in duration for some one that feared for his life after walking into his own room and encountering one or more persons there that he neither knew nor invited into his home. I would just think that if I were in fear for my life it would have looked like world war three had torn through this place."

"Ok, but where are you going with this?" asked Jamison.

"Not really sure yet, but I wonder if the substance found on the floor where some kind of a chemical that could be used to help subdue someone. You know, like a tranquilizer or sum such thing?"

Cline stepped in for this one and said, "Any form of medication that I am aware of used for that purpose would be delivered in the form of a shot. However, if they did indeed have such a shot and the victim moved while in the process of delivering the sedative it is very likely that some of the medication could have been ejected onto the floor."

Looking impressed with his young detectives discovery Jamison added, "Well done Hart, we will have to keep an eye out for that lab report when it gets done. This may very well be our first real lead in this case.

CHAPTER 21

"Hurry, hurry get the fuck out of there!!!!" I said to Jill as we run for what seems to be our very lives.

Ok, I suppose I should back up just a little bit, this way I can tell you how exactly it was that we came to be in this little pickle that we now find ourselves in.

A couple weeks had gone by since we sent Albert the kiddy porn punk to wherever it is that people like that go when they die. We had several discussions on the crime and neither of us seemed to be of the mind that anyone, anywhere, would really be any worse off by the people that we killed not being around anymore. At least, no one other than maybe his immediate family that is. Even then, if the family had found out what he had done, maybe even they would not be missing him so much. Who's to know really who values who at any given time anyway.

"So, you ready to take on a real big task my dear?" I asked her one night as we sat in bed doing our normal things prior to drifting off to sleep. I read the paper or watch Fox News on my iPad, and she reads medical journals on hers—really lame now that I think of it. It really is funny how the older you get you tend to slow down and just enjoy life the easier it can get. If I looked at myself at the age I am when I was a teen and seen what I was doing I would have probably said something like, 'Oh the hell I will' or 'I'm going to be having sex with all kinds of women that love me because I am a famous something or other'. I can guarantee you that I would not have seen me and my wife sitting on the bed just chilling out prior to getting a good nights sleep. Then again, I would also not have believed that I would have been responsible for multiple murders and now my beloved and I were a serial killer team. Like I said, funny.

Anyway, back to Jill and I talking about the next gig we were going to do. "Before I asked you into all this business, I was dealing with a group of human traffickers. I wanted to see how you would do under fire so to speak, before I drug you into anything else." I said to her.

"So how did I do, Drill Sergeant?" Jill said with a grin.

"I think I will give you a meritorious advancement in rank and allow you to sleep with me."

That got a raucous laugh out of Jill followed by, "Oh my king, may I please be at your side always, being ever present in times of coital need your greatness." We both laugh as she attempted a curtsy.

"So, as I was saying, this next group of assholes, two of which I have already dispatched have their fingers in all kinds of nastiness—human trafficking and all that it includes—everything from forced labor to prostitution. All the things that I just mentioned are not gender or age specific. They take them all and use them all," I told Jill.

"So, let me get this straight. You managed to infiltrate a human trafficking ring?" she asked.

"No not infiltrate; I simply was going to take out one of the guys on my list that was involved with the trafficking. I had found him the same way that I target and find all my selections—unfair criminal punishments or a straight lack of punishment for whatever reason. So, I picked this guy, and in the process of watching him in preparation of taking him down I followed him and discovered that he was part of something much bigger."

I continued to talk to her about this gang of traffickers and my plans for them. "So essentially we are going to do what with these guys?" Jill asked.

"Well, my plan was to remove as many of them from the face of the earth as possible and then give the location of their area of operations to the authorities and let them deal with the rest," I said. I saw the look on her face that always means that she is thinking about something. This is usually reserved for thinking about a problem she is having and needs to solve. "What are you thinking?" I asked.

"Well, I say that we continue on with your plan but critique it just a bit."

"Ok, but how do you want to make it better? I say better because I have rarely seen that face on you, and whatever it is that you where chewing on always comes out better than before you started thinking about it."

She went on to say, "I think we should use our children's above average ability to use computers, then, when and if we get a chance to break into the place, we take any and all computers and see if we can expand our target pool in order to get as many of these bastards as we can."

"Whoa, whoa, whoa, you want to involve the kids in all this crap?" I asked her.

"Easy, Tarzan, only on a superficial level and only if we need them. Shit, we have a young Bill Gates and Steve Jobs combined only a few floors below us. The hardest part will be protecting them from what they might see when they crack any security protocols."

I sat back and wondered if that was a good thing or not and said to Jill, "I understand where you are coming from and agree that they could be useful. So let me just think on it a bit. For now, can we go after the bad guys and see the viability of even getting into the place?"

She looked at me in the way that only she can and said, "You are a great father and husband. It would be foolish of me to ask something of you without allowing you to first think it over." She spoke as she ran her hands down my chest and slowly to my groin.

"You know, sexual favors will get you everywhere," I said to her with a great big grin on my face.

To tell you that the sex was anything but absolutely outstanding as always would be nothing but a flat out lie. We have always had a vigorous intimate relationship ever since the very first time. However, like the night I came home after one of my kills the sex seemed even more intense. With both of us involved in the game, the sex is just absolutely mind blowing.

I waited a day or two and thought over the use of my children as a source of information for the advancement of my crime spree. While I thought that I could keep them safe, I worried that as smart as they are, they would eventually catch on to what it was that their mother and I were up to and end up hating us forever or joining in on the chaos and possibly ruin their lives forever. It was really more of a moral decision than it was anything else. Some of you out there may say, "But you're a killer, how can you possibly have a moral objection to having your kids kill people." Again, an easy question to answer—BECAUSE I AM A PARENT.

No matter what you do, unless of course you are a psychotic, or a sociopath or combination of both, you will love your kids unconditionally. There is absolutely no way of describing the desire to keep your kids safe; it's just there. Another point to be maid is that I may be a killer, but I never started out wanting to kill anyone. Did I lose a piece of me that lead me to this point in my life? Maybe, but what I can tell you is that I did get very tired of people getting away with things that they had not been appropriately punished for. We can argue about who gets to make the decisions as to what punishment is appropriate and whether or not a person has learned their lesson or not. That is fine, let them, but as long as there are people getting off easily after committing horrible crimes then there are going to be people that are going to take the law into their own hands and finish what the law didn't.

"So, darling. We need to fine tune this next job that we are going to do." I said to Jill one night as we sat in bed.

"Have you thought about using the kids to tear apart any electronic devices and hard drives we may find if we can find a way into these people's compound?" She asked.

"You know, I have indeed thought about it a lot. I think we can use them however we need to groom them a bit. By groom them, I mean that we need to ask them what their feelings are about the law and people that receive a less than acceptable punishment for their crimes. Does that make sense to you?" I said to her.

She looked at me and I saw the love that she has for the kids and I and she said, "Yes I can indeed see where this would be a good thing. My guess is that you are worried about their safety and future. I agree with you and would like to keep them as far away from the actual business as possible until they are able to make their own choices as whether or not to join us in our little venture."

Knowing that she is right about my concerns and loving her even more for it I said, "That is totally correct about the why, and if they choose to or choose not to join us in the future. I feel that we should allow the thought of vigilant justice come up all on its own in their life. If it does come up in the context of conversation repeatedly then we can broach the subject at that point."

She nodded her head and said, "I agree that feeling them out first is a great idea. For now, as to bringing them in to help with the computer aspect I say that we lean toward a crime solving hobby. The crimes we are investigating and trying to solve are real and need solved. This can get them more actively involved if they think they are really making a difference."

"I like it," I said.

"Let's say we call it a night." I tell her and we both get under the covers and fall fast asleep.

The next day we just treated as a normal day. I went to work and Jill did the same, kids go to school and life is as it normally is. When the kids got home from school, we called in some Chinese food and sat down for some television. Being a Friday night, the kids don't have a real bedtime to speak of. We have all been fans of shows like

Law and Order, CSI, Hawaii Five O, NCIS, and various other crime shows. That night, we sat on the couch and watched the latest episode of our favorite show. Jill and I decided that we would watch our children's reactions to the shows more closely and try to read what may or may not be going through their heads. We also decided to inject some well-timed suggestions and reactions to certain crimes in order to get a response from them.

"Dad?" Thomas asked. "Why is it that some people go to jail for a very long time for the same crime as a person that virtually gets off scot-free? That doesn't seem at all fair, not fair to society or the people that were harmed by the act itself."

Jill and I looked at each other and tried our best to explain. "Well Thomas, the law, in all its well-meaning intentions doesn't always work the way we think it should. Our law has been dissected to a point that it's almost laughable." I said to him.

"Dissected how exactly?"

Jill stepped in and took that one. "Thomas, we have laws to protect us against numerous crimes—crimes that covered us against both physical and non-physical crimes. These laws in their simple form worked well, however, as we proceeded forward into the future, crimes changed, and people got accused and punished for crimes that they did not commit. So, in response to this, the law makers were forced to critique the laws in an attempt to help protect the innocent. Sometimes however, with the best intentions in mind, the lawmakers have fine-tuned the laws to the point that there are loopholes that you can drive a truck through."

In response to this Thomas said, "So essentially it boils down to whether or not you can get through the loop holes? Whether your guilty or not only plays part of the whole judicial process. Money and influence can also play a real part it looks like. Does that sound about right?"

I looked at my son and said, "As much as it pains me to say, yes, that about sums it up bud."

We went on the rest of the night and had some stimulating conversation with our children about the law and how easy it seems to virtually get away with just about anything given the right circumstances. Just then, Charlie piped up out of the blue, right in the middle of an episode of *NCIS* as the judge in the case had to let a guy go due to a flaw in the case. Charlie said, "Someone should take that guy out back and put a bullet in his head."

My wife and I both looked at each other and smiled. I said to Charlie, "What was that all about?"

Charlie looked back at me and said, "Well that guy was clearly guilty, and a simple thing like not allowing the jury to hear a crucial piece of evidence due to some stupid law that allowed it to be inadmissible is a bunch of crap. I can see if there was something that was mishandled, or some evidence was deemed mishandled and therefore inadmissible, but something that could not be admitted due to a lawyer not giving opposing council a heads up that it was coming is a load of crap. It is either evidence or it is not evidence, who cares when it was given to whom? If someone needs more time to prepare due to a foul-up like that, call a recess and resume the trial when both sides are ready."

I had to admit he made a good point. Some of the things people get away with, do to improper handling and/or storage of some pieces of non-organic evidence is indeed a bunch of crap. "Well Charlie, that is how thing just work sometimes. I know that it is stupid as you say, however, sometimes that is just how it goes."

Charlie responded to this shaking his head and said, "Yea well it shouldn't just work that way. Someone should take care of the people that the law can't seem too."

We all nodded and looked at each other and all the sudden I found myself saying, "Boys, as a parent I should probably not be telling you this." As I said that, I got a look from my wife that later we would laugh about. "As much as I believe that we must have a society with laws, sometimes those laws are manipulated by people to work in their favor. When this happens, I have to agree with you and your thinking that sometimes the law should be taken into our own hands and bad people should be punished."

We rounded out our evening with some ice cream and pie that we had picked up at the store. After a while, we went our separate ways—the boys to their rooms and Jill and I to ours.

We had since gone to using burner smart phones that we could pay cash for and throw away to do any searching on the web for our little kill club. "I found the blue prints of the building which that group of traffickers is held up in. At least a lot of them are held up in —if not the headquarters itself," I said to Jill.

"I say that we do some scouting and in two weeks, if able we break in and see what we can see. Do you think that we can snoop around without being seen or have someone become suspicious of our returning presence?" Jill asked.

"Funny you should ask that," I said.

"Funny how?" she replied.

"Remember that drone thing that the kids wanted so bad last Christmas?"

"Oh yea, that 4 propeller thing that has a camera on it and is flown by remote control?" she said. "Exactly, I have seen some new drones that are way smaller and a whole lot quieter yet still have the capability to send back real time video of what they are seeing as they see it." I sat back and contemplated what it was that she was saying and realized that it could actually work.

"So, what you are suggesting is that we wait 'til an approximate time and attempt to fly this drone into the building and get eyes on what it is that we are after, and in doing so, we can also see just exactly what we are facing and whether or not we can do it. What ways may be occupied and/or may have security measures, and whether or not there is a way around said measures. Sound about right?" She looked at me with a knowing smile and I realized that, indeed that was what she was suggesting. "I like it," I said to her.

The next day turned out to be a beautiful day and we both decided to go to work for half the day and meet downtown around one o'clock. I met her at little bistro we often frequent and had lunch. We discussed our plan for the drone surveillance and chose two places that had the highest ratings on Google for selling the best surveillance and counter surveillance equipment in the area. Not exactly sure how to approach the store and stay out of reach of the cameras, we wore baseball caps and some loose- fitting clothes and entered the establishment.

"Welcome, how may I help you today?" came the surprisingly friendly voice of the person behind the desk. "Oh boy, virgins." He laughed out loud as soon as he caught a look at our clothes. Jill and I looked at each other and we too began to laugh.

"You caught us," I said to him.

"Hard to miss you," he replied and then went on to say, "I wouldn't have a very successful business selling this type of merchandise to the type of people that want to purchase it if they walked in and the first thing most of their paranoid eyes see is surveillance cameras, now would I?"

Jill looked at him and said with a smile, "No, I guess you wouldn't."

The man informed us that he is the proprietor of the establishment and asked, "So, what can I get for you all today?"

I looked at Jill and she nodded at me and I said, "Well, we want to buy a drone. A real quiet drone that we can use to locate bad people. Then we want to kill them."

I waited a second for a response, and after a few seconds he said, "So, like that vigilante serial killer does? Well shit, why didn't you just open with that? This guy is making me all kinds of money."

We laughed it off, and I told him. "Actually, I want to use it to follow my nephew and see where he is getting ecstasy from. While I believe that he is a big boy and can make his own mistakes and should also pay for those mistakes if caught, I do not believe that selling that shit to others is ok. Does that make sense?"

The man behind the counter nodded his head and said, "Yes, I do understand. I also have the perfect machine for the job, The Parrott Mambo," he said as he reached into the cabinet behind him for the flying device. "This little beauty can be controlled from your phone and has a flight time of around 9 minutes. I realize that that doesn't seem like a long time but if you wait to deploy it until you absolutely need to, the flight time will be more than adequate to get some very good pictures of the subject in question for identification purposes."

We both looked at the little device. "It fits in the palm of my hand," I said.

Jill looked at me and said, "We should get two. That way we can come at him from both sides. This gives us an ability to see him if he happens to catch on to what is going on and turns to run."

I nodded my head in agreement. "We will take two," I told the man. That of course put a smile on his face as he turned to the cabinet to retrieve a second machine.

"Thank you so very much for your business and please stop in again anytime." We nodded our heads and walked out the door.

We took the crafts home and studied them in our rooms. The controls seemed simple enough, and as the store owner said, when fully charged the craft had a flight time of 9 minutes.

"We will have to take these out and test fly them," I said.

Jill agreed with me and we made a plan to do so the next day. We went to one more store and found a couple computers and some top of the line investigative software with the ability to cover its tracks after a person has probed into a place and retrieved the info that they were after. Those two items were for the boys to help them get into the whole investigative thing. We decided that we would create a fake company that tracks down and finds members of suspected human trafficking and various other crimes committed against persons.

"I think if we present this company to our children and use it as a decoy, it should keep them out of harm's way, at least as it pertains to the law."

One evening as we were sitting on the bed I said to Jill, "So, I will get together some official looking corporate papers and make a business prospectus. We can show that to them and if ever the shit hits the fan, they can pull that out and say that as far as they knew they were doing legitimate work for their parents."

"I like it," she said. "Let's get some sleep and get ready for tomorrow." We both turned out our lights and called it a night.

CHAPTER 22

The next day turned out to be a great day. The sun was out and…blah blah blah. Sorry, I must have gotten all caught up in the book writing thing. Like you all give a shit what the weather is like on the day we plan to take down a ring of human traffickers.

Anyway, back the real story. Jill got up and the day started as they all do—shit, shower, shave, get the kids off to school and start our day. However, this day would be one filled with planning and discussions on when and how to surveil, gain entry, gather evidence, and get out of the building without getting killed or caught. If we could get that far, then we would gain a whole lot of new targets to choose from. From those new targets, we hoped to get both known members of this hideous group of assholes, and if we are really lucky, a list of their clients. I have to say, if you like fucking children or any person against their will, I will find you, it may take a while but have no doubt it will happen.

"So how do we get the drone inside?" asked Jill.

"I have been studying the blueprints and noticed what appear to be skylights on the roof of the building. These will work, but I think the nine-minute range on the drone will play against us. In a pinch we can pre-plan a route to go to where we think the best location may be for their computer operations and take our chances that we are right."

She looked at the small drones and then at me and said, "That's a good back up plan, but I say when we get there we see if the place has those windows that have those small openings on top of them, as some older industrial buildings do."

I looked at her and she could tell that I had no clue what she was talking about. Noticing that I was completely lost she said, "Ok, picture this." I nodded my head. "You have those tall glass brick looking windows. These windows have a hinge like device in the middle of them so if needed you can open them up outward and essentially have the whole window space open to the outside for air flow. At the top of these windows, there is an approximately two-foot high by the width of the window long second window of sorts on top of the window space. This window can be opened independently of the large window. Why this is that way is a complete mystery to me, but if I had to guess I would say it was to let small amounts of heat out in the winter as heat rises."

I nodded my head and said, "So... a window on top of a window?"

She looked at me cross eyed, "Yes."

Starting to laugh I said, "Well why didn't you just say that?"

"Say what?" she said.

"It's a window on top of a window."

By then I was laughing out loud. "You are a real shit, you know that?" she said.

I tried to contain myself and said, "Yes, I know, but I am a shit that really loves you."

Smiling, she said, "I know. Now can we get serious?"

We spent the next few hours deciding where to approach the building and how to gain access to the roof if needed and inside the main structure to snatch the computers. Having decided that having Jill along with me was indeed a good idea, no, a great idea, I wondered back and thought how much more I would have gotten done if I had just seen what she thought of the idea in the first place. That however was just a thought and the past is the past. We decided on the east entry way to the establishment and the rear fire escape if we needed to gain access to the roof. We decided that this weekend would do well for us to pull off our little escapade.

The rest of the week went alright in terms of everyday life, got up, ate, worked, slept and so on. When the weekend had finally rolled around, we were more than ready to do it. In fact, I do believe that we may have even been a little giddy if that is possible. I can understand where some people might say, "Psychos." However, I assure you that it was not that kind of giddy. It was the kind you get when you know that what you are doing is going to please someone. The kind of giddiness you get when you know that not all people may agree with what you are doing, but what you are doing is right—at least right in our minds and some of the minds of those that have been hurt by the perpetrators we were hunting.

The kids had some kind of event that they wanted to attend with some friends, so after we saw them off, we went to the garage. After a final check of the gear we headed off to do our little deed. Of course, we did still have a spare junk vehicle that was parked at storage unit that had what you could call a less than honorable service record. By this I mean that, for a few coins a call could be made, and a certain thing or things would come up missing from that storage units. For example, a well-used vehicle, get the drift?

After transferring our gear over to the junker, we left the unit and headed to the industrial area to see what we could see. After doing a drive by of the block, we noticed that it was actually rather quiet that; what that meant was unclear.

"Why do think there is so little activity tonight?" I asked Jill.

"My guess is that they are either in the middle of a sale or…well hell, I don't have a clue," she replied.

"Ah, good answer." I went on to say, "at least we should be able to send the drone in the window without anyone outside seeing us."

Jill nodded and said, "While that indeed will be nice, there is one thing that I do worry about. That one thing is if they are doing something inside, how many people may be in there to see the drone do its little fly through."

I agreed with her and we moved ahead with the plan, knowing that it may be tougher than we had first anticipated.

We parked the junker a block away and headed toward the building. After identifying a suitable window that was close to the area, we believed our quarry might have had their main area of operations, we launched our little friend and sent him on his way.

"Four minutes and twenty seconds to go 'til we have to turn around the drone," I said to Jill. She of course having coined the idea of using the drone, got to fly the thing, at least that time anyway. I had a shrunken version of the building's layout in my hands and I guided her toward the area of interest. Jill kept the drone close to the ceiling to avoid being seen too easily by a passer-by.

"Turn left at the next hallway and look for the third door on the right," I said to her.

"Time?" she asked me.

"Two minutes and forty-five seconds to go," I said to her.

She reached the desired door, and to our surprise, we had yet to encounter any people wandering around. The door which we would like to have seen on the other side of was closed. However, just as the windows on the outside of the building, these windows also had a small transom above them for whatever the desired purpose was for. The window above the door appeared to be open just enough to fly the drone through. Jill did this very carefully and the drone sailed through without any trouble.

Once inside the office she did a quick fly around to get the lay of the place. She clicked the record icon on the screen of her phone so that we could have a record of what we saw for later if needed.

"Two minutes," I said to her as she completed the circle of the room.

"We have either hit the jackpot or this is where they all sit and jerk off to porn," Jill remarked as she pointed the drone back toward the window above the door in order to navigate it back out toward safety. Once clear of the door we saw a light from ahead as the hallway lit up in an instant.

"Go high and hover," I said to her.

She did, and we watched as a group of women were led down the hall from one room to another. "Holding room to sales room or vise-versa," she said to me.

"I think you are right," I said, nodding my head in agreement. Just then across the screen of her phone blinked a battery icon indicating ten percent battery life left.

"Oh shit, let's get a move on. Head toward the nearest window and head to the roof," I said.

"Why the roof?" she's asked.

"Because we can retrieve it from the roof for sure. If it drops to the ground, we may lose it, or it may also be discovered."

She found a window and got the drone clear and went vertical. Just as she cleared the lip of the roof the picture on the screen of her phone went blank and we lost contact with the drone.

"We have to go get it," Jill said the moment we lost contact. "We also have to help those women."

"We will, but we will not go running off half-cocked to the roof of a building with no plan. We still have time to think about how to do this, let's sit back and think of the right way to do it." Obviously distressed by what she had seen, she was ready to charge into the place and save the world, I know the feeling.

We decided that going around to the back of the building would be the safest most out of sight way to retrieve the drone. "There is the fire escape," Jill pointed out as we walked close to the back of the building to keep as inconspicuous as possible. We looked at the fire escape and realized that the ladder as in the up position and the real possibility of a rather annoying screeching may project from the rails as it was pulled down into place.

"What do you think?" I asked her. There was only one way to find out. Faster than I could object, Jill jumped up and grabbed the bottom rail of the access ladder and down it came. *SCREETCH*, the ladder made a horrendous metal on metal sound for the first second and then tapered off to low moan until it hit the pavement and came to a stop.

"What the…" I looked at her with a 'what the fuck' look on my face.

"Look at the amount of rust on that thing. There is no way in hell that thing was coming down quietly." she said.

"That may be but damn. Give a fella a little warning next time, would you?" I said to her.

She looked at me with that little smile she has that makes it impossible for me to be mad at her and said, "Ok, I will next time. Can we talk about it later? For now, let's get up there and let's go get our drone and get the fuck out of here, so we can plan on how to save them women." I nodded my head, and we started to climb.

We got to the top of the fire escape and jumped onto the roof. Feeling more confident that no one heard us, I walked with Jill across the roof to where we believed the drone to be. "There it is," I said to Jill.

She looked in the direction I as pointing, and we headed that way. "Doesn't look any worse for the wear," Jill said.

I nodded, seeing that indeed our little drone had made it onto the roof unscathed and said, "Now if we can only stay in one piece ourselves, all will be great."

We got to the edge of the roof and got ready to go back down when I saw someone climbing the access ladder and heading our way.

"Well shit," I said. Jill peeked over the edge and then looked at me. We both looked around and realized that the roof offered almost nowhere to hide.

"I have an idea," Jill said.

I looked at her and said, "I'm all ears."

"Pull your pants down," she said. Before I could ask or even disagree, she had my button undone and my pants around my ankles.

With my back to the ladder as the man reached the top I heard, "Hey, you two, do not move. What the fuck you do up here?"

I couldn't quite place the accent, but I believed that it was from somewhere that used to be Russia, Yugoslavia, or there about. We both froze. Jill was on her knees and I had my pants down around my ankles. As I stood there bare assed, we heard the man walking closer.

"Why you pants down, you…." He was apparently unable to finish what he was saying.

Jill poked her head out from beside my legs and said, "One guess, and I sure hope that you get it right." She said it with a smile on her face that only my wife could pull off. Many years of being a doctor and having to put on a face that suited the situation had trained her well.

The man's face changed as he began to shake his head. "No guess, you need to leave roof. Get hostel or car or whatever, but no sexing up here. Is this understand?"

Unrelenting and playing her part to a tee, Jill said, "Can we at least finish? You can watch." The man cocked his head in that way you often see a dog do when it looks as though it is trying to figure something out.

"NO FINISH, NO WATCH!! You go NOW!!" As hard as it was to comprehend, we had just gotten away with this thing, this time anyway. I pulled up my pants, turned around and lowered my head as I walked by. We tried to look as though we got busted and as though I were embarrassed—not that I had to try too hard given the bared ass thing and all.

Jill had stowed the little drone in her ample bosom in hopes that as we left in a hurry the person would be too much in awe to really look past her tits and see a small bulge where there should not be one. As we climbed down the fire escape and walked toward the car, I said to her, "You my dear are one smart women."

"I know," she said.

We got back to the car and both took a deep breath of relief, feeling safe now that we had reached the car. "So, when are we going back to get the electronics and try to save some of those girls?" Jill asked.

Seeing that she is indeed serious I said, "Tomorrow night. First we need to stock up on tasers and bullets."

She looked at me and I saw a skeptical look on her face and asked her, "What?"

She looked at me and said, "Tasers, why tasers? Not a single one of those assholes deserves to live. Not after treating those women like animals, salves, and sex toys. Fuck the tasers."

I chose my words carefully and told her, "I don't want to accidentally hit any of the prisoners or run out of bullets. If we have to run while under fire, we'd be leaving anyone that survives the joyous luxury of going to jail. I planned on calling the cops as we were making our escape and let them do the asshole roundup."

We agreed to come back the next day and saw about getting the girls and anyone else that we came upon free of their bondage. The plan was to go in via the roof stairway entrance that led into the interior of the building. You may be wondering why we did not just utilize that route for escape last time. The reason is, we did not want anyone to be the wiser that we were anything else more than two weirdo's out for some different style of sexual eroticism. So the roof access would be the place that we would gain entry to the building.

Once we gained entry, we would proceed to the computer room and at all times remain vigilant to our surroundings, to both find the people being held against their will and for the people holding them there. Our first line of defense would be the tasers, followed up with our weapons if needed. Our hope was to get in and get out as fast as we could in order to save as many of the people as we could. While I to wanted to kill the bad guys, there were plenty of them to kill and we would be killing more of them. For now, however, our main goal was to free the enslaved and get out with our lives.

We told the kids that we were going out that night and would not be home until late and to just do as they always did on any other given night. They nodded their heads and carried on with whatever it was that they were doing.

"So, are you ready for this?" I asked Jill.

"As ready as I can be, given we are about to do what only a hostage rescue team or S.W.A.T. Team might do, just without the training. Other than that, yes."

Not really having anything else to say in response to that, given she pretty much covered the entire situation in that one statement I said, "Very well then."

We retrieved the beater car and headed over to the building where the people were being held. With the can of gas and a road flare in the trunk for a fast disposal of the car should, we left the car and headed to the back of the building and up the fire escape. Luckily for us, the guy that almost caught us the other night never put the access ladder back into its upright storage position when he left. Maybe he just couldn't get it to go back up, either way it was good for us. We made a cursory scan of our surroundings and headed up.

Already knowing how we would be getting out, we headed inside and straight for the area that we thought the prisoners were being held. "This is not it, there is no one in here." I whispered to Jill.

"Only two other rooms make sense, unless they are holding them in one of the wide-open work spaces that was used for a factory floor when the place was active," she said to me. We continued our search, and wouldn't you know it, the last door we came to, was the one we were looking for. However, there were not half as many people in that room as we had seen walking down the hall last night.

As we walked into the room, a group of young girls huddled up into a tight group in the corner of the room. They were obviously terrified of any one that came into the room under the assumption that they were only here to do them harm. Jill moved closer and held her finger up to her lips in the universal sign of quiet and spoke, "Does anyone speak English here?"

One girl stepped forward and said, "I do, a little."

Jill turned to her and said, "That's good, you are very brave to come forward. We are here to help you get out of this place. It seems however that there are a lot less of you that there were last night, is there somewhere else that they keep you all?"

The girl said without hesitation, "There is room close to where the bad people use computers that they keep some of us to be moving. You can help them too?"

I could tell that my wife was trying to hold back the tears as she spoke to the young girl. "We will try very hard to get all of you away from here, ok?"

"Ok," replied the girl.

We had the little girl translate the best she could our plan that we had to get them out of the building and how we would need to stop and get the computers on the way. We also had to tell them that there may be gun fire and a lot of danger along the way and to just do their best to stay strong, and we would do all that we could to get them free. There was a little bit of skepticism in the eyes of the captives. But knowing what lay ahead of them if they were sold however, was far worse than the possibility of freedom.

The girl that was translating did what I can only assume was her very best. Seeing a few nods of the other people's heads, I had to guess that the directions were passed along, and a sort of understanding was met. If they were afraid, it didn't show. However, not knowing what they had been through up until then, I could only guess that just about anything was better than that.

"You ready darling?" I asked Jill.

"As ready as I can be."

Just as we were ready to head out, I felt a tug on my shirt sleeve. I looked back and saw a young woman or maybe even as young as sixteen, not sure exactly.

"What's the matter?" I asked her.

With a tear in her eye and a mix of emotions on her face she said, "tank you."

I am not really an overly emotional person, but that one got to me. The words may have been in very broken English, but anyone that had ears could have understood her meaning.

"You are very welcome my dear. Now keep your head down, and let's see about getting you to safety and maybe even home." The young lady looked at me and nodded.

"Ok, let's go."

We rounded the corner of the hall heading to the computer room. Knowing exactly where the room was, we got there without delay. "Given the time is close to that of last night, I can only hope that again there is no one manning the computer room," I said to Jill.

"Let's hope," she said.

I gave the door knob a twist and found that it was not locked. I continued to turn it when I heard from the other side of the door.

"Wait, wait, wait," I looked at Jill and we both suppressed a laugh.

"I think someone was sorting the family Jewels." Jill scrunched up her face and shook her head.

"You are nasty," she said.

In my best Russian accent—well to be honest my only Russian accent I said, "You have to be joking, Yes? You no able to keep that thing under control till later?"

Jill and I let out a laugh. From the other side of the door we heard. "Go fucking yourself."

Then we heard footsteps come across the room. I looked at Jill, and she pulled out her taser. The door swung open and she nailed him with fifty thousand volts of 'oh fuck that's gotta hurt' and he hit the floor like the big-ol sack of shit that he as. I grabbed his hands and pulled him into the room as Jill retrieved the taser barbs, not very gently either I might add.

I saw her giggle a little bit and asked, "What is so funny?"

Jill replied, "You know those shows that you see where people get kicked in the nuts or hit with a baseball or even fall off a pier into the water during their weddings?"

I nodded my head having a feeling I already knew where this was going. "Yes, I do."

She went on to say, "Well, I think that they should have a bit on there where they show people being tased. That is some funny shit now, straight up hilarious." I nodded my head and kept pulling Mr. taser into the room, also laughing a bit to myself.

CHAPTER 23

The girls waited in the hall, and while very nervous, agreed to keep watch as we went in and grabbed the computers and any other information in plain sight, without doing too much of a search and possibly compromising ourselves or that of the girls. We quickly rounded up the laptops and stuffed them into a backpack that we brought with us for that very reason. Thankfully the thugs in that ring of assholes had decided to move into the new age of computers. A lack of any style of paperwork meant that we got all the good stuff or that the crap we got was literally just used for jerking off and internet use.

Given the fact that they had all these women just hanging out against their will and the fact that they had no respect for human life—selling said women—makes it hard for me to believe that if the urge should come upon them, they would not hesitate to use one of their captives to itch any scratch that they may encounter. If indeed we are lucky, we just found something more to make this whole thing worthwhile instead of just saving the girls. Ok, so that came out all wrong. Saving the girls was top priority, however, bringing down this ring of slavers is also very important.

As we continued down the hall the girl that was interpreting for us said, "We need right at next hallway, place that others is are down there."

I looked at her and nodded my head in thanks and we moved off in that direction. Outside a set of double doors, the translator stopped us. Behind those doors was where we could find the rest of the abducted girls. Knowing this, I communicated with the wife and we got ready to make entry. Jill pointed to the chain strung around the handles and the lock holding the chains together at the end. I nodded in acknowledgement and reached for the lock. As I grabbed the lock it unlocked with a small pull. I instantly looked up at Jill and smiled.

"Guess you can depend on people being lazy in all aspects of life." I said to her.

She nodded her head back at me and indicated that we should go in. "Wait!" Jill says quietly.

I stopped undoing the chain and look at her. "What?" I asked.

"Let's take the girls in with us this time. They may be able to keep the others calm as we come in, as opposed to being terrified and accidentally making enough noise to alert the guards."

I nodded and said, "Good idea."

With the chain removed from the doors and one of them held open, I motioned to the girls to go in first and tell the others that it is ok, we are here to help, but they need to keep the noise down. Our translator did her thing and we walked into the large room that had been converted to a dorm style holding area. What we saw made us want to kill all those bastards in the worst way imaginable.

In the poorly lit room, were about 15 girls of varying ages. All were laying on the floor with nothing more than a small piece of egg crate foam as mattress along with a sheet to cover up with. Most of them must have sat up the moment they heard the door chains rattle, expecting the worst as they had become accustomed to. Our translator spoke to those that she could and others that didn't speak her language but understood the translation of the translation looked at us.

"I'm not sure if they are happy to see us or wondering if there are more coming." I said to Jill.

"I am sure that they are hoping on the latter, so instead of letting them ponder it too long and loose hope, let's get them the hell out of here," she said to me.

"Ok all of you, let's get you out of here," I said to no one in particular. I led the way and the girls followed while Jill brought up the rear. Knowing that we have to go down one more floor in order to get to the exit, we headed that way.

"Why the hell haven't we run into anyone yet?" I heard Jill ask me.

"I was just wondering that myself," I said back to her.

We all made it down the stairs and thought that all was well when from around the corner came two people walking down the hall. 'Guess our luck just ran out,' I thought to myself. They were both engaged in a conversation in a different language thus giving us a few extra seconds to figure out what the hell to do. I indicated to the women to get down when the two looked away from each other and saw us.

They seemed startled to see for a second, but only for a second. When they caught a glance of the girls following us, the shit hit the fan. Unlike in the movies when the good guys meet the bad guys and they instantly begin a dialogue, these guys came out firing. The same time they began to fire, Jill and I also began to fire our weapons in return. Having already had our weapons out and ready in that very lucky few seconds that the two were jaw-jacking helped us to get the upper hand but not without some casualties.

Jill put several rounds into the chest of her target, while I managed to get two in the chest of the other. Watching the two fall and knowing that we had essentially sounded the alarm, we started to move, but we realized that one of our girls was hit and down. I ran back to her and heaved her up and carried her. Jill took the lead, and in only a few seconds, we heard people coming up from behind us screaming at us to stop.

Jill stopped for a second at her end of the hall and stared at something. n

Not sure what it was that she was doing and still carrying the girl I yelled, "Hurry, hurry, let's get the hell out of here."

She turned and looked at me and snapped out of whatever had her distracted ran for the exit. Again, she stopped but indicated to the girls that they should keep heading for the door and keep going straight down the road and we would be right behind them. Scared but smelling freedom they did as she said.

"What are you doing?" I asked her.

"Get them out of here," she said, "I have a small can of nitrous oxide."

Shrugging my shoulders, I did as she said. I looked back and saw her turn the valve wide open and toss the open bottle down the hall at our assailants. In that instance I realize what nitrous was—laughing gas—the added bonus to what they call laughing gas is, in the right amount the lights go out for a bit. Ok, anyone of you that didn't catch that, it means good night bad guys, especially in that amount.

"Awesome work, darling!" I said to her with a huge smile on my face as we approached the door.

Her face went from happy to oh shit in an instant, and she screamed, "Look out!!"

Already reacting to her face, I was turning around trying to see what it was that got her panties in a bunch before I heard her say look out. The same moment, I got completely turned around, but before I can react, I felt what can only be described as being kicked in the chest by a horse. The next thing I knew I was on the ground completely out of breath. As I lay there wondering why the hell I couldn't breathe I heard gunshots, shouting, and lots of footsteps. When the shooting stopped, I felt hands underneath me trying to help me to my feet.

Having agreed to never say each other's names when on a job is one thing, but even the best laid plans have a way of going to shit in the heat of the moment. "Jack, Jack, can you hear me? You are going to be all right. Jack, Jack, look at me." I heard Jill saying as I finally started getting my shit back together yet somehow still moving at the same time.

"What the..." I said.

Jill interrupted me and said, "No questions right now, just help us help you keep moving there are still two of those assholes after us."

With that info sinking in, I realized that the occasional zing that I heard going by my ears was not a bug of some sort after all, but the occasional bullet just missing my thinker by a matter of millimeters.

"Where is the girl that I was carrying?"

"She is being helped by the other girls, now make the call!" I heard Jill say to me as the girls and I continued to run for our lives. Somehow for the most part we were still all together.

"I'm on it," I said and grabbed the burner phone from off my hip and called nine-one-one.

"Nine-one-one, what is your emergency?" I heard through the ear piece as we continued to run down the street into an abandoned industrial complex.

Having already programmed a voice distorting app onto the burner, making my voice sound like a twelve-year-old girl I said, "Help me, I was kidnapped and have escaped but they are after me. Please help me, please."

The nine-one-one operator signaled her boss and immediately started to track the call. "Stay with me dear, I have help on the way."

I continued to act as the scared little girl. The nine-one-one operator asked her to help give the responding officers as much info as possible. "There are several of us, I think you all call it trafficking, please hurry."

If they were not already in a hurry, I was fairly sure that the sound of the gunshot that my wife let loose to helped give us more time to run really lit a fire under their asses. "ARE YOU ALL OK?" I heard the operator ask.

"Getting tired and afraid they will catch us, please hurry."

"They are six minutes out sweetheart, just hang in there, we have you on our GPS and you should start hearing the sirens soon."

I told her thanks and stopped for a second and let off two shots. One of the shots caught one of our assailants in the throat. I watched as he stumbled and grabbed for his neck as bright red blood started gushing from the wound. Just then I heard the first sounds of sirens.

Guessing that the other guy also heard the cops or just stopped to help his colleague I said to the group, "Hold up for now They have stopped chasing us and the cops will be here any second." The group stopped, and we all gathered around. The injured girl didn't look all that great, but I knew that EMS would be with the cops or right on their heels.

"We are not what you would call working on the right side of the law, so please do not describe us to anyone. If they need answers tell them that the people who help rid the city of the bad people helped you and leave it at that. Please be good and try to have a better life and enjoy every minute of it."

They all tried to give us hugs when Jill, hearing the sirens getting louder, said, "Come on, we have to go now."

After wiping down the burner phone I gave it to our little translator girl and told her to keep it on her till the cops came. She nodded and grabbed me in a big hug. Jill grabbed me, and we ran like hell in the opposite direction of the sirens.

We ran until we felt mildly sure that we were safe, circled around back to where our car was and casually headed toward the more, seedy part of town. Yes, it could get worse than where we found the girls. We left instructions with the translator girl to tell the police all about their capture and treatment at the hands of their captors and which building exactly it was that we ran from. We hoped that anyone who hadn't already left and any evidence that we hadn't gotten might be recovered and used to capture and prosecute the perpetrators of that hideous crime ring.

We found a nice quiet spot to torch the car, after stripping off our clothing. I watched as Jill took her outerwear off then turned to assist me with mine. Let's not forget the horse kick earlier. Had it not been for the fact that we both found some used police issue bullet proof vests and decided that it would be a good place to give them a test, I may have been back there with that horse—or should I say the slug that the horse threw at me.

She looked at the spot at where the bullet made impact and slowly took off the vest. The wound site was already beginning to bruise, and Jill informed me that it would be an impressive bruise at minimum. We put the clothing we wore during the break in into the car, doused it in gas and set it ablaze. We made our way back to our good car, hopped in and headed to the house with our bag of treasures for the kids to try to hack and discover what they could about what or who they found on it.

As we drove home neither one of us really said anything. When Jill finally broke the silence she said, "If we do something like that again, it needs to be planned out a bit better."

I looked over at her as she smiled, I too began to smile. We both break into gut-wrenching laughter, all be it for me only lasted for a fraction of a second as that damn horse reminded me that he had kicked me.

"A bit better you say?" I said, nearing the point that I almost had to pull over from tears in my eyes that were preventing me from seeing the road clearly.

"What!" she said.

Still laughing and cringing I said, "Bit, in reference to the amount of planning we need to do is indeed one way of putting it."

She just sat there laughing and nodding her head. We drove for a bit longer and when we got settled down Jill looked over at me and said, "We did a good thing tonight didn't we?"

I looked at her, smiled, and said, "I would like to think that we did. The law may have a different opinion on the subject concerning the several dead bodies we left them, but as far as I am concerned, they had their chance. So yes, we did do a good thing. I just hope that those girls find happiness in the rest of their lives. That will make it even more worth doing what we did." Jill nodded in agreement and we continued our journey home in silence.

CHAPTER 24

A loud ringing noise stirred Jamison out of what was turning out to be a pretty good sleep, at least until that damn phone started ringing. Reaching for the phone still half asleep, he found it on the end table, brought it to his face and accepted the call. "Jamison, and this better be good."

"Boss, it's me, Hart."

Jamison got a less than impressed look on his face and said, "No shit Sherlock. I was pretty sure it wasn't Abby from *NCIS* here to take me out to dinner and fulfill my every desire. What the hell do you want?"

Hart started laughing, "Damn you are grumpy when you get up. But anyway, you will like this, so put your phone on speaker and get dressed because we may have a break in our case."

Jamison hopped out of bed and put the phone on speaker as he threw some clothes on. "Keep talking asshole," he said to Hart.

"And pick me up some coffee on your way in, would you pal?"

"Oh, now it's pal is it," Hart said to him.

"Pal, asshole, BFF. What ever gets me some coffee is what I will call you right now."

Snickering, Hart said, "How about handsome man."

To that Jamison responded, "Fuck off, I'll get my own damn coffee."

Hart began to laugh, "No worries boss, I already got you some and am almost to work."

"Good job you ugly bastard." Jamison also started to laugh.

As he pulled up to the station, he saw that Hart and Hanson were there, but Cline had yet to arrive. Wondering to himself how it was exactly that everyone seemed to get called before him, he scrolled through his phone's missed calls log. He saw that not only did dispatch try calling him three times, but the call that he did answer from Hart was his second attempt at reaching him. 'Well shit fire and save the matches, I guess there is a first time for everything,' he thought.

He walked up the stairs and into the task-force space and said to the two detectives, "What we got? Where is Cline?"

Hart grabbed the first question, "Well, a little after three thirty this morning, nine-one-one received a call from what sounds like a scared girl approximately twelve to fifteen years of age. When the nine-one-one operator asked her what her emergency was, she claimed that she and several other girls, and by girls they vary from age fourteen to twenty-five years of age."

Jamison broke in and said, "How many exactly are we talking about?"

Hart continued by saying, "Last I heard there are twenty-three."

Hanson stepped in and said, "Of those twenty-three, all but one was for the most part uninjured."

Jamison opened his mouth to say something when Hanson held up a finger to indicate that Jamison wait one second. "Let me finish; I am sure I will answer most of your questions. These girls were found in the old industrial park area; you know the place. It's where a lot of the Russian mob does their business and the place where we found the two bodies that looked like they were killed using a bow and arrow."

Jamison nodded his head as Hart took over from there. "After the first responders arrived on the scene a little Philippine-a girl with a decent command of the English language tells the officers that they were just rescued by two people that, and these are her words. 'Do justice for ones that don't get it'."

Jamison tried to take it all in and said to the others, "So we are thinking that these two are our vigilantes, and if so, why did they do this type of job. What was their motivation?"

"Damn that is a lot of what's for one sentence." Cline says as he walks into the room.

"Nice of you to show up. Out trying to conquer the world and lose your phone or what?" Hanson chided.

"Nope, I was staying the night at a friend's house on the other side of town."

No sooner than Cline realized he had made a mistake with that statement the room broke out into an oooohs, aaaaahs. Jamison broke into the conversation and said, "Who Cline is fucking is not pertinent to the matter at hand, now let's get back to it." Hart and Hanson were both laughing by that time and even Jamison had a smile on his face.

Let's back up again for just a second so I can give you a little bit of Clines story.

When he heard his phone, Cline reached over grabbed his phone off the table next to the bed, "SA Cline." He listened for a second and then replied, "Got it, on my way." As Cline hung up, he heard the phone ring again, "Cline. Hello, hello." He looked at his phone and realized that it was not his phone that was ringing.

Amanda said in a sleepy voice, "This is Dr. Moore." Cline watched her as she said. "I'll be there in approximately an hour." She then hung up the phone and turned to look at him. "Well good morning handsome."

He smiled at her and said, "Good morning to you too. Is it actually morning or what?"

Amanda looked at him and said, "Just the beginning for some, but it is for certain our morning."

Cline reached over and gave her a kiss and promptly rolled out of bed and threw his clothes on. "You catch the industrial area case? I only ask due to the fact that our phones rang nearly right after each other."

She nodded her head "Yes I did. So, we on for dinner this weekend?"

Cline was trying not to trip as he was putting on his shoes and trying to answer her at the same time, "That sounds great, that is of course if our work allows it." He ran over and gave her a long deep kiss, "Until we meet again ma-lady."

She smiled at him, made a feeble attempt at a curtsy and said, "Indeed good sir." They both smiled at each other as Cline walked out the door.

"Yeah, yeah, yeah," Cline said to the guys as he took his seat, "Yuk it up ass-hats."

The room finally returned to some form of normalcy and Jamison cleared his throat in that 'listen up' way that some people do. The detectives all turned to face him and listened, "Ok, this is what we have. If this is indeed our guy, or as it has been made aware to me that it may be more than one person, then we are entering a new type of what the fuck situation. I say this because it is unlike any other serial killer case that I have ever heard of. PERIOD!" Jamison took a pause to think about what next to say or even where the hell to start.

"Cline? Do you with all your brain shrinking wisdom have any ideas as to how the hell to deal with this?"

Cline stood up and addressed Jamison and the rest of the detectives. "Honestly sir I am at a loss, not to be mistaken as not having an idea, but just at a loss as to how this is all unfolding."

Jamison made a face at him, "AND?"

"Sorry, the way I would go about this is two-fold. One being that we have a vigilante, this is known. The next is that he/she or they have a soft spot for people in general, not that it prohibits them from taking a life but over all a caring for human beings and doling out the proper punishment to those that cross a certain line and harm their fellow man and do not get properly punished as they see it, regardless of the law." Cline went on, "One or both of these people have had something bad happen to someone close to them, and this person that perpetrated the crimes did not get punished the way that these people felt it to be appropriate. This being said, they have decided to dole out punishment as they see fit. I believe that this last take down was centered around the trafficking angle. I don't think that they started out to take them down but stumbled into a hot bed with too many people there for them to just turn their back on."

Hart stood up and asked, "So with this new angle, how the hell do we go about finding these people?"

To that Cline responded, "Good question Hart, the simple answer is, the same way you solve all your other cases. This time however you take into account that you have to be looking at it from two separate angles. Both angles have different threads that will ultimately lead to one piece of string which is our team of killers."

"Right, so that just fucked me all up." Hanson said.

Cline looked over at Hanson and began to say something when Jamison stepped in, "Don't worry about him Cline. Hanson could get confused by someone telling him to go stand in the corner in a room full of corners." Cline and Hart just laughed while Hanson stood there flipping them off.

"Ok you all, here's what I say we do. Hart and I will take the inside of the crime scene on the main floor, while Martha Stuart and her ball of yarn take care of the second floor and the roof. If anyone finds something, please use your radios to notify the other team. Oh yea, there are some fatalities so make sure you don't get in..."

Jamison went over his notes that he got from dispatch. "Ah, here we go. So, do not get in Dr. Moore's way at the scene. Just ask her and as you all know she will give you permission, or she will tell you to fuck off, we good?" Jamison looked all around and made sure that there were no questions and said, "Good, now let's get over there and see about catching us a killer." They all headed toward their cars and headed over to the crime scene.

"Cline?" asked Hanson. "What in the hell did you mean by strings and threads?"

Cline looked over at Hanson who was driving. "You were really confused by that?" he asked.

"Well maybe just a little, I think I have the basic idea, but I want to make sure I am on the same page as you all."

Cline nodded his head, "Well, think of it like this. You have a lake, you want to know how the lake got there. Was it, manmade, spring fed, or formed by a river. You set out to see, and you run across two rivers on two different corners of the lake. You could stop there and say ok, it is river fed and call it a day. However, you are more curious than that."

Hanson looked at him and said, "I am?"

Cline looked over at him said, "Yes you are."

Hanson nodded his head. "Ok."

Cline gave a little laugh and continued his story. "You choose a river to follow in hopes that it will lead you to its source. Half way up the mountain you see that the river branches off and heads back down toward the lake. You follow the branch of the river, and indeed it does end up at the lake just down from the spot where you went up to follow the first one. Again, you could assume that the whole thing is fed from one river and call it a day."

Hanson jumped in, "But I am more curious than that, right?"

Laughing some more, Cline continued, "Again, correct. So, you go back up the hill alongside the river you just followed down and again you meet up with the second river. Now you follow the one river for a long while till you almost come to the top of the mountain. You crest the top, and what you find is greater than all that you have seen befo......"

Hanson again broke in, "Olympic size pool filled with hot chicks in the nude with my name tattooed on their bodies screaming out in desire for the one thing that they don't have. ME."

With a puzzled look on his face and a crooked smile Cline said, "While indeed that would be an out of this world find, sadly no. However, you find a lake is the source of the rivers that is the source of the lake below. This lake just so happens to be fed by a huge underground spring."

Hanson looked at Cline and said, "So what you are saying is not to jump to conclusions, but follow every lead no matter how trivial it is, because you never know, that may be the one that leads you to your conclusion."

Cline looked at him and with wonderment on his face he said, "Yea, that is exactly right. How in the hell where you confused by the first one and not by this one?"

"I wasn't, I was just fucking with you to see if you would tell me another story for the trip over to the crime scene. Would you look at that, we are here."

Hanson climbed out of the car and headed toward the building. Cline sat there shaking his head. "Are you coming or you just going to sit there and keep the seat warm?" Cline began to laugh and headed off to catch up with Hanson.

They met up with Jamison and he told them that the good doctor was almost done with the body. They could go ahead and go up to the second floor but to start on the roof in order to give the crime scene techs some time to finish.

Cline stopped next to Jamison and said, "Did you know that Hanson knew exactly what I was talking about when I had made my analogy earlier at the station?"

Jamison looked at him, "He is a fucking smart ass, genius, but a smart ass. I stopped wondering what he does or doesn't know a long time ago. He always gets his guy in the end. He got you to tell him a story on the way over-here didn't he?"

Cline nodded, "Got me with that one also." Jamison laughed and walked toward the door while Cline jogged to catch up with Hanson.

"Hey, doc? Anything interesting about this stiff or is he just another dead bad guy?" Jamison asked.

She looked over at him and said, "Ah, detective Jamison, how nice to see you again. I see your way with words has gotten more eloquent since last we spoke."

Jamison looked back at her with a smile on his face, "Nope, still the same-ole foul mouth gutter trash as before. It is nice to see you again however, princess."

They both laughed, and Dr. Moore said, "Nothing particularly interesting about him. As you put it, just another dead bad guy. Looks like he caught a round with his neck, and that as they say was that."

Jamison nodded his head and looked around. "I noticed some blood on the way in and it looked like there was some more in the hall behind you. Not exactly what you would expect from the injury this guy received. Did you find any other victims?"

"No, however there was a little girl that was injured while they were making their escape. She is being treated at County Hospital now. I believe that is where the blood that you speak of is from."

"Thanks, doc," Jamison said as he and Hart headed down the hall to start trying to make heads or tails of things. They were now thinking it may be one of those cases that takes a career to solve.

"So? Two guys, guy and a girl, boyfriend girlfriend, or husband and wife? What are you thinking boss?" Hart asked.

"Honestly Hart, I don't know. We are going to have to take this one step at a time until it's over or we are reassigned, retired, or dead. We will get them, just don't know when or how."

Hart nodded his head, "Back to the basics then? Good old-fashioned, police work, pound the pavement and look at all the angles till they lead somewhere. I am guessing that the one thing that I think will give us the biggest ass ache is the fact that this team is not crazy. Well, least not crazy as we see it. They don't need to kill, they are doing it to satisfy what they think is right."

Jamison looked over at him and just stared for a bit. "What?" Hart asked.

"You know detective, you may be right on the money."

Hart, looking confused said, "Ok, I would love to say thank you and I agree, but I don't know what I am on the money about."

"Yeah, yeah, yeah. Thanks, are for later." Jamison said.

"Boss?" Hart said.

Jamison looked over at him. "What?"

Hart looked right at him, and without hesitation said, "I realize that there is a lot going on in that big brain of your right now, but what in the hell am I supposedly on to?"

Jamison looked right back at him and said, "We need to drop all the 'find them easy' stuff and go back to the basics, just like you said."

Nodding his head, Hart answered, "Well yea, I don't think this will be one of those things that can be solved by a VICAP (violent criminal apprehension program) or any other alphabet acronym system. I think that we will literally have to start plotting the crime scenes on the wall and attach strings to each site and see if the connect anywhere for start. Then if not, we need to find something to match all the victims together other than they are or have been criminals. I mean, just because these two are killing people that hurt or take advantage of women and children doesn't mean that is all that there is to be done. To me it just means that this is what has them occupied right now."

Jamison looked back at him and then down the hall looked at Hart and said, "Do you think they just got exceptionally lucky this time, or do you think they were trained in a former life so to speak? To me it looks like the gunfire, while well aimed still doesn't look like that of a professional hitter. Maybe an ex-soldier of some type, but not an avid shooter. Hey, Doc?"

Dr. Moore looked over at them and raised her eyebrows in a 'Yea, what's up' motion. Jamison pointed at the wall by where the one victim was laying and said, "You see that spray pattern on the wall there behind your vic?"

Dr. Moore replied, "Kind of hard to miss."

"True, but in your professional opinion do you think that this particular pattern could have been made while the victim was on the run or do you suppose that the killer or killers where on the move while taking the shot?"

Dr. Moore looks at the wall and then at the victim and then at Jamison. "Detective, we have known each other long enough that you know that I am not about to make that kind of a call on scene. However, if I were to make an unofficial guess, I would say that the victim was most likely shot in place or simply walked into it."

Jamison looked at Hart then said, "Thanks, Doc. Hart, let's get up to Cline and Hanson. I think I know what may have happened."

"Rodger that boss."

They reached the second floor and waved Hanson and Cline over to them. "What's the what, boss-man?" Hanson asked. "This case is going to bust our balls. Not only are we nowhere closer to solving it, but as Hart and I were discussing, I think we have to start from the beginning and hope we get these two before they can cause to much more death. However, I don't think it will be easy or soon. Let's get back to the station so we can start over and get a fresh perspective on things." They all loaded up into their cars and headed for the precinct. None of them knew just what lay ahead of them in this case or whether or not they could stop these killers.

EPILOGUE

The task force room was quiet as everyone was absorbed in the conversation that the Captain and Jamison were having about the change of tactics in the Vigilante serial murders. This was the foremost topic of conversation around the station and slowly crept out into the public after the takedown of the human trafficking ring only a few days ago. The purpose of the reworking of the team was a must, not based off of performance of the team members but more due to the fact that this team of killers was not your ordinary killing team. As with conventional means of tracking down a murderer and bringing them to justice, lawful justice that is, the law enforcement officials gather information, track down leads and follow up on any evidence that they may gather in the pursuit of the criminals. If they get lucky, the criminals make some kind of mistake and end up giving the police something that gets them caught.

"The oddest thing about this team in-particular was that the only thing any of the victims had in common was the fact that they were criminals themselves, not just criminals, but criminals that had caused grievous harm to their victims. The harm in which I speak of was usually that of a sexual nature. That was the case at least until the trafficking ring which had its own type of sexual aspect to it," Jamison said to the captain.

The other detectives just sat and listened as though they were actually part of the conversation. "Do you suppose that they forgot that we were here?" Hanson asked Cline.

Just then the captain turned to the group and said, "I know you have heard what we have been discussing, and no Hanson I did not forget that you all were here." The rest of the detectives chuckled. The captain went on to say, "Sorry for the lack of focus on the rest of you. This case is just one of those ones that can really put a wrench in the machine. As for the rest of the story, the only odd duck in the group was a man…"

He referred to his notes then looking back up said, "Mr. Resnik who was selling those fake life insurance plans and various other money-making schemes. When caught received a rather light sentence. The killers, and this is where it gets a little weird given Mr. Resnik never mentioned more than one person, kidnapped him and after demanding that the gentleman give them enough evidence to put him away for a very long time, turned him over to the police along with said evidence in exchange for his life. This is very odd to me that someone can take out people at random, sometimes quit gruesomely even then spare someone so easily. Cline do you have any advice on the psyche of these two?"

Cline stood up to address the rest of the room and said, "Honestly captain, these two are looking more and more like a couple. Now by couple, I mean boyfriend and girlfriend or husband and wife. The way they are so in tune with each other and leave absolutely no evidence indicates they are a very close couple; this is why I believe it to be a married couple. As for why Mr. Resnik only mentioned one person in his statement, I believe that is because I think that the second person became part of the team after Resnik was turned over to the police. Now I realize that doesn't do much in the realm of helping the case, but I do have to believe that they are a couple with means, or should I say, they are not hurting for money in any way. As I said before,

I believe is that all the murders prior to the child porn dealer were done alone."

The rest of the detectives looked at him with slightly puzzled eyes. "I thought that might get you all fuckered up as Hanson might say," Cline said with a smile on his face. "Let me explain. Before the child porn distributer there was a more escalated form of violence, assault, bruising on the vics body, etc. When the kiddy porn man was killed the coroner found a healthy amount of a tranquilizer in his system. Now I am not sure why this was done, but given the fact that the murders prior to that there was no indication of any drugs at all, but a healthy dose of violence indicates to me that the other half of the team had a good back up plan in the event the victim was tougher than anticipated, indicating two different styles of thinking."

"Where do you suppose the Ketamine came from? I mean, I realize that you can buy almost anything from a dealer these days, but Ketamine...isn't that like some kind of horse tranquilizer or something?" Hart asked to no one in-particular.

Cline answered and said, "Its primary purpose is during anesthesia and as a pain killer. Doesn't really mess with heart function or breathing, but it will knock the living shit out of any pain. It can also cause memory loss."

"Ok so where's it from? I ask because it seems like a viable point in which to start or is it something that is out there and just not popular around here?"

The captain jumped in at that point and told the group, "I will let you all hash out the particulars, I am going to call the DEA and ask that very question about the Ketamine, Hart. I also believe that that may be a good starting point. For that matter, it may be a place for us to start this thing and maybe, just maybe if we are real lucky get some kind of a grip on this investigation so that we can bring it to an end."

Meanwhile, back at Vigilante HQ—yeah, yeah, I know. poor humor. But I always wanted to say that. Besides, it's my book, and I can. Now, back to the story. Yes, I just did it again.

"Jill, what is the weather supposed to be like this weekend? I can look it up, but I was just curious if you had heard yet." She said something to me from the other room at the same time the microwave signal went off letting him know that his breakfast sandwich is ready. Not remembering just exactly why it was that he was wondering about the weather, he shrugged his shoulders and took his meal out. He went to the table where his I-pad was on the fox news page where he left it to go heat up his sandwich.

Jill came into the room, poured herself some coffee and sat next to him. "Anything worth reading about?" she asked, just before taking a sip of her coffee.

He looked up and finished chewing his bite of food and said, "Just reading about that trafficking ring that got brought down the other day in the news."

Early on, when they had decided to work together, they both agreed to talk about anything that they may have done or been involved in as though it was done by a third party. That way they didn't have to worry about a slip of the tongue around anyone, especially the children.

"I heard a little bit, but what is new with the case?"

"It seems as though there are no real leads in the case, at least as it pertains to who killed the person inside the building or who was actually responsible for the girls escape from captivity. As for the group themselves, it would seem as though the more senior of the crew were out on a 'scouting mission', if you will, for new product."

Jill made a scrunched-up face and said, "Product? They actually called them product?"

Realizing the can of worms he had just opened unintentionally he reiterated. "Not the news, the persons that were taken into custody and the girls themselves stated to one reporter that the girls where called product."

Jill shook her head and continued to drink her coffee.

He looked her right in the eyes and said, "Do not worry my dear, the people behind all this will get caught and properly punished for their crimes. You can mark my words."

At the same time as I was finishing what I was saying to Jill, Thomas came into the room and said, "Yea, sure they will Dad. I mean, sure they may get caught and tried by a jury of their peers, but as for justice, well let's just say that anyone that can buy and sell or kidnap and sell another human being has no real form of punishment that I can think of. Heck I say we round up all the rapists, child porn or child molesters and traffickers, line them up behind the court house and shoot the lot of them. Save the taxpayers some money, but that is just an opinion that the first amendment of our constitution as a citizen of the United States of America allows me to make. Oh yeah, good morning."

Jill and I just looked at each other and grinned. "Good morning to you to sunshine." Jill responded then whispered to me, "Must be in the DNA." I smiled at her and went back to my iPad and the news.

Later that night found us doing our normal routine of reading or watching something on our iPads as we sat in bed and relaxed before going to sleep. Sometimes, our best laid plans came from those sit downs as we were comfortable, less stressed and quiet. Well, we were quieter than the rest of the house, given that it was our room and all.

"So, about the comments that Thomas said earlier?" I said, laying on the bed facing the ceiling.

"Yes, about that," Jill replied. "Yea, I am a little perplexed about what to do. I think that he too will eventually be part of all this, however, I can't help but think that if he does get involved with it, we will be robbing him of his future. I mean, we already have a successful life and careers, and I don't want to take that from them."

Jill looked over at me and said, "I agree with you on that. Is there a way that you can think of that we can involve them in this but only subject them to the lighter side of things?"

"What lighter side?" I asked her.

"Well for instance, there is intelligence gathering and surveillance of the individuals that we choose to remove from this planet for the betterment of society. We could do the actual deed of the removal while Thomas and Charlie, if they so choose, can work at finding the bad guys and if possible gather enough evidence to put them away for good. We will have to sacrifice a few kills in order not to draw attention to ourselves, but I think we can manage to still do some good."

I nodded my head in agreement and said, "So maybe steer them toward intelligence gathering and/or the law, and maybe open a private investigations type company of sorts that focuses primarily on gathering intelligence and using said info to help prosecute those that we find. If they are charged and then let loose than we can make them disappear, so they will not be able to re-offend."

We decided to let the bad guys take a break from dying for a while and got to the workings of an information gathering agency going in order to make it official. We also decided that the laptops that we grabbed from the human traffickers would be used as our first case. We would decide how to explain how we got the laptops later or not at all. If absolutely necessary, we could say that any and all information we obtained came from confidential sources.

Thomas and Charlie decided that they were interested in the investigations career and focused their school work around the law and the enforcement of the law. Charlie, being more scientifically inclined, decided to also throw into his studies, forensic investigations and all that it entailed. Thomas, on the other hand, had a love for reading and a knack for memory retention. So, while Charlie turned more toward the forensic side of things, Thomas decided that his interest was in the opposite direction, the law itself. Not really having a strong desire to become a lawyer, Thomas decided to study the law as it pertained to the investigation side of things. For example, he would be learning what an investigator can and cannot do verses what a cop can and cannot do.

We all decided that private security was the way to go with an emphasis on investigating unsolved crimes and cold cases while also assisting the law enforcement officials with active cases if possible. As for how to rid the world of the unpunished, well we were not going to stop doing that.

We would however have to be more careful not to tie ourselves or our new company to the vigilante crimes that we committee. With a little thought and some time, I was sure that it could be accomplished.

With the boys getting ready to graduate and head off to college, I settled into the start-up of the new company and brought an end to my current one. First thing was to find a buyer for the engineering company. I was sure that my father would have rolled over in his grave if he could see me selling the company. However, I think he would understand my need to right the wrongs that were going on in the world. If not, he would find a way to return from the grave and kick my ass.

The wife had her own decisions to make. She decided to sell her part of practice, giving the explanation that she would like to go into volunteer work at some of the clinics that service the homeless and less fortunate of or city. Doing that would free up her time and not keep her bound to a schedule and obligations of private practice. With all our new ideas in motion, we anticipated an interesting new future, maybe not the type of future that most people would plan for themselves, but a future that both Jill and I believed would be a good one that would serve the human race as well.

Till next time, yours truly.

VJT (Vigilante Justice Team).

P.S. If you can't do the time, don't do the crime. No one can return from the grave, and the grave is exactly where you will end up if you so choose to forego your punishment and continue to re-offend.

OTHER TITLES BY
BLKDOG PUBLISHING

Arthur: Shadow of a God
By Richard Denham

King Arthur has fascinated the Western world for over a thousand years and yet we still know nothing more about him now than we did then. Layer upon layer of heroics and exploits has been piled upon him to the point where history, legend and myth have become hopelessly entangled.

In recent years, there has been a sort of scholarly consensus that 'the once and future king' was clearly some sort of Romano-British warlord, heroically stemming the tide of wave after wave of Saxon invaders after the end of Roman rule. But surprisingly, and no matter how much we enjoy this narrative, there is actually next-to-nothing solid to support this theory except the wishful thinking of understandably bitter contemporaries. The sources and scholarship used to support the 'real Arthur' are as much tentative guesswork and pushing 'evidence' to the extreme to fit in with this version as anything involving magic swords, wizards and dragons. Even Archaeology remains silent. Arthur is, and always has been, the square peg that refuses to fit neatly into the historians round hole.

Arthur: Shadow of a God gives a fascinating overview of Britain's lost hero and casts a light over an often-overlooked and somewhat inconvenient truth; Arthur was almost certainly not a man at all, but a god. He is linked inextricably to the world of Celtic folklore and Druidic traditions. Whereas tyrants like Nero and Caligula were men who fancied themselves gods; is it not possible that Arthur was a god we have turned into a man? Perhaps then there is a truth here. Arthur, 'The King under the Mountain'; sleeping until his return will never return, after all, because he doesn't need to. Arthur the god never left in the first place and remains as popular today as he ever was. His legend echoes in stories, films and games that are every bit as imaginative and fanciful as that which the minds of talented bards such as Taliesin and Aneirin came up with when the mists of the 'dark ages' still swirled over Britain – and perhaps that is a good thing after all, most at home in the imaginations of children and adults alike – being the Arthur his believers want him to be.

Fade
By Bethan White

Do you want to remember?

Do you want to forget?

There is nothing extraordinary about Chris Rowan. Each day he wakes to the same faces, has the same breakfast, the same commute, the same sort of homes he tries to rent out to unsuspecting tenants.

There is nothing extraordinary about Chris Rowan. That is apart from the black dog that haunts his nightmares and an unexpected encounter with a long forgotten demon from his past. A nudge that will send Chris on his own downward spiral, from which there may be no escape.

There is nothing extraordinary about Chris Rowan...

I Know Where the Bodies are Buried
By Chris Bedell

17-year-old Carson believes his former "boyfriend," Billy, didn't commit suicide by jumping off a cliff and into the ocean. Billy's sweater and suicide note might've been found, yet a body was never discovered.

So, Carson befriends, and "dates" his classmate, Dean, on the possibility that Dean knows something about Billy's death. Dean and Billy both belonged to the same community service club (Charity Now) where Billy devoted his time to.

Clues soon unravel, though. Like an eyewitness seeing members of Charity Now in the woods near the cliff before Billy's suicide, a diary entry, proving Billy lied about his father being homophobic, and a hazing incident involving a student's death—that Billy might or might not have been responsible for. However, Carson doesn't only have to grapple with Billy's duplicity. Genuine romantic feelings for Dean emerge. Except Carson will have to finish his sleuthing if he wants closure about Billy's death.

Soul of a Vampire
By Silencio Marquez

Kris Kellman is a vampire living in Calgary, Canada who works as a detective at the Magical Laws Division. It's his job to solve crimes committed by magical people like himself. When his former lover, Zeke Yonah, shows up on his doorstep covered in blood and asking for help, Kris is conflicted. Is he a vampire first, or is he a cop?

As he begins to investigate the murder that Zeke doesn't remember committing, things get really complicated when Kris realizes that Zeke is being set up for murder.

Charles Anderson is in charge of the vampire community, and he has a plan to enslave all mankind. The only thing standing in his way are people like Zeke and Kris, a vampire whose loyalty can't be bought. Kris's ridiculous dragon-shifter boyfriend isn't making things easier either.

Kris realizes that if he can't stop Charles, it will mean war between humans and vampires. He knows that it's not just humans that will suffer, but vampires like him who won't just sit by and let Charles get away with genocide.

**Arc City Stories
By various authors**

Welcome to Arc City.

A city that exists in a world beyond governments, where war and climate change have destroyed the old order. Corporations are now the authorities of the surviving city states. The elite live in luxury above the clouds in their towers, everyone else lives further down, based on their corporate and economic worth.

Arc City Stories is an exciting, action-packed collection of nine cyberpunk tales, written by eight authors, of various citizens each trying to survive, in their own way, this brave new world.

A Storm of Magic
By Ashley Laino

Being brought back from the dead is an impressive trick, even for magician Darien Burron. Now he must try and use his sleight of hand to swindle modern-day witch, Mirah, to sign her power away, or end up a tormented demon in the afterlife.

Meanwhile, sixteen-year-old Mirah is starting to lose control of her powers. After an incident at her aunt's Witchery store, Mirah is sent to a secret coven to learn to control her abilities.

While away, Mirah meets up with a soft-spoken clairvoyant, a brazen storm witch, and the creator of dark magic itself. The young woman must learn to trust in herself before she loses herself entirely to the darkness that hunts her.

Consumed
By Justin Alcala

Sergeant Nathaniel Brannick is trapped in Victorian London during a period of disease, crime, and insatiable vices. One night, Brannick returns from work to find an eerie messenger in his flat who warns him of dark things to come.

When his next case involves a victim who suffered from consumption, he uncovers clues that lead him to believe the messenger's warning. Despite his incredulity, he can't help but wonder if the practical man he once was has been altered by an investigation encompassed in the paranormal. That is, until he meets the witch hunters, and everything takes a turn for the worse.

Click Bait
By Gillian Philip

A funny joke's a funny joke. Eddie Doolan doesn't think twice about adapting it to fit a tragic local news story and posting it on social media.

It's less of a joke when his drunken post goes viral. It stops being funny altogether when Eddie ends up jobless, friendless and ostracised by the whole town of Langburn. This isn't how he wanted to achieve fame.

Eddie knows he's blown his relationship with rich girl Lily Cumnock. It's Lily's possessive and controlling father Brodie who fires him from his job - and makes sure he won't find another decent one in Langburn. And Eddie doesn't even have Flo to fall back on - his old nan died some six months ago, and Eddie is still recovering from the death of the woman who raised him and who loved him unconditionally.

Under siege from the press, and facing charges not just for the joke but for a history of abusive behaviour on the internet, Eddie grows increasingly paranoid and desperate. It's Sid who offers Eddie a refuge and an understanding ear. But she also offers him an illegal shotgun - and as Eddie's life spirals downwards, and his efforts at redemption are thwarted at every turn, the gun starts to look like the answer to all his problems.

BLKDOG

www.blkdogpublishing.com

9 781913 762476